'Andrew Pippos has wr[...]
Australian humour and G[...]
Such skill and heart and love pulses through this debut!'

ALICE PUNG

'From the first pages of this debut novel, it is clear that we are in the hands of a wise, perceptive, and highly-skilled story-teller . . . The writing is fresh and fairly crackles with energy. *Lucky's* is one of the best Australian novels I've read in years!'

EMILY BITTO

'A gorgeous novel of wonderful characters, *Lucky's* is the real deal and I didn't want it to stop. I was so caught up in the casual charm of this book that I kept being sideswiped by the excellent turns of its plot, and the wise, sometimes disturbing things it has to say about fate, luck and family over the sweep of decades.'

RONNIE SCOTT

'A sweeping, sprawling family epic of heartbreak, hope, and redemption. This is the debut of a born storyteller.'

LIAM PIEPER

'Affecting, authentic and tender, *Lucky's* reminds us that serendipity and salvation can be found in the best kinds of fiction.'

REBECCA STARFORD

'Crisp and evocative.'

RICK MORTON

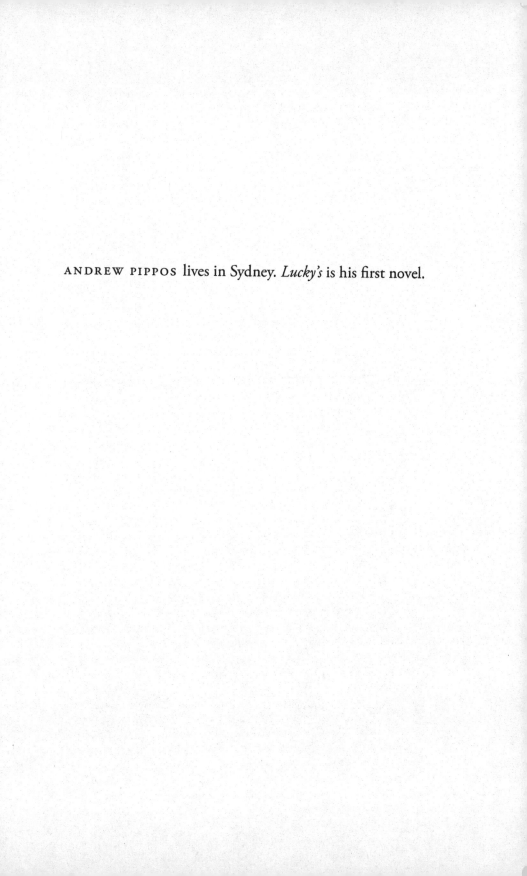

ANDREW PIPPOS lives in Sydney. *Lucky's* is his first novel.

LUCKY'S

ANDREW PIPPOS

PICADOR
Pan Macmillan Australia

First published 2020 in Picador by Pan Macmillan Australia Pty Ltd
1 Market Street, Sydney, New South Wales, Australia, 2000

A catalogue record for this
book is available from the
National Library of Australia

Typeset in 12.2/17 pt Adobe Garamond Pro by Post Pre-press Group
Printed by IVE

For Renee

Thus Don Quixote becomes a knight . . .

– Simon Leys

2002

1.

HE STILL HAD time to make changes. Not to his nickname, which he could never shake, and not to his appearance, and there was little prospect of changing the flaws in his character, since the time had passed for great internal transformations, but Vasilis 'Lucky' Mallios supposed he could fix his own story—to be specific, how it ended.

Lucky sat tucked at his kitchen table, newspaper spread across the surface, stripping rigani from the stalks. The herbs had hung inside a cupboard for a week—not long enough to properly dry—but he couldn't wait; this old ritual was necessary. It offered a moment's accord with the past. He placed the stalks to one side and picked through the heap of flower-heads, plucking out grey twigs, as the smell drifted up like the spirit of someone dead. The apartment now otherworldly, dense with human life. He told himself we all have missing people: our dead parents, or the spouse who left too soon, or the lover who betrayed us, the sibling who deserted the family, the friend we never found, the friend who walked away, the child we didn't have, the person we couldn't become—the life we should have led. Or the missing person might yet arrive: the child we still could have, the family we were about to find, the lover or destroyer coming to the door. Lucky could briefly accept that his world was incomplete, and he waited for this moment to end before he switched on his television.

That afternoon he had rushed home from the bank appointment and straightaway cut down the rigani from the cupboard near the kitchen window. The expansive new apartment complex opposite looked like a tower with its pockets turned out. Lucky's own building reminded him of a motor inn.

The Suncorp Bank loan officer had been kind when rejecting his application. The officer cited Lucky's lack of income in the past twenty-four months, without stating that he was too old anyway to take on substantial debt. He possessed no assets; there was no loan guarantor. The officer said she liked the idea of a person starting over. She couldn't be more sympathetic. Her parents, on special occasions, used to take the family to Lucky's former restaurant in Stanmore. She remembered the jukebox, the fat chips, the decor like the set of a TV show. And she acknowledged Lucky's later history, referring to 'the tragedy in your life'. If only Suncorp loaned on those grounds. At the end of their interview, Lucky admitted to the loan officer that her bank was the last in a list of lenders he'd approached. 'What does that tell me?' he said as he thanked her for the appointment, feigning concession, not wanting to come across sore, but what the final stop on his unsuccessful circuit of loan applications told him was this: the banks in Sydney were too conservative.

The light from his muted television faded and flared in the lounge room. An advertisement for a sports betting company ended and the middle segment of *Wheel of Fortune* began. They'd finished with the pointless speed rounds. The three contestants today all looked startled. They appeared miscast, thrown together behind the scoreboard. Lucky solved two puzzles before one of them even touched the wheel. Food: *Bacon bits*. Phrase: *To go in pursuit*.

Lucky Mallios scooped the rigani into a spiral jar and balled up the newspapers, sending green dust into the air. He got up when the phone rang, his eyes not moving from the television screen. Five beeps and a delay: an international call. 'Lucky's!' he sang down the line.

2002

1.

EMILY MAIN STOOD at the corner in a grade of sunlight she associated with photographs of people at the peak of a mountain. The blue sky tinted the windows of cars as the traffic moved in a series of jolts through the intersection. Emily no longer felt exhausted: the breeze set off a thread of energy. It was the middle of the day. Somewhere in transit between London and Sydney the wheels had buckled on her suitcase, and they produced an abrasive sound when she crossed the road and entered the hotel.

Her flight had circled over Sydney Harbour, over the Lichtenberg figure of the northern suburbs, and from the air she had seen bushfire smoke in the distant south-west, where streams of grey roved into the sky and tabled over the horizon. Isabel, at hotel reception, mentioned the smoke smell that drifted into the city. Brightening suddenly,

4

Isabel said there would be rain soon: at night she heard frogs in her backyard, a sure sign. The hotel's airy lobby smelled of vanilla candles and appeared to be filled with the style of furniture displayed in the windows of stores across the road: white sofas and leather cushions, tubular lamps, mid-century carving chairs, enormous white seashells on the blue marble coffee tables. The floors were oiled and bare wood, dark as soil, faintly scratched. On the walls were blown-up photographs of native flora, the prints grainy as old fabric. Isabel asked if this was Emily's first time in Sydney (no, a long time ago), if she required wake-up calls (no), and whether internet access was necessary (yes).

Emily was expecting an email from Michael, her husband, though last week he'd used the term *partner* when introducing her to someone they bumped into on Chamberlayne Road. Later, when Emily asked him about this description of her, Michael said he'd misspoken, that's all. There was nothing in it. She didn't absolutely take issue with the term: what bothered her was everything else Michael had done and said in recent months. The introduction of the term *partner* suggested to Emily that he somehow felt differently about her status and their marriage, which had indeed shifted (against her will, as though by the orders of a tyrant) into a mostly impassive and practical conjunction. Emily tracked the change back to last June, or thereabouts: the month they began trying to fall pregnant. When they did have sex, it was the kind that involved a minimum of touching. When their time together wasn't admin-minded, it typically involved drinking. Michael liked wine and beer;

Emily cider. He told her: 'I've come to prefer slightly drunk sex.' Some nights they stayed up late and talked and talked about how to fix their marriage until Emily went to bed so exhausted and stupefied that the next day she barely recalled what they'd said to each other. And yet, she thought, they hadn't tried couple's counselling. They hadn't gone on a proper holiday. She told Michael that most marriages go stale (or whatever the hell had happened), but couples could salvage and thrive again, better than before. Whole shelves of the bookstore charted such recoveries. And here she cited friends and acquaintances who'd overcome what she suspected were the same problems. Michael grew his hair down to his shoulders, which looked very becoming.

'He's obviously depressed. He needs to speak to someone,' she told her friend Liam.

Liam and Emily had known each other since their second year at Goldsmiths, where they both took a class on the Central European novel. She'd already heard of him before that seminar, when a friend in common said Emily ought to meet this clever Irish boy called Liam, since she'd like him, platonically. And she did, right away. After graduation, Emily and Liam (now friends) shared a two-bedroom flat with sloped floors in Ladbroke Grove. Liam convinced the landlord to let him paint the bedrooms dark red. This was the late eighties. They would both remember Ladbroke Grove as a good period, four years long. With a great deal of uncertainty—about his own talent, about losing touch with friends—Liam broke their lease and left London to work as the Berlin correspondent for *The Guardian*. In his new flat near Oranienplatz he was relentlessly unhappy and drank to excess but never failed to find good stories. Some weekends he'd fly back to London and sleep on Emily's couch, bringing her German smallgoods and small quantities of excellent acid, which he'd hide inside a tube of toothpaste. Occasionally she'd post him an article she'd written for the *Evening Standard* or *The Independent*, or a short story she couldn't make work.

Liam had been in Berlin for six years when the *New Yorker* offered him a job as a non-fiction editor, and by that time he'd grown distant to the pleasures of writing and said he'd rather edit other people's work: he hoped to never again go home at night worrying about a detail or quote he might have screwed up in a story filed that day. Liam went to New York. Probably he'd never leave. Emily married Michael, a social worker, whom she met at a small dinner party in Harlesden.

Now Liam and Emily spoke once a month, if not more often, and they still confided in each other utterly, like they did when they'd sat up late in their kitchen, years ago, smoking cigarettes and drinking strong cardamom coffee. Some friendships stayed viable because they stayed much the same.

Liam said: 'I'm guessing your husband's girlfriend is named Sandrine.'

'Don't joke about Michael having an affair.'

'I'm not joking.'

'Don't be serious either,' said Emily.

It turned out the girlfriend's name was Therese. Even the way Michael said 'Therese', as if drugged, made it perfectly clear that they, the lovers, had a meaningful union. In the middle of the night before Emily's flight from Heathrow to Sydney, Michael had decided to tell his wife of seven years about his affair. Wearing scarf and gloves, he'd woken Emily at 2 am, standing statue-like above her. He spoke a little louder than he needed to. They were never partners in sleep, husband and wife: she went to bed early, he stayed up late.

'Sorry to wake you,' Michael said, 'but there's something I need to say before you go to Sydney. I'm in love with someone else.'

'What? Repeat that.'

'It came as a shock to me, too. Her name is Therese and I've known her about six months.'

Emily sat up in bed. 'You idiot.'

'We need to talk about this more, but not now. I'll send you an email tomorrow.'

'You're going out in the middle of the night?'

'I should leave, don't you think?'

'You tell me you're in love with someone else and then rush out the door to fuck her?'

'Jesus, Emily. My timing is bad, I know that.'

'Bad timing?' she said. 'Bad timing is when you drive over a level crossing and a fucking train kills you.'

Michael left the bedroom door open, the hallway lights on in their Kensal Green flat. For the rest of that morning, Emily lay in bed trying to convince herself of the inalterable actuality of what had happened to her marriage. She stared up at a light fixture in the shape of an armillary sphere until her alarm sounded, then she got out of bed, into the shower, out the door and onto the tube automatically, on a trajectory already assigned. At the terminal she had the terrifying thought she might be pregnant—for a moment her mind seized up and split helically as it had the night before (what felt like five minutes ago) when Michael told her about beloved Therese. At Boots she bought ClearBlue, and in the departure gate bathroom she peed on the strip while a cleaner slopped water over the floor of the next cubicle.

Three minutes later the test came up negative. The previous month a negative result wouldn't have produced this heavy surge of relief—a bitterly underlined form of relief. The image of one solid line on a stick drenched in piss, Emily thought, said more about the Michael situation than she was presently capable of expressing. Her neck hurt. They called her flight for boarding.

When she took her seat on the plane it seemed wrong that she wasn't still at home, furious, because she felt thrown into abeyance, cheated out of a full response. Michael would be relieved she was leaving the country. He must have viewed the trip as a convenient break in their routine, the coward, and timed his confession to avoid a proper confrontation. Over the plane's intercom an air steward announced the current time and temperature in Singapore—Emily's layover on the way to Sydney—while she swallowed twenty-five milligrams of diazepam and opened a *New Yorker* magazine and closed it again as the plane shot up in what felt like a sequence of jumps.

~

Last September, Emily had been made redundant from her subediting job on the features desk of *The Independent*. No reason was given as to why she'd lost her position instead of some other colleague. No one at the paper had ever faulted her work—or not in her presence. Occasionally her headlines were changed down the line, because she hated puns and some section editors felt differently, but that was no big deal at a broadsheet. She put clean copy to the page. In a five-minute meeting, the managing editor thanked Emily for eight years of service and explained that advertising revenue had been falling. When Emily asked why they didn't sack someone else, the managing editor said they had to choose *someone*, and it had to be a full-timer on the subeditors' desk. When Emily asked again why *she* was that someone, the editor said Emily was being made redundant yet she wasn't literally *redundant*, in a professional sense, but rather out of a job.

In the months after Emily's departure, she received emails from ex-colleagues, subeditors and reporters, whose messages seemed more probing than well wishing, as if they were worried they might be headed towards a similar fate. To one email she replied: 'I'm feeling fine. And let's be honest, half the office will be out of a job in ten years.'

She applied for full-time work she didn't get. She wrote to production about gaps in their casual roster. During her five months of unemployment Michael did not once mention their rent. He did not suggest a new career. He did find her a fortnight of temping shifts at the social work branch where he was employed as team manager. All day, as Emily discovered, he sat at his desk with a gelid expression on his face, absorbed in email and phone conversations and client interview transcripts. Even with his wife present, Michael ate lunch in front of the computer. Emily was surprised by how little he moved from his desk; it was like sanctuary for him, like an escape, like a parallel life. During lunch hour on her last shift at the social work office, she pitched an article to her dear friend Liam. *You probably expected one of these emails*, her message began. She'd always wanted to write something for the *New Yorker*. She intended to write an essay about an obsolete restaurant franchise in Australia, its rise and catastrophic fall. Emily wrote the pitch in fifteen minutes, which was her way of underinvesting in the *New Yorker* fantasy, and in return she expected a kind rejection email from an old friend.

Liam called her that night. 'Emily,' he said, 'I think this is going to work.'

2.

Her first day in Sydney, the summer light slowly growing out of noon: with the curtains drawn in their recessed track, the dim light in the Darlinghurst hotel room was orange and abject. From the desk, Emily picked up the menu, sticky with fingerprints, and cleared away the tent cards that offered instructions about room service and the minibar. She plugged in her laptop and sat on the bed, removing her clothes while the computer started.

An email from Michael:

Em,

I don't know how to explain what's happened in my life. Not being able to express myself is the best expression of how I feel about Therese. Is that a cop-out? She came as a surprise to me, too.

I'll move out before you get back to London. This month's rent is all sorted. And good luck, I know this article will turn out well.

Michael

Emily presumed that when Michael wrote, *I know this article will turn out well*, what he really meant was: *Your ideas are mediocre and that mediocrity is one of the reasons I fell in love with someone else*. Perhaps he felt galvanised by the end of their marriage. He was already deep in a long retreat from their relationship, the stupid bastard, while she was left to feel—something else. She deleted his email and picked up her blouse, a thirty-sixth birthday gift from Michael, throwing it into the bin. How much of her life would he and Therese spoil? It felt as though the hotel room door was wide open and the two lovers (Emily hated that word) could storm in and take whatever they wanted.

On their first date, Emily and Michael shared dinner and went to a pub, where he told her about his elder brother, whose body he found one afternoon at the family house in Coventry. This catastrophe—this meteorite on the family—occurred after the brother had been through drug rehabilitation and moved home and found a job cleaning the windows of shop fronts in the centre of town. Michael came in from school and found his brother dead of an overdose in the bathroom. And Emily told him about her father, whose suicide she witnessed as a girl. She had a sense of these stories joining, of their histories clicking into place. They had seen the same things. They knew the same sorrows. That night in the pub on St Giles High Street, Emily felt certain that she and Michael would fall in love; that they were already together in grief, and now they would build a happy life together.

In the shower, Emily turned so the water hit between the shoulder blades, almost knitting her together again. She asked herself whether she and Michael had made a terrible mistake going to bed at different times, never doing what she supposed better couples did, always rising with each other. From the start they had kept separate hours. A doctor specialising in sleep problems told them Michael suffered from delayed sleep phase disorder. It's like you live in different time zones, said the doctor, different countries. Michael was prescribed melatonin and warned it might wear off in six months (it did). But if he and Emily had gone to bed at the same time, one of them reaching for the lamp at 10.30 pm, if they'd done this every night, then she wouldn't have certain memories, Emily's happiest, from those Saturdays when she rose early to jog her two-mile route, shutting the front door loudly when she came home, calling his name, then running into the bedroom and jumping onto the bed, stripping off her clothes, laughing.

3.

The restaurant franchise Emily proposed to write about was called Lucky's. In fifty years, the franchise menu barely changed an item, the decor stayed as fixed as a photograph (the awnings yellow and gold, the floors chequerboard) and the opening hours were long and uniform across the chain. The franchise was named for its founder, Lucky Mallios, a Greek American who'd migrated to Sydney after the war. (In her research, Emily could not anywhere find an explanation of his nickname.) From America the restaurants took their diner-style interior, the novelties of the soda fountain and jukebox, the sundae and milkshake; from Britain they borrowed the greasy spoon menu of main dishes; from post-war Greece they obtained most of their staff. Lucky's restaurants—also described as cafes—numbered forty-nine outlets at the peak of the business, but they had fallen out of style by the 1990s. What Emily would frame in her story as 'the death of the franchise' was a shooting in 1994: an incident commonly known as 'the Third of April', in which a gunman killed nine people inside the last Lucky's restaurant in Sydney.

Liam wanted to run the piece in the annual food issue of the *New Yorker*, scheduled for the last week in May. 'Would be great if you found a new angle on the shooting,' he said. 'I want to know what happened to the survivors. Focus on the long-term effects of the Third of April.' One other thing, said Liam. He'd been booked to speak about the magazine at a Melbourne university in February. Why didn't they plan to be in Australia at the same time, and he could pop up to Sydney for a short visit?

4.

That day in the Lucky's restaurant, two chefs tried to fight off the shooter, Henry Matfield, and he shot them both dead. Customers hid under tables, but Matfield found them. There was one survivor—a waitress, Sophia—and she later wrote a first-person account of the massacre, published in the local suburban paper, the *Inner-West Courier*. The restaurant's manager and proprietor, Lucky Mallios, wasn't present; he was sixty-seven at the time and rarely worked a full day anymore. While the shooting took place he was at home watching *Wheel of Fortune*. This fact, Emily noticed, found its way into several contemporaneous news reports of the Third of April, as if the gameshow detail revealed something important about Lucky.

Henry Matfield was discovered three days after the shooting: hikers came across his body in a national park on the south coast. By the time the state coroner ruled Matfield's death a suicide several weeks later, Lucky Mallios had closed his final cafe. A chain of discount pharmacies later purchased the building.

5.

Lucky had seemed pleased to hear from Emily when she'd called him from London. He came across as excited, moved—relieved, even—and said he'd be happy as hell to help with a story for the *New Yorker*. 'Most people have something to hide,' he claimed, 'but not me, not anymore'. He was at last ready to spill his guts, as he put it. Lucky's abundantly energetic voice was a mid-Pacific mixture of a kind Emily had never heard before—the American accent after fifty years in Australia. He'd been easy to find: the online White Pages listed his number. The company that bought into the franchise was also listed in the yellow pages. These two contacts would lead to others, Emily supposed, and through them she'd discover the piece she wanted to write, since even the most closely crafted pitch was only a good guess at the final product. She could no better imagine the story than she could, at this point, imagine her own future, guessing where she would live, if she would be alone for the rest of her life, if she would grow bitter and cruel like the people she avoided. Just as well, she thought: dwelling on the future would be like walking into quicksand.

After her shower, Emily decided, what would make her feel better was to hire a small car and get to work. 'Shall we meet this Lucky?' she said to herself. Shall we secure his trust? Shall we pretend that Michael isn't in love with someone called Therese? She hated that name now: it seemed fine before, homely even, but now she hated it on a deeply personal level. 'What the fuck, Michael?' Emily said loudly. 'What the *fuck*?'

The article might be the beginning of her new life. The commission was some kind of blessing, a second chance, a good thing in a bad time. Isabel at reception arranged for the rental to be brought to the hotel on Victoria Street. Emily called Lucky and asked if he were available for a brief interview that afternoon.

'Come over!' he said. 'I haven't spoken to a soul all day.'

Driving down Cleveland, glancing around, the sun in her eyes, she thought the street was architecturally pretty one moment, ugly the next. The terrace houses were painted egg-carton colours. Each of the pre-tuned radio stations shouted at her.

Lucky lived under the flight path, on a long street in the suburb of Tempe. The parked cars were the colour of dirty running shoes. Cockatoos picked themselves up from the powerlines and flew north. In the middle of the street the road shone with tiny glass particles. Emily sat in the car outside his building, a few minutes early for their meeting, and in one hand she held her mobile phone, in the other a Go Bananas calling card that offered discounted calls to thirty European and North American countries. She wanted to tell someone that she'd arrived in Australia, but it was 2 am in New York—too early to ring Liam. They'd spoken last week, after Condé Nast's travel agent had booked flights and a hotel for Emily. 'This will be fabulous,' he'd said, before adjusting his evaluation. 'I mean, it's a good premise,' he continued, and here Emily could picture him sucking in his cheeks. 'Not without risks, but no doubt you'll luck on to something in Sydney.'

He had a few suggestions: he asked Emily to situate the Third of April within the country's history of mass murders by firearms, ending with the Port Arthur massacre in 1996, after which the federal government further restricted gun ownership. He said American readers were interested in gun control legislation. 'We're intrigued by the shooting,' he explained. 'And, to be honest, without that element we might not be keen on the article.'

'Do your colleagues have reservations about this commission?'

'No, no. I passed around your clippings and people liked them. They made approving sounds.'

'You still have the clippings I sent you? From a hundred years ago?'

'I've kept them. Is that weird?'

If it was 2 am in New York that made it 7 am in London. Emily called Michael instead, because she was still, somehow, in love with him.

'It's me,' she said.

'You're in Australia?'

'I don't know why I'm calling.'

'You must be exhausted. It's such a long flight!'

'Where is Therese? Is she staying at our flat?'

'She's not here.'

'You must think you're a good liar.'

'I'm not lying, Em.'

'Blah, blah, fucking blah!' said Emily, and she ended the call, left the car and walked down the footpath. Her footsteps made a distinct sound: nup, nup, nup, nup. Maybe, she thought, Michael will have some kind of breakdown and stop turning up for work and Therese will leave him and he will spend all day writing letters of contrition to Emily and their friends. And well, then what?

Lucky lived in a four-storey apartment building with shirt-pocket balconies of rendered concrete. The windows had bare aluminium frames, dull eyes. A tight car park instead of a large courtyard. Emily buzzed inside near the driveway and Lucky, in a first floor flat, came to his door in a white shirt tucked into corduroy pants. He wore long sideburns and had a full head of stray silver curls.

'Are you all right?' said Lucky, noticing her unhappiness. 'Would you like wine or coffee? Hey, I could fix you some food?'

'I did nothing but eat and drink on the plane.'

The front door opened onto a narrow hallway and they walked past a bedroom and bathroom to a dim kitchen that smelled strongly of coffee. Emily sat at the kitchen table and locked her feet together on a patterned rug—a faded red field of concentric medallions that seemed to proliferate. A sideboard held silver sundae dishes and milk jugs and sugar bowls leftover from the franchise, glittering like Lucky's grail. The paintwork showed blisters and scales here and there, but for the most part the walls were crowded with framed photographs of old restaurant outlets. Lucky looked sideways at Emily, as if reacting to something she'd said.

He asked: 'Probably the first thing you want to know is why I live in a dump like this when I used to be a big-time franchiser, yes?'

'It's not a dump.'

'As you'd know, I sold the franchise in the 1970s. That was a bad deal, no question. They paid me peanuts, took the businesses, took my name, and left me with one restaurant, which I ran independently. Two people named Sam and Shirley got hold of the other restaurants. Sam and Shirley: they probably sound like people in a country song.'

'Like a couple in a sitcom.'

'The worst decision I ever made, selling. I wasn't too smart. People muck things up at weak moments. And after the shooting I made bad money decisions,' he said. He took a breath and, as if confessing, continued, 'Some days I couldn't get out of bed. I developed mental problems.'

This would be a difficult subject, Emily recognised. This was an inadequate explanation of how Lucky lost control of the franchise, how he lost his money, how he ended up here. But she could revisit the question another day. For now, instead, she would offer him a story of her own. On the one hand, it might be a way to establish trust and intimacy. On the other, it might make him uncomfortable.

At home, in her bedroom, hung a small painting of a Lucky's restaurant, a picture made by her late father, copied from a postcard, and given to Emily for her seventh birthday. Michael used to say the bright, running colours reminded him of melted plastic. It was a portrait of what Emily took to be a typical Lucky's franchise in an Australian country town. A red dirt road, red evening sky, and gambolling children in green school hats, the shop's signage in royal blue. Emily kept the picture in her bedroom, more or less hidden away, because she didn't want to explain its presence to visitors.

She didn't want to tell them that her father, Ian Asquith, had killed himself when she was seven years old. She had her stepfather's surname: Main. She didn't want to invite questions about her father because she did not have all the answers. The painting, and perhaps the Lucky's franchise, might have been meaningful to him, but that meaning was private, entirely lost to his daughter. Some mornings, when getting herself ready for work, the picture was another small object in her field of vision. But sometimes she looked at the painting on the bedroom wall and remembered the last day she spent with her father; in her mind she was again visiting him on an autumn day in 1971. Sometimes she tried to tell her seven-year-old self: he's not going to live for long. Hug him, hold his hand and make him feel better and he won't kill himself. Enjoy his company, or pretend to enjoy it. Maybe you can change his mind.

How could she explain this painting to Lucky when she hid the thing in her own bedroom, when she couldn't explain it to herself? But maybe he was the right person to tell. Maybe he would take the picture at its simplest value: a representation of a building on her wall at home. Not a haunted picture. A representation of Lucky's legacy, not her father's. Maybe Lucky could transfigure the image, modify its power.

'In a sense, I've been thinking about Lucky's for a long time,' Emily began. 'I've a painting of one of your restaurants in my home.'

'No kidding! I should have a painting like that. I got photographs, as you can see.'

'My father painted it. He gave me the picture not long before he died.'

'What was your father's name?'

'Ian Asquith.'

'Never met anyone with that name.'

Emily could practically see the lie: there it was in the lights of his eyes. Why would Lucky lie, of all things, about her father? She reached into her bag. In a pocket of her purse was a photograph of Asquith; the photo had been buried in the minor compartments of consecutive purses. Years had passed since she'd showed her father to anyone.

'Definitely, the resemblance is clear as can be,' Lucky said. 'That's nice to see, the likeness between parent and child.'

'I needed to ask whether you knew him,' Emily said with too much emphasis, swallowing forcefully.

'I'm sorry that I didn't, but I'm pleased you're here,' said Lucky. 'Now, about the shooting—I'm sure you'll want to address that event in your article. It goes without saying that what happened was a terrible business. It's tragic what happened to my franchise. But the whole truth, the full story, the entire sweep of its history, in many respects, is a happy thing indeed and I hope you recognise that. See, we need each other. You need me to cooperate for the article, and I need you to tell the totally true, evenly considered and comprehensive story of the franchise. The final word, in a high-profile magazine.'

'I'm not eulogising the business,' said Emily.

'And it's too early for a eulogy! I'm going to revive the

franchise,' said Lucky. 'I'm going to give that business a good ending.'

'How do you intend to do that?'

'I'll explain soon. A few details must be worked out. But I can't talk long today—I should have mentioned that on the phone. For now, here's a souvenir.' And Lucky reached into a linen bag on the kitchen table and handed Emily a rolled-up T-shirt. She held it up and read the slogan printed with a Hellenic-style font: LUCKY'S FOR US.

1945

1.

LUCKY MALLIOS PRETENDED to be someone else. Pale and clean-shaven, his hair parted on the other side, he sat dressed in another man's uniform, inside a military jeep nosing out of Railway Square. On the back seat next to him lay the most important prop—a clarinet. In the front passenger seat was his accomplice, Gregor, and behind the wheel sat a US Navy pool driver, a nice guy, who'd asked Lucky and Gregor for a cigarette and then offered them a lift. Lucky had a round face, wore spectacles, and fell outside what *Yank Down Under* magazine described as the ideal weight-to-height ratio. People said he resembled the big band musician Benny Goodman.

When the car reached speed, the driver passed back a slip of paper and Lucky signed a counterfeit autograph, his hand shaking. He always kept a Dixon pencil in his shirt pocket.

'Nice to have a bona fide genius in town, Mr Goodman,' said the driver.

'Thank you,' said Lucky, disclosing a nervous cough. 'It's my first time in Sydney.'

The imposter Lucky and his accomplice Gregor were on a two-week furlough from an Army Air Force base in Bankstown, where they'd held low-status, danger-free hospitality jobs for eight months. Mallios was a mess steward: twenty-one years old, no family. The airmen liked to call him 'Benny'. It was their idea of an insult. As a joke—though it was barely that—the pilots invited 'Benny' to play at the barracks or they suggested he perform at the dance hall for the locals. To these requests he usually responded with a shrug, saying he couldn't play a note. At times he kidded along and told them sure, he would, he'd perform the night after next, and the airmen laughed at the incongruity between a famous guy and a worthless mess steward.

To the other mess kitchen auxiliaries, Lucky said if he did resemble Benny Goodman, then he was sick of hearing about it all the time. Another thing—he told his mess steward buddy, Gregor—he, Lucky Mallios, used to play the clarinet, and the trumpet on occasion, for a union-sponsored big band in Chicago. His bandmates gave him the nickname 'Lucky' because they said he was lucky to ever get the job. After a few months they kicked him out. That's rough stuff, said Gregor. Music is an unkind scene, said Lucky. He joined other bands, and the nickname followed him, but he couldn't fit in with other musicians, whom he considered either swine or aloof. They all seemed to think themselves more talented than Lucky. Still he was sturdy, self-believing: he thought he was good enough to one day join the Glenn Miller Orchestra, for example. Such self-belief mitigated his music-related disappointments.

In the air force, he introduced himself as Lucky, claiming that the nickname referred to his luck in poker; he intended to take ownership of the slur, to wheel the dumb joke around on all these jackasses. And at the base in Sydney he might have responded to the airmen's false offers with an actual performance, he could have played for these puffed-up pilots, but he imagined the scene would do him few favours; it would be a naked display of cornered indignation.

One night, after they'd incinerated a discouraging amount of dinner waste, Lucky stayed up late with Gregor in the mess hall kitchen. They drank dark coffee in the billiard-hall glow of the room, and there Gregor outlined his big idea: in February, they would take leave and tour a few eastern cities in Australia. It would be a fake United Services Organizations tour, a solo event and thus modestly publicised. Lucky would play Benny Goodman, and Gregor his manager, and no one would ever find out their true identities.

At least Gregor—who would die at the age of twenty-six, knowledgeable only in quantity cooking—needed no convincing of Lucky's artistic ability. For some time,

Gregor had believed that cooking and making music were associated fields, and he hoped one day to test this connection himself on either piano or string instrument. With a certain glare and steady tone of voice, Gregor described his plan as if it were perfect, as if Lucky would easily agree. They did not like their lives. They were bored stewards. Something needed to change.

Gregor said: 'Worst that can happen is we get caught by military police who throw us into jail for a spell, and later we get court-martialled. But y'know what? That ain't gonna happen.'

'That's a terrible worst case.'

'We'll be real careful,' Gregor said. 'All we need to do is to get our hands on a good clarinet. It will be damn hard to find one in Sydney.'

'How well do you know the place?'

'Just what I hear,' said Gregor.

'And what do you hear?'

'It's not a town bursting with brass.'

'You mean woodwind.'

'Woodwind, then, sure,' Gregor said. 'You agree then? You'll run this caper with me?'

Lucky looked around the kitchen, taking in the cleanliness and order he and Gregor brought to the mess: the meals, the service, the cleaning.

'I don't know,' said Lucky. 'We'd be deceiving other people.'

'Screw other people,' said Gregor. 'They should know better.'

'I don't want to go to jail.'

27

'Look where we work. Look at this shit. The guys we serve don't even know our proper names. What are you doing here? Killing time?'

'Not killing anything. Staying alive.'

'Don't you want something more from life? Don't you want to be someone else for a while—someone who isn't the butt of a joke?'

Lucky had joined the army air force because his elder brother, John the Terrible, joined the infantry. Their boyhoods had long mingled in relentless sibling conflict over who, between them, came first at school and at games, at accumulating friends and winning praise and provoking fear. John (born Yiannis) was the most sadistic boy in Greektown; he might have been the most evil kid in all Chicago. He had the habit, after he won a fistfight, of holding down his opponent and cutting the boy's legs or arms with a paring knife, because that's how they used to conclude duels on the Eptanisa, the seven western islands, or so he'd heard from the old guys who worked at the Marathon Diner with John's father. But Lucky's parents wouldn't hear a word against John, wouldn't accept or acknowledge that he terrorised weaker boys and that, during fraternal disagreements, he would grab Lucky's genitals and threaten to cut them off. Their parents saw only a first-born son who was handsome and spoke confidently, who believed in God. John the Terrible believed he would one day be rich and mother and father would share in that wealth. They celebrated John; Lucky observed this celebration. Their parents spoke Greek to John, but English to Lucky.

The younger Mallios knew he was a better person than his cruel sibling, but he needed to prove this point; he had to enlist, he couldn't let big brother get away with it. Lucky couldn't stay at home in Greektown, playing and failing in swing bands, while John fought in the 25th infantry. The army air force assigned Lucky to mess duties while John the Terrible was in combat on the New Georgia Islands.

Lucky told Gregor: 'Sure, I want to be appreciated.'

'You feel like you have something to prove,' said Gregor. 'You want adventure, not this tedium all day. Yes, fine, you're not a hero like your brother. Not everyone is cut out for the battlefield. You're a musician, you're a romantic deep down. Act like a romantic then.'

Lucky said: 'It does a person good to get away with something, doesn't it?'

'Thing is,' said Gregor, 'you *do* look like Benny Goodman. You don't look Greek. Not much anyhow.'

It was resolved. Lucky intended to prove that, despite his nickname, despite his fortunes, he *was* a real musician. He could play like a famous guy—he could well *be* a famous guy. The perilous game of being Benny Goodman would prove his worth beyond question, to other people, to himself.

Gregor bought a clarinet for three pounds plus ten US dollars from Maeve Doyle, a friend of sorts, whose fiancé had died in France the previous year. Gregor had met her at the hotel in Canterbury where she worked, but Maeve wasn't interested in romance and straightaway told him so—in a friendly way. He worked in an air force mess; he could be useful to her as an agent of regular trade in basic items. He brought her rationed goods, such as nylons and spaghetti, biscuits and bacon, matches that didn't break, toilet soap and toothpowder, tinned ham and herring, and also one alarm clock, the scarcest of items. In return she gave him fresh sauces, sweets, baked food. She found him novels—westerns and thrillers, chosen simply for the preposterousness of the author's name.

Gregor came out to meet Maeve at the Bankstown Airport gates. She had the clarinet inside a suitcase, cushioned with a green velvet scarf.

'Will you tell me why you need this thing?' she said.

'If you keep it quiet.'

'Not a soul, friend.'

'My buddy is going to impersonate a famous musician on tour.'

'A bold plan!'

'It's been well thought out and we're confident nothing can go wrong. You should come along to a concert.'

'I'm going to wish you well.'

Lucky and Gregor applied for leave: the leave was approved. Every night for the next week, after dinner service, Lucky walked from the barracks dormitory to a dry stockroom inside a yard controlled by a vicious dog that had lately mauled a hungry pilot. But the dog loved Lucky, the man who never failed to bring food. In the storeroom, he practised arrangements from *Roll 'Em* and *Swing into Spring*. His newly acquired folio of sheet music, *Benny Goodman's Recorded Clarinet Solos* (Bregman, Vocco & Conn, 1938), was not well-bound: Lucky let the challenging booklet flop open at random pages and he played what he saw. In the daytime, when a musical idea came to him, he stopped and went to the storeroom and played for a few minutes. Meantime, Maeve got hold of some uniforms. She supposed British army khakis might pass for USO dress.

2.

In their first substantive act of fraud, Lucky and Gregor took a train to Central Station and outside, in character, approached a jeep in which the driver sat sunning himself. Gregor introduced Benny Goodman and asked for a lift. The driver said sure thing, he'd be real honoured.

The jeep's excited driver steered with one hand and with the other flaunted his knowledge of Sydney as the eastern suburbs brushed past Lucky's nervous eyes (terraces, churches), until the tourists graced their destination: a community hall. The driver reminded Lucky of a movie villain; he couldn't remember which film.

'Odd thing,' said the driver as he stopped the car, 'but there was a military police car behind us a couple streets back.'

'And where's it now?' asked Lucky.

'Can't see 'em. Maybe they're for your protection?'

'Yes,' said Gregor. 'That's it.'

Out on the footpath, Lucky said: 'I suspect that guy knew something.'

'He didn't know squat,' said Gregor. 'Stay composed and we'll get through this.'

A few weeks earlier, Gregor had written twenty near-identical letters to hotels and government clerks in the two largest Australian cities, proposing a short concert. He did not write to the service clubs, the American Red Cross Society or official USO clubs, or the Booker T. Washington Club or the Trocadero, because these were places where frauds might easily be detected. There were a million Americans stationed in Australia (the figure Lucky cited from the *Sydney Morning Herald*). One million uniformed men (or perhaps fewer), and Lucky and Gregor feared them all for their knowledge of popular music. In his letters, written on US Army Air Force letterhead, Gregor made clear the shows were for civilians only: 'a small thank you for so much hospitality'.

There were five requests for a concert and an itinerary was devised: Sydney first, then Melbourne. The imposters would take trains of various gauges to Victoria and back, unless they could talk their way onto military flights. Which Gregor was determined to do. A depressing pattern, they'd heard, of a thousand miles of harsh countryside and stations with sinking platforms and green verandah roofs was not something you submitted yourself to, if you were a great musician.

To the left of the community hall was a funeral parlour. On the right, beyond a vacant lot, stood a brick home surrounded by cypress trees. Lucky held the clarinet case with both hands, thinking of the first tune he'd play. Breathe with the diaphragm, like making yourself fat.

Two men in uniform came out of the hall and waved to Gregor and Lucky.

Gregor said: 'You know these guys?'

'Let's walk away.'

'They've seen us already—we'll talk to them. You're Benny and I'm your manager. It's going to be fine.'

The two men wore expressions Lucky found startling, comic up to a point. One of the MPs was tall and broad with thinning black hair. The other had large ears and said: 'May I have your autograph, Mr Goodman?'

'No problem at all,' said Lucky.

'Hell of a joke,' said the MP with big ears.

'What do you mean by that?' asked Lucky, looking up from the scrap of paper on which he'd made a mess. The false signature was not at all natural.

'We heard about your little concert today. You ain't Benny Goodman.'

'I damned well am!' said Lucky.

'And I'm Gary Cooper. And he's Wallace Beery. It's funny the shit you end up doing in a war.'

'Benny is who he says he is, got that?' said Gregor. 'Now we must leave. We have an engagement.'

The big guy countered: 'We can say for sure you're not Benny Goodman.'

'How do you know?' asked Lucky. 'I'm only asking out of curiosity.'

''Cause we're MPs and there's a thousand Americans leaving Sydney each week, give or take, and hardly anyone new coming in. We'd know if a big personality like Benny Goodman was arriving.'

'And you look nothing like him,' added his colleague.

'Sure he does!' said Gregor.

'Kid, I know what Benny Goodman looks like. The man is a star.'

'We must be going,' said Lucky. 'I'm late for something.'

'You ain't late.'

Gregor said: 'Come on, we're all Americans. We're good people here.'

'Right there, yep, that's changed my mind.'

'I tell you what's going to happen now,' said the other MP. 'The four of us are walking to our vehicle and we're going for a drive.'

'Absolutely not,' said Lucky. 'We're not going anywhere.'

Lucky sat rigid in the sedan, reluctant to ask questions about how they were caught or what would happen next, in case such queries invited answers he didn't want to hear, in case the two strangers hadn't yet decided what they were going to do with the Benny Goodman imposter and had only cruel, by-the-book remedies close at hand. Lucky decided to say nothing. He was still in that space between being caught and being punished, when a reprieve seemed like the obvious and best solution for everyone. That way he'd still get to play Benny Goodman. They, these trumped-up police, couldn't understand what lay behind the fraud; it wasn't another scheme, a dumb prank—it had meaning.

On the ride westwards, he absorbed as many details as he could: a face in a shop window, fabric tangled in a poplar. Each detail appeared oddly distant, mocking his present situation. A slate-grey morning leaned on the European trees along a boulevard. The military police asked how Lucky could have dared to impersonate Benny Goodman. Goodman was a famous person!

They stopped on a short street. The man in the back seat, the marginally more aggressive of the two MPs, produced a revolver when he exited the car—he was a small-framed but large-eared man with a cold red complexion, whom Lucky would later refer to as 'Frank', since he never gave a name. The other MP was a minotaur with a square forehead—he would be known as 'Harry' to his pair of captives. The prisoners were ordered to the doorstep of a two-storey building behind a leprous wooden fence. Harry assisted Lucky's passage with a helpful punch in the back, before he opened the front door and led the imposters down a long hallway to a dark room, locking them inside.

Lucky and Gregor both swore gently. They felt their way around in short introspective steps, their boots scraping across the unswept concrete floor. There was one dormitory bed, one sad toilet, a light globe fixed to the wall. A golden bar of light came from under the heavy door.

'You know, it's bad,' Gregor observed, 'but is this a cell?'

'I think indeed it is a cell.'

Gregor sat down, claiming the bed. 'You're supposed to be doing a concert right now!'

Lucky stood in the corner underneath an air vent—a grille cut into the brickwork, through which strained the soubrette laughter of a woman somewhere outside.

'You scared?' asked Gregor.

'Sure, I'm scared.'

'I'm not, funnily enough.'

'That's because you're not smart.'

Lucky hadn't fully appreciated how difficult the USO fraud might be, how ill conceived, how inappropriate a sidekick was Gregor, and he acknowledged such shortcomings as he floated about in the dimness of their cell. Lucky's next idea: to appeal their detention. With the pencil he'd used to sign a Benny Goodman autograph, he composed a plea on the only paper he possessed: a folded piece of six-by-nine-inch, torn days ago from the mess kitchen pad, on which he'd meant to compile a list of songs to play. He wrote:

Dear Sirs,

We believe there has been a big misunderstanding and that our detention here is unlawful. I think that we can come to an agreement, whatever the problem may be, as soon as we are released. We hope that occurs soon.

Many regards,

Lucky

Lucky posted his note under the door and passed the night awake. Gregor slept a good eight hours, just about. In some ways the night encompassed much for Lucky: rage, regret, confusion, fear, the swearing of oaths to certain changes (for example, abandoning his childhood delusions about music). But he knew these feelings well. He knew they would soon pass. Imprisonment might be a less transient condition. Lucky and Gregor stayed in the ad hoc jail for six nights.

1913–1939

1.

THE CAFE ACHILLION played a precursor role in the story of Lucky's restaurants: it was the prototype from which Lucky worked; it was the home he corrected. His restaurant franchise reproduced the architecture of the Achillion and its colours, the style of silverware, the window displays, the oval plates and menu. Even the idea of a franchise did not begin with Lucky. That dream—a proliferation of Achillions—first belonged to Achilles Asproyerakas, whose destiny warrants description. The regulars called him 'Mad Achilles', though never to his face, never within earshot. To some customers, Achilles functioned as a bogeyman, a child-frightener, the devil's substitute in the suburb of Bardwell Park, Sydney. Parents told naughty children that if their behaviour did not improve quick smart they would be sent down to the cafe, where Mad Achilles would punish them in the terrible ways that people suffered in myths and fairytales.

Achilles had left the island of Ithaka at the age of sixteen, carrying his father's amber worry beads in his pocket. His uncle, a Sydney fishmonger, offered to sponsor the boy as long as he lied about his age to immigration officials. Achilles' father explained that the offer amounted to peonage, that the first few months in Sydney might be harsh. He was a fisherman and each month went further and further out into the Ionian Sea: on the boat he spoke broken Italian in an attempt to fool the fish into thinking he was bad at his trade. 'The sea is a secret underneath,' his father said. 'Much better to work in a fish shop than to ever be a fisherman.' Achilles' mother, who agreed, told her son that he must stay unmarried, pay off the debt to his uncle, succeed in Sydney, and come home to remove his parents from the peasantry.

When Achilles did return to Ithaka, twelve years later, on a second-class passage, he was class IV bald like his father. His worsted suit had been purchased with money made cutting cane on sugar plantations in southern Queensland, where Achilles worked after quitting the fishmongers in Sydney, tired of being exploited by casually cruel blood relatives. Most important, he brought back a large opal ring he thought might impress someone—somebody who wouldn't realise or mind how desolate he was inside. Achilles wanted two things: a wife, and money to build a cafe. He hadn't bothered to bring back presents for his family. In a paper shop in Circular Quay he'd looked at postcards and considered these as gifts, but thought better of it. Did anyone in Ithaka send him cards? Did anyone anywhere? By now his parents had long ceased to harbour expectations of Achilles as a provider in their old age. Whole years had passed in which he did not write to them, and they thought he was out of reach, his life itinerant. At times they feared he was no longer alive.

If the village of Vathi had changed much, Achilles could not tell. He did not care. His parents' home was a square building of whitewashed walls with a pitched roof and a yellow front door that faced Mount Neriton. He sat down and told his mother and father what he'd been meaning to say for a long time: they sent him away too young. He wanted them to look guilty and squirm; he would have thanked God for the sight of his parents sobbing. They did not weep.

Sitting at their dining table, a felt hat hooked over his knee, Achilles made little effort to hide his disapproval of everything (their table was unsteady, his coffee not sweet enough), and it occurred to his mother that Achilles might have been angry with them on a day-by-day basis, year after year, when they'd spent that same time in various degrees of worry and regret over him. Now this was the result. The three of them could hardly have a conversation. To Achilles, the rain on the village and the dark condemning sky approximated his feelings and offered him a kind of support.

'You should be ashamed of sending me away,' he said.

'We wouldn't have done it if we'd known you'd be this unhappy,' his mother replied. 'But you're here now. Why don't you make a life in Ithaka or even Kefalonia?'

'It's too late for that.'

By this time Achilles had acquired the heated, brisk tone of voice that would characterise him for the rest of his life. A marriage was quickly arranged with Eleftheria, the artistically minded daughter of the village tailor, and they were wedded on 22 August at The Chapel of the Transfiguration of the Saviour in Vathi. The combination of her dowry and his savings would give them enough money to start their own cafe in Sydney. Achilles already had the spot picked out.

Achilles' block of land in Bardwell Park allowed for a shop, an adjoining home behind and a large yard, where he intended to plant olive trees, figs, oranges, lemons. Most important of all, he planned to grow grapevines, under the shade of which he might one day sit and feel content, no longer driven so unhappily by ambition, by anger.

The cafe building went up in six weeks.

'What does your last name mean?' asked one of the bricklayers, a man named Tom.

'Asproyerakas is a white hawk.'

'Then change your name to White or Hawke,' said Tom, as if solving for Achilles some problem they'd been working on for weeks.

He had no intention of altering his surname. Not all early Greeks were convinced to abbreviate or Anglicise: he followed the examples of Kalokorinos, Varvaressos, Papadamatis, Morfopoulos. As for the name Achilles, he'd already modified it from Achilleas: he thought this by-the-letter allusion would only aid his aspirations. The hero of *The Iliad* was uncompromising, singular, no one's employee, not a person to be cheated.

Achilles—who wore the Greek-Australian service industry uniform of grey shorts, white shirt and long white socks—liked to tell Eleftheria of his determination to never again work for someone else, to rather kill a man than work for one. He taught his wife English and ignored most of her attempts to communicate in Greek. When she teased or taunted him in their first language, Achilles responded in English, because he didn't want a word of Greek spoken in the cafe: he said using a foreign language in front of customers was rude, terrible for business.

As a new husband, Achilles felt disposed to remain wilfully ignorant of his wife's emotional life; he reckoned they had time to get to know each other. He didn't want to hear what Eleftheria missed about Ithaka, didn't ask her questions about her past, didn't want to spend any time on matters that might inflame her sadness and bring it into the open. To him, she remained an immensity of private feelings.

Eleftheria gave up speaking Greek but did not abandon her artistic inclinations. In spare moments stolen from the cafe, and for reasons Achilles couldn't understand, she sketched what her husband considered to be the most unremarkable objects in the cafe, things unworthy of representation, barely deserving of notice: the shop fittings, boxes of powders, stacks of aluminium ashtrays, the clock, jars of fat. Yet she made not one sketch of their two daughters. Achilles worried that Eleftheria's unfathomable interior life was somehow coded in these drawings, that each picture was an expression of disgust.

'Why do you draw?' Achilles once asked.

'I don't know,' said Eleftheria. And she left her still lifes in a pile on the side table in their bedroom.

'What will you do with these pictures?' Achilles would ask.

'Nothing,' she would say. 'I have to make them, I have to put them somewhere.'

When Eleftheria was especially unhappy she'd tear up and dispose of these sketches. The next week she'd start drawing again: the same objects, the things that stuck up like icebergs in her visible world. They were yet to properly fit together, Mr and Mrs Asproyerakas. Maybe one day they would make a good life possible for each other: this was how Achilles thought of his marriage, as cold stuff that would slowly melt into some better shape. But Eleftheria died before any such transformation could occur.

In 1938, during her last days at Prince Alfred Hospital, in a room to herself, with cancer in her bowels and lungs and liver, Eleftheria kept returning in her mind to the problem of her marriage.

She asked the nurse: 'Why my parents make me marry that man?'

The nurse said: 'I don't know. Arranged marriages aren't the custom here.'

Eleftheria's two daughters, Valia and Penelope, were both children at the time they were bereaved. That commonplace notion—that each of us grieves idiosyncratically—was true for the Asproyerakas family, but one dilemma was the same: none could say they truly knew the wife of Achilles.

2.

Nineteen thirty-nine. At the hottest time of day, Valia and Penny, twelve and ten years old, climbed onto the corrugated-iron roof of the Cafe Achillion. The gauge on the verandah read thirty-eight degrees Celsius. Achilles was inside, behind the stove, watching bacon crisp. There were customers in the cafe, and the girls trod lightly. Valia and Penny stood at the midpoint of the cafe's pitched roof, a feature that Valia associated with pictures of the prows on ancient boats. A few rocks had rained onto the iron: they assumed these came from the Anglo-Celtic boys of the suburb.

The sisters removed their shoes and stood facing each other on the corrugated iron, one bare foot on either side of the roof arch. They wanted to see who, between them, could stand on the hot metal surface for the longer time. If you could bear the burning sensation, if you could forget about its sting long enough, you won the game, the test of your capacity for pain.

'What will happen to us without a mother?' Valia wondered aloud on the rooftop.

'I don't know! My feet are hurting already,' said Penelope.

What always happened then duly happened: Valia succeeded. Penny sat down first on the roof, making the sounds *ow ow ow,* and plunged her feet back into shoes.

'Don't make so much noise,' said Valia. 'There are customers inside.'

Valia enjoyed the sight of jacaranda trees in the distance: she'd come to know what it felt like to appease her own wilfulness.

3.

That year, at the outbreak of war, Achilles told his daughters that he had queued at the recruitment branch like all the other men—like other fathers, he wanted to do his duty—but the army did not have a service shirt to fit his broad chest, and the stupid army people had refused to enlist him.

'It's done then,' Achilles said. 'I'm not meant for war.'

At night the sisters convened in Valia's bedroom to discuss their father. The eldest Asproyerakas daughter believed the recruitment branch story was poorly conceived in several ways. She told Penelope that widowers were not allowed to serve in the military, and even if their mother were alive he wouldn't leave his business. Achilles couldn't leave his daughters because he believed they belonged to him; he thought men owned women, that families were possessions created by transactions. Their beloved mother had brought a dowry. But Penelope disagreed: she suspected that her father told the truth—yes, he did try to enlist. Probably he wanted to fight; he wanted to hurt people.

It didn't matter to Achilles whether they believed him. That he had made the effort to lie and save face was enough.

~

He objected to the popular idea that all Greek-owned cafes in Australia were copies of one another, identical in architectural design, offering the same dishes at similar prices, served on creamy, oversized, oval plates. But he never convinced himself that his own establishment was a thing of originality. There were times when he looked at the large sign that hung above the kitchen door—

OUR MOTTO: CLEANLINESS AND CIVILITY

—and was reminded that an identical motto was installed at cafes run by the Economos family elsewhere in Sydney, and the Koutsakis family in Melbourne (who owed Achilles a favour). They followed each other in the fledgling sense of a new tradition. But Achilles held on to some sense of distinction: for example, no one cooked as well as he did. And he had in mind an enormous chain of cafes—a franchise of outlets all named the Cafe Achillion. First: a few more years of profit at the Achillion in Bardwell. Second: a loan for a sister business. Then: great success and many outlets nationwide.

On the main street, the Cafe Achillion neighboured a weakly lit pharmacy—all drawers and cabinets, no open shelves—run by a Catholic family who held moral objections to contraceptives. Such products could be easily and discreetly procured from Achilles, at the cafe, so long as you approached the man himself and not his eldest daughter. Special customers popped in and took away large paper bags of Dunlop condoms, and it dismayed Achilles that

45

many of these men were clearly odd. Even mad bastards had a lot of sex. At the other side of the cafe was an empty allotment that nursed brown weeds and crawlers that ensnared flyaway newspapers, cigarette butts and pet dogs. Achilles was appalled by the vacant plot and the imaginative and entrepreneurial vacuum that allowed it to exist, but he rarely went onto the street and could forget about the eyesore for weeks at a time, until its presence came to him in a passing rage.

The entrance to the Cafe Achillion was one boundary of what might be called Achilles' world, outside of which he felt vulnerable and alien.

You entered through tall saloon doors set on a terrazzo entrance step. On either side of these doors, shallow awnings came down like brows over the windows. The Cafe Achillion's two window displays were bedded with coloured tissue paper: the left display was reserved for fruit and vegetables (only legumes in ration times) and the right for tobacco products and small items associated with male and female grooming, mainly creams and brushes. The cafe, Achilles told customers, had the largest selection of combs in suburban Sydney, no competition. Valia took care of the displays and Achilles appreciated her eye. The cafe's slate floor, crazy-paved with cream tiles in brown mortar, had been sold as a Cubist design and one fashionable in Europe. There was no pattern remotely like it in the southern hemisphere. This was true. You got used to the floor. Along one wall were seven booths, appropriate for five adults each, and along the other wall was a long counter—this space was

Valia's domain. Behind the kitchen was a windowless central hallway that terminated in a living room with a back door to a verandah. The bedrooms lay off the passageway. There were three bedrooms: Penny's, Valia's and Achilles'—but Achilles hadn't slept in his room for years, since Eleftheria's death, preferring to rest on the back verandah, which he had enclosed with louvre windows and canvas curtains. Instead, he used his former bedroom to keep bread and packets of cigarettes; things that would spoil or be stolen if stored outside or behind the counter. In the yard was a shed for dry goods, an overgrown olive tree, a kitchen garden with radishes and herbs, an enclave of grapevines, lemon trees and, amid this, the stump of a banksia. (Achilles found the large native tree ugly and obstructive; he left the stump in the ground because he found it aesthetically pleasing. Also, he liked signs of his own governance.) From underneath this dead banksia slab, during rain showers, huntsman spiders ventured forth into house and cafe. Achilles devoted his spare time to pest control, fearing the cafe would be overrun with bugs, that something terrible would happen to his family.

2002

1.

ON EMILY'S FIRST day in Sydney, Lucky told her nothing about the Benny Goodman fraud, or the Cafe Achillion, or where he'd found the funds to start the franchise, or how he'd find the money to open a new restaurant. The interview was brief. Lucky promised to talk at length another time. He walked Emily down to her rental car and she allowed any pauses in conversation to hang in the air between them, hoping that Lucky might feel pressure to say something, to offer information. And he did; as he raised his voice to compete with the rumble of a plane overhead, Lucky recommended she get in contact with a detective, Peter Popescu, who'd attended the scene at the cafe on the Third of April. Popescu, who had since left the police force, Lucky said, was the sort of cop who liked to give his opinion. He now worked for a company that sold medical supplies to clinics and hospitals.

A few months ago the former detective had called Lucky out of the blue, and contacted also the survivor of the shooting, Sophia Cootes, to see how they were doing many years later.

'I'm still in touch with Sophia,' Lucky added. 'She's the daughter of Valia, my ex-wife. The child of her second marriage. I wouldn't say she's like a daughter to me, because that sounds corny, but I like Sophia and her kid. I don't see them often. We're all busy, I guess. Different times of life.'

'Do you have children of your own?' Emily asked.

'No family at all,' Lucky said, grinning broadly, as if everything had worked out for the best, as if this fact about his life had happened according to plan. 'Do you have kids?'

'I was going to have a child, but now I'm probably not,' she said, opening the car door. The possibility had been extinguished—she tried to build a family home and the walls came tumbling down. She felt like a cartoon character who'd smartly pursued something across the desert only to be squashed by a dumb object. Oh well, she thought. Oh fucking well.

2.

The midday streets behind the beach clattered with prams and bicycles and the clap of thonged feet. Cars could barely move. A tourist helicopter veered inland and white gulls floated above the water. The sea, as the tide receded, dropped like loose freight onto the sand, leaving behind little curls of sea vegetation. Emily leaned on the promenade wall and felt herself abstracted by the movement of

49

the ocean and thousands of accumulating bodies. The sun shone as if stuck.

Peter Popescu would be good at interviews. Probably he'd conducted many of them, even hundreds, with victims and perpetrators, with high stakes. He might be better at interviews than Emily. Maybe he would be a prick about it. She saw, again, how the world could turn hostile all of a sudden: one moment she was looking at a beautiful beach—the spectacle of all those people *there* in the experience—and the next minute she might be asking for information from someone who hated her tone, her accent, her questions, someone who thought she'd come all this way to make a mess of things.

He had suggested they meet in a park behind Coogee Beach; since it was a weekend, he said, and a shame to be anywhere else. He would be wearing a green sort of fishing hat, and Emily, who'd arrived early, spotted him almost as soon as she turned her gaze away from the water. He sat sedately on a bench, a folded magazine in one hand (the *New Yorker*). There was a large black circle on the cover, like a portal to someplace. He stood up and then sat down when she did the same.

'I'm a subscriber,' Popescu explained. 'I always bring a copy down to the beach with me. It's not for show. I sit right here. So I reckon you've been reading about the Third of April?'

'The coronial findings, the psychiatric report. Everything I could find from old newspapers. The major dailies, anyway. What I'm looking for today is your perspective. How you see things almost eight years later.'

'My ex-boss won't like it, but too bad—I work private sector now. He thinks ex-police should stay quiet, out of sight; I think we should have a voice.'

This comment made Emily wary. People who believed themselves silenced could cause a scene when given the chance to speak. 'Tell me about Lucky's restaurants,' she suggested. 'The last one in particular.'

'There was a time when the Lucky's restaurants were associated with migrant culture, mostly Greeks emigrating after the Second World War and the Greek Civil War. The occupation damaged that country. The civil war wrecked it again. I knew some cafe Greeks and they'd often talk about the famine during the occupation. Then they came out here to cook enormous meals for Australians. I think of the franchise as an offshoot of the Greek-Australian cafe, which were diner-style restaurants. Mostly gone now. By the time Henry came along with his gun in '94, Lucky's was reduced to one cafe. The country was more diverse, racially and ethnically. At the final restaurant a couple of the staff had Greek heritage. One of the chefs was Chinese-Aussie, another Tongan. We're not talking about an exotic setting. It's modern Australia. The food they served was Anglo-American stuff.'

'Okay,' said Emily, and she was reminded of how much she disliked that conversational tic, saying okay. 'What do you think the media and the official reports got wrong about the Third of April? Is there something they missed?'

Popescu closed his eyes, as if trying to remember some distant detail, and Emily waited through these waves of thought.

He said: 'With Henry, there was enough discussion about his mental health, and his access to firearms, and the fact he was not well socialised. The *Daily Telegraph* ran a story about Henry being bullied for a time at school. He was a disturbed man, yes. You read the psych report: he was diagnosed with schizophrenia in his late teens, but later there was disagreement about the diagnosis. Another doctor found he suffered from severe depression. But if you ask me, what was not properly addressed was his extreme sense of entitlement.'

'Entitlement to what?'

'To everything he wanted. Henry was reacting to a perceived slight when he planned and committed the murders. On the day of the shooting he visited Lucky at home and asked for a job. After Lucky said no, Henry went to the restaurant and shot up the place. He wasn't desperate for work; he already had a part-time job with a demolition crew. But he felt entitled to a position at Lucky's.'

'Have you studied psychology?' asked Emily, and Popescu looked at her like this was a personal question.

'No, but I have plenty of experience with psychologists and psychiatrists, believe me.'

'Okay, so according to the coroner, when Henry visited Lucky's home a few minutes before the shooting he was only delaying what he was going to do. The gun was likely in his car already.'

'Yes, some shooters set up a distraction that will soon be exhausted. It's their way of playing with the world, of asserting their power. Henry devised a brief meeting that would likely convince him to go through with his plan.

It wasn't the first time he'd asked Lucky for a job. He knew what Lucky would say. I believe Henry saw himself as a victim of the world. He believed other people, all of us, treated him unfairly.'

'What makes you think this?'

'The violence was latent in his relationship with his parents. He didn't have a history of extreme displays of anger—no assault charges, no destruction of property. But he regularly threatened suicide, and well into his twenties he subjected his parents to screaming rages, typically over something he didn't get, like a job, or a person he thought was a fool, who'd thwarted him somehow. This anger was part of his defence mechanism. Henry's violent fantasies—which we can assume he nurtured, given the planning that went into the Third of April—made him feel less inadequate in the face of his disappointment. He had no friends, no partner. He frightened his parents. He probably had many rejection experiences because people could see there was something wrong with how he faced the world. When Lucky knocked him back for a job, the perceived slight amplified a defence mechanism that was already there.'

'What was driving that entitlement?'

'He believed he was better than other people,' Popescu said. 'It's obvious.'

Popescu removed his fishing hat: his hair, parted over his right ear, and his grey goatee beard made Emily think of football coaches and boxing gyms and vasectomies. He grew the beard, she presumed, after leaving the job.

Emily said: 'It was confronting for Henry whenever

53

someone challenged his belief that he was better than other people. But why was his violence so extreme after the rejection at Lucky's?'

'Henry was a regular customer at the cafe before he asked for a job. It was a world he knew, a world he'd chosen—but it didn't want him. It was a place he inhabited. Perhaps he thought of the cafe as a second home. And he responded to that rejection with incredible violence. He couldn't get what they had, so he took their lives, staff and customers.'

'What does Lucky think of this interpretation?'

'Ask him. And ask Henry's mother.'

'I want to interview her,' said Emily. 'Do you have a number?'

'I won't share contact details with the media. That's a rule of mine.'

He waved at a barefoot couple who passed by, each eating a packet of crisps, different flavours. Emily asked whether Popescu lived in Coogee and he said yes, until last year, he had a house back up the hill but he'd moved out of the family home and now lived a few suburbs away.

He said: 'You've met Lucky I guess? He's broke these days.'

'How exactly did that come about?'

'When he sold the franchise in the 1970s he was in debt. He must have run the business into the ground. Then he was left with one restaurant. After the shooting, he developed a gambling problem and lost everything.'

'He didn't mention gambling the other day.'

'Here's my tip: Lucky's unreliable, he won't tell you the whole story. I got to know him a little.'

'He plans to get back into business.'

'Lucky wants to start over in life? That doesn't surprise me. Reality is too small for him. But it would be a complete disaster. He's Don Quixote.'

'He said you called him recently. Are you friends?'

'Not friends. But he sounded happy to talk. I called Sophia, too, but she didn't say much.'

'Why would you call them?'

'You develop interests in the job. It's harmless. It's not obsessive. It would be a shame if people mistook kindness for being a creep,' said Popescu.

'No, Lucky vouched for you.'

'You know, I've thought of writing about the Third of April shooting myself, but I'd have to take time off work. Writing a book is the kind of work that costs you money to pursue. I have two houses to pay off. And I've never written anything. Maybe when I get long service leave.'

3.

Emily worked at the hotel. She made phone calls, she wrote notes, she scripted logical sequences of questions. Going through the motions took on a new significance when going through heartbreak. Everything work-related was a relief—not happiness but, for a few moments, a break from unhappiness.

Even before she lost her job and Michael confessed that he loved someone else, Emily had become aware that confidence was draining out of her, that somewhere along the way she'd changed, she'd grown out of her youthful self-possession and her sense of self hadn't been adequately replaced. She'd been parked on the subediting desk years ago, and she would have stayed there forever, her career decided. Now and then the editors would commission a sub to write a short review or a travel story—a sweetener to keep you on the copy desk. The last time she'd been on assignment was 1999, when *The Independent* sent her to the Venice Biennale for two days. Her brief was to produce an article from the perspective of someone for whom the Biennale was a new and strange experience, someone who didn't have art-world knowledge to retail and professional criticism to offer, since the paper had already run two such articles by regular critics. At a pavilion in the Giardini she'd got lucky and witnessed a fistfight break out between German performance artists and heckling audience members. One of the artists appeared to break his hand in the shouty toing and froing; Emily noticed there were a few teeth on the floor, but she couldn't tell to whom they belonged. No one picked them up. Emily was sitting with her notebook on her lap, describing the scene, when the Carabinieri arrived. 'Looks like this piece basically wrote itself,' said the features editor. But he never commissioned another word from Emily. No one did. No one accepted her pitches. In the newsroom the features editor was known as Uday, as in Hussein—a nickname coined by Emily—because he had a bad temper, shaved irregularly, and his father was the editor-in-chief. Uday's eyes were also large and reddishly tyrannical. Emily coined

several other unflattering nicknames in the newsroom of
The Independent, and the epithets never failed to take hold.
Two examples: a boozy subeditor frequently absent from
his desk was called Red October, after the Russian sub that
went missing; a self-important reporter named Donna,
who ate dinner late at night, became known as Kebab (or,
in full, Donna Kebab). Only in their absence, in safety, out
of earshot, out of the office, were they referred to as Uday,
Red October, and Kebab.

During her months of unemployment, Emily concluded
that Uday had heard about his nickname, its origins, and
pushed for her sacking.

Last week Michael had said that maybe all the petty
newsroom politics and the stasis of subediting, of
correcting the work of reporters and columnists she didn't
respect—maybe it wasn't bungled life but preparation for
this Sydney assignment? Michael, all that time, bending
over backwards to cheer up his wife while still making time
for his girlfriend.

More than once she'd asked him if her story idea was
good. He'd said all her ideas were great.

4.

Her father's suicide left seven-year-old Emily with an
impression: that she wasn't enough for him. That she wasn't
enough to keep him alive. Why would Ian kill himself
when he had Emily as a daughter? Maybe she'd said or done
something that she couldn't recall and couldn't identify as

coldness or misbehaviour given how complicated the adult world was, given her inability to understand why people did the weird things they did. As a teenager, she began to second-guess herself in class and around friends. At night she replayed conversations in her mind to identify when she'd misspoken and what she might have said otherwise. Her self-doubt interjected whenever she began to feel confident. One way she concealed this lack of confidence was by never asking for affirmation, by pretending not to care for other people's opinions of her.

As Emily grew older she became ever more curious about Ian Asquith, to her mother's obvious disappointment. She intended to be a good historian of her life. But the Asquiths, supposedly her kin, wanted nothing to do with the girl. Ian had two siblings, a brother and sister, both in Buckinghamshire, and when she was sixteen Emily wrote to each of them. Neither responded. And Emily's mother offered only a few flat stories about him, none that satisfied, none revealing enough, unless Asquith was in fact a flat person. Emily came to the view that her mother was withholding information that would have been unpleasant to discuss. The mother wanted to move on! The daughter could not.

Emily's mother, Heidi, would say the following: There was only so much you could know about the past. Only so much you could know about your own story. Emily found it difficult to accept these loud conditions.

It had occurred to her that the article about Lucky's was a substitute for the real story of her father.

Sometimes, at night, she would close her eyes and her dead father spoke to her. She imagined him saying what she needed him to say. I'm sorry. I made a mistake. We are alike, but you won't end up like me. You won't have a life like mine.

5.

A card slipped under the door of Emily's hotel room. Michael had called twice while she was out. *Please call home*, was the message.

'The thing is,' said Michael, 'I do love you.'

'No you don't. You really don't.'

'I'm in love with two people at the same time.'

'I don't think you are!'

'My relationship with Therese was entirely unavoidable. It's something that *happened*.'

'Yes, it certainly *happened*.'

'All right. Look, your mother called,' said Michael. 'She forgot you'd gone to Australia. Have you told her about . . .'

'About you fucking this girl? No. That's a conversation I can look forward to sometime soon.'

They spoke like this for five minutes or so, while Emily stared out the window at a man walking up and down, perhaps looking for an address, until she'd had enough of the conversation and ended the call.

There had been many times, years ago, when Emily tried to counsel heartbroken friends who had separated from a lover or spouse. The most crucial condition of that friend's former relationship or marriage, she said, was the reciprocal nature of the love. Once that reciprocation ended, the friend was in love with a lie, with a person who existed in the past and was now a product of invention. It was *impossible*, she'd maintained, to remain in love for long with an object you knew to be false. In Sydney, Emily reminded herself of this advice, but it gave no comfort at all. She sat at her hotel room desk with a newspaper and a glass of cold water, barely reading the paper, and sipping from the glass as if it were liquor. She went to bed and pulled the sheets to her chin, before getting up again and mooching around her room. She thought of Michael and Therese in the flat in London; she thought of them naked on the carpet between the couch and the television, and she could hardly bear to imagine this scene, yet there it was, pronounced in her mind like a memory, and Emily could not picture herself entering the flat in London and sitting on that couch again, knowing what they might have done, how they must have felt.

After sending Liam a three-sentence email—*I'm here. And you were right about Michael having an affair. He's in love with someone named Therese*—she emerged from her hotel room, blue-skirted, white-bloused. She ate Balkan food on Crown Street. She drank wine in a bar. When Emily looked at the faces of strangers in Sydney—and the same thing often happened in other foreign cities—she was reminded of people back in London, seizing on some resemblance: everywhere she saw the Australian doubles of ex-colleagues and old friends, her mind mitigating the distance from home. In Emily's stomach a wheel of anxiety turned whenever she saw somebody who looked like Michael.

On the way home from the bar she stopped on a footpath, transfixed, alone in the spectacle, as dozens of enormous bats circled a tower in what looked like delirium.

1945

1.

AFTER SEVERAL DAYS in the cell, their food and water brought to them with barely a word from their captors, Lucky and Gregor ran clean out of subjects to discuss. To break the silence Lucky whistled or hummed one of the Benny Goodman tunes he'd intended to perform, such as 'Why Don't You Do Right?' or 'Don't Be That Way'. Sunlight strayed through air vents high in the wall. Their worsening body odours crammed the air like balls of fat. On the final morning of their captivity, Gregor said in a shaky voice, 'Oh fucking hell,' and it sounded to Lucky's ears like someone far away crying out: '*I'm stuck in a well.*'

'Keep it together!' said Lucky.

'What are they doing to us? This is torture!'

It might have been another two hours, maybe three, when the door opened. One of the MPs asked for 'Benny', and soon there he was, Lucky, in an adequately lit room at the back of the building. A plate of mutton and squash had been set out for him. Also on the table was Lucky's pleading letter from a few nights ago.

'We can talk while you eat,' said the MP whom Lucky and Gregor referred to as Harry.

'Thank you.'

'We know your name's Vasilis Mallios. Awful name. I'd hate my parents—'

'Call me Lucky. And you would be?'

'You don't want to joke with us.'

'How long you been in this country, Lucky?' asked the other MP, Frank.

'Eight months.'

'You a draftee, Lucky?'

'No,' said Lucky.

'Most of the draftees are dipshits, thought you'd be one.'

'You won't be playing no concerts,' said Frank.

'Except for the Collins Hotel tomorrow afternoon,' said Harry. 'This city closes early, which means you start early. You'll be appearing as Benny and we'll charge an entry fee. Your buddy will collect the money on the door and hand it to us. The owner wants fifteen per cent. You get zero per cent.'

'We need to think about it,' said Lucky.

'Then think about it right now. Here, I'll remove this distraction,' said Harry, taking Lucky's unfinished plate of food off the table.

Lucky said: 'And after the concert we're free to go?'

'We'll see.'

'If I'm going to be forced to play, I'll need my bags and clarinet—I have to practise. And I should practise out here. It's too dark in the cell.'

'Done.'

Lucky changed the focus of his gaze from Frank to Harry. 'And we need to wash.'

'That's acceptable.'

'And a bottle of liquor. And cigarettes.'

'Just looking at you makes me angry,' said Harry. 'Benny Goodman is a great musician. And you're an ass.'

Harry roughly helped Lucky up from his seat, though no help was required, and they walked back to the cell. The imposter asked his captors to leave the door open, please.

2.

That afternoon, while Lucky napped and Gregor sat at the edge of the cot in the dark, fidgeting and smoking, a woman named Valia Asproyerakas boarded a train to Central Station. Seated at the carriage window, aft-facing, she caught herself in reflection. Her most prominent feature was her bare arm, olive against the blues of her long dress. Along her forearm were little scars from excursions deep into the cafe oven. She resumed reading *Jude the Obscure*. Valia saw her own conditions reflected in Thomas Hardy's Wessex: a place of crushed men and brilliant but thwarted women, of predetermined lives, wet statues and children turning in their beds. Tears almost came to Valia's eyes when something bad happened to Hardy's people.

Valia was taking a brief holiday from her father's small business, and from the home he built behind the cafe. Achilles Asproyerakas had decided that his eldest daughter ought to spend her unmarried years serving customers in the family cafe while Achilles worked in the kitchen from 8 am to 9 pm; each day their lives folded and folded again behind counter and stove. Valia used to be warm and charming with customers, because she wanted to show them how much she loved life. And she did like the work; she was good at it. But by 1945 the long hours had distorted her enjoyment of labour, and lately she just smiled and showed people the menu. Her younger sister, Penelope, still at school and useless in the cafe, was spared from any duties in the family business, at least for the time being.

Their mother had died at the age of 31. Two grandmothers also died young. Valia discerned this pattern of early death and believed holidays could save her sanity, and probably her life (Achilles opposed regular time off). Sunday afternoons were the extent of her free time. She didn't know how to confront her father, not yet, but he could be managed and manipulated.

She planned to stay at a hotel in the city for the weekend, to be alone, free to be another Valia—a double, an avatar, a Valia with a different surname. To escape for the weekend, she told her father she'd been called up for compulsory weekend exercises with AWAS—the Australian Women's Army Service. Achilles' ego deferred to the war. He assumed his daughter had no choice, was legally compelled to attend this AWAS training exercise, or whatever jumble of letters she was throwing at him.

'How often can this happen?' Achilles said. 'I need you in the shop.'

'I'll tell them you object.'

'Explain your mother is dead and there's just you and me to run this place. Don't mention Penelope—they'll take her next!'

'I've already written and explained our situation.'

'What kind of country drafts women?'

'They don't give us guns.'

'This affects our business!'

'It's for one weekend.'

'This might be a busy month. Explain that to them.'

'I'll say I have to work and maybe that will be the end of it.'

'But don't be cheeky or pass remarks against them.'

'Definitely not.'

'And where will you stay?'

'A dormitory for women.'

'You go then! And we endure.'

The train crawled down the platform at Central Station. Valia stepped off early and walked alongside the slow-moving carriage. The sky was lifting: it had recently rained. First, she'd find a coffee and cigarette. Then the Collins Hotel. The future turned with each tiny decision.

3.

People came early to the hotel, which rose on the street corner in a de Chirico arrangement of open windows. The composition of the Collins audience was entirely civilian.

At the entrance Gregor sat with his money bag, collecting entrance fees and turning away servicemen, as per the admittance policy. Civilians only. Nobody made a fuss. Benny waited in a tiny back room, sweat lurching down his back, his performance nerves made worse by the hubbub of people waiting to see him, the sustained barrage of their voices coming closer. Intermittently, Lucky had a powerful urge to abandon his buddy Gregor and leap out the first-storey window then—all being well—run like the devil away. The scoundrels, Harry and Frank, came in and out unpredictably, checking on their man. They'd come to be amused by the sight of Lucky fiddling with his clarinet, and were especially tickled when the club's manager, party to the fraud, leaned on the doorframe, hands in pockets, and told Benny that a total of four hundred and six people were somehow squeezed inside the venue. The manager said he'd guessed the capacity at about three hundred and fifty, never before getting the chance to factor in significant compression.

Goodman would be playing without accompaniment, sticking to the nicest melodies in his most popular arrangements.

Frank ran a flat hand over his own hair. 'You better enjoy tonight,' he told Lucky, 'because tomorrow you might be back in jail.'

The manager introduced Benny to the crowd.

Some people don't know what they're capable of until they put on the right mask. Some people need to hide a part of themselves to perform. On stage, before the applause died down, Lucky began the show with a wrong note:

C instead of B sharp. The tune he played was a stitched-together 'Don't Be That Way', and it was opened and shut like a box. The next song he rushed through with a similar spirit (get it over with). Third down the list was 'Stompin' at the Savoy' (he could play that dead). As the tune ended and the performance continued, Lucky drew more and more on bites of exhilaration whenever he felt in his stomach the magic of heavy, honest applause. He played for much longer than expected. Each composition was stretched and nervously disentangled and bumped to an end. No one in the audience knew Lucky wasn't Benny Goodman; they would never know. When these people applauded or turned and spoke with excitement to the person next to them, they were saying what Lucky wished he'd heard, before the war, when he played in those unfriendly bands. His performance, as Lucky would remember it, possessed the glory of a lie that was nearly as meaningful as the truth.

Coming off stage he returned to the back room, where he was unable to stand at rest. He swallowed air in hungry gulps, his eyes moving like two gnats.

'The people here are nice folk,' he told Gregor.

Gregor, who missed the show, was bleeding from the blade of his nose. He said: 'I'm busted up at the moment.'

Lucky said: 'For sure you are.'

'Frank walloped me. He got angry when I brought him the money. He said I pocketed some.'

'Did you?'

'Damn right I did. This whole thing was my idea. Why should they be the only guys to profit?'

'Where are they now?'

'I don't know. I think something popped inside my nose.'

'How about we stick around, meet some people?'

'But what about my face? Am I presentable?'

'Clean up first,' said Lucky. 'Then come find me.'

A young Englishman, perhaps in his twenties, waited in the hallway outside the room. His black hair was wet-hard with coif cream, slicked back in the airman's style (though he was no airman). This fellow wore a Glen plaid blazer and an adoring expression. Lucky looked forward to more praise from the audience; the wish was more than equal to his fear of being found out.

'Mr Goodman, that was utterly superb,' the man said. 'I thank you.'

'You think so . . . even performing without a band?'

'This was the most fun I've had the whole war. You were—' and the man paused here '—brilliant. Unique. Indeed, I liked you very much.'

'No one's ever been that nice about my work.'

'I doubt that. You had the whole audience licked to a custard.'

The man steered Lucky towards a booth in the hotel bar but did not himself sit down. He soon returned with drinks, holding out the tray as if presenting a prize. It was another minute before Lucky understood that he'd got away with it, that he was free of Frank and Harry. The police played no further part in the story. They'd taken the money, left the hotel, and allowed Ian Asquith to meet Benny Goodman.

4.

A half-hour later, or so it seemed, Gregor came to the table and introduced himself as Benny Goodman's manager, never bothering to explain his red and swollen nose. Gregor sat next to Asquith and listened to what he had to say about Benny Goodman's 1938 Carnegie Hall recordings. Meantime, Lucky finished four glasses of booze, after which he refused all further drinks. (There was a time, before he enlisted, when Lucky tended to overdrink, because only in a drunken stupor did he believe he was a real musician.) All three of them smoked Asquith's cigarettes. The bar was full but nobody approached Benny Goodman.

'Here, I've decided something,' said Gregor, when Asquith had finished his critique. 'I want to join a submarine crew. What do you think about that?'

'Bravo,' said Asquith. 'Very brave indeed to leave your current duties. I don't think it's foolish at all. You know, I've been in Sydney since 1940. Rather a quiet way to spend the war.'

'I may die in a submarine,' said Gregor.

'It's a real possibility,' said Asquith, now turning to Lucky. 'Tell me, Benny, if it's not too awkward a question, what is it like to be a success?'

'I don't often think of myself as a success.'

'Oh, come, how does it feel?' said Gregor. 'We need a full and fitting answer.'

'Some days I feel lucky, privileged, like I've gotten away with something but with the permission of people who could take it back at any moment. If they did take it back, I would go be a mess steward, or a soldier, or I'd work at a diner. At times I see only the mistakes I've made. Those mistakes tell me what I should do better next time. I know I've got a ways to go, and maybe I'll think like this when I'm an old man still. On the best days I feel like I've paid some debt to myself. I'm meeting the terms of my personal contract.'

Lucky did not find it difficult to imagine what being a person of exception might feel like. You well know your dreams, whether possible or impossible, banal or extravagant, abandoned or tightly or foolishly held.

'I wonder about the terms of my own contract,' said Asquith. 'I wonder what I'm supposed to do better.'

Occasionally, as the evening progressed and the conversation returned almost by default to the subject of Benny Goodman's career, or at some point paused to take in the scale of the great musician's opinion, Asquith looked over and patted Lucky on the shoulder, emphasising how much he enjoyed his company. Other music enthusiasts, mostly men, now found the courage to approach Benny Goodman and they timidly stood over the table, making small talk and giving Lucky a look of near-sexual love, until Asquith read discomfort on Lucky's face and politely dispatched them, saying Mr Goodman was fatigued.

Gregor had started to complain about the war department's plans for demobilisation—he didn't understand why the US Army wanted to start discharging GIs before Germany had surrendered: they'd all signed up for the same deal, duration plus six, and the air force and navy were still drafting—when Lucky and Asquith were distracted by Valia Asproyerakas, who sat by herself at a high table, under a tangerine glow. Her long hair, a perfection of black, came down and twisted around the strap of a blue beaded bag. She perched her chin on her hand, and gave out the confidence of a woman in a portrait painting; she appeared amused by the theatre of the room, crowded with strangers.

A tall Australian man, a person who seemed composed of larger and cruder molecules than Lucky, approached and spoke to her until he got the message. Asquith kept an eye on this exchange, waiting for its conclusion.

'Excuse me,' said Asquith, calling out to Valia. 'Would you like to meet Benny Goodman? He's entirely pleasant, more than one might suppose.'

'I would like to meet him,' said Valia.

'I shouldn't presume too much,' said Asquith, 'but you're Greek, aren't you?'

'Yes, up to a point.'

'May I ask your surname?'

'It's Asproyerakas.'

'Then you must be Kefalonian.'

'No, Ithakan.'

'Is English your first language?' Asquith asked.

Valia nodded, not impressed with the question.

'Perhaps you would like to attend this gathering I hold once a month at a hall in Elizabeth Bay. We read ancient Greek. Next is the play *Choephori*. After that *Eumenides*. It would be a novelty to have someone with Greek heritage present. You might find you have a good time.'

'I don't know those plays. And I don't know you?'

'My name is Ian Asquith. Incredibly pleased to meet you. I'm second secretary at the British High Commission.'

Valia asked: 'What's the difference between the first and the second secretary?'

'That will take a great deal of explaining.'

'Then forget I asked the question.'

Asquith laughed. 'I like your bottle.'

'Would you mind sitting with us?' asked Lucky.

Asquith monopolised Valia's company with minor personal questions, inserting these queries from across the table whenever Benny and his man spoke directly to each other. On several instances Asquith spoke Greek, and what he wanted in these exchanges, Lucky figured, was a special channel of exchange, an intimate connection.

'My Greek isn't too good,' Valia whispered to Lucky.

'Nor is mine,' said Benny Goodman.

'There's something not quite right about the people at this table,' she said, again in a low voice. 'I get that feeling.'

'What do you mean? And whatever it is, does it worry you?'

'No, I'll stay.'

Lucky let the other three talk. Maybe this was something you did if you were a professional artist: you put yourself in the hands of other people. They made something of you. In strange cities you sat down with people you hadn't met before and hoped it worked out. Lucky tried to understand a public role he would never hold. Why was it touching to him, seeing that gleam of appreciation on Asquith's face? Would it have meant anything to the real Benny Goodman? That evening he confirmed an old suspicion: Lucky believed the successful person lived a much simpler life.

All the other people in the Collins Hotel, the audience, were leaving. They were saying goodbye to Benny Goodman, offering a word or two and asking for a handshake on their way out.

'That was real music!' said one person.

'Will you come back?' said another.

'Next time I'd like to see Benny Goodman with his band.'

Eventually the hotel looked like a depopulated dream. There was the sound of doors being shut upstairs. Gregor and Valia spoke quietly to each other, and Lucky tried to display an attitude of sangfroid, but really he felt alarmed by the idea of never seeing Valia again. Asquith left to find the hotelier, in the hope their small but important party would be permitted to continue. From the bar you could hear booms and shudders in the hotel plumbing. Lucky's sneeze was so loud it sounded out of character. Valia linked her arm in his, and she and Lucky and the seat all seemed to creak at the same time. The table at their booth was made of marble, patched with cement. In a low voice, Lucky said: 'It doesn't feel right to deceive you, or even to try for much longer. I'm not Benny Goodman. But I think you already figured we're fakes.'

'Perhaps I didn't,' said Valia. Her chin dipped as she smiled; her eyes drifted over the room. 'Why would you pretend?'

'To be someone else for a change. To go beyond ourselves.

To have fun. Until tonight it hasn't gone much to plan, though.'

'I think it's amusing,' said Valia. 'And Mr Asquith believes everything.'

'My real name is Vasilis.'

'Then we have the same name. Valia is short for Vasiliki.'

'There is a Greek myth—I forget which gods were involved—about all lovers being the same person split in half. We look for the missing part of ourselves. And something strange and good happens when we find it.'

'That is a silly myth.'

'I wasn't sure whether to mention it.'

'I like that you owned up to your Benny Goodman deceit, even if it might cost you.'

Lucky addressed Gregor across the table: 'I've told Valia the truth.'

'Hey, it's your show, pal,' Gregor said.

'We are sharing this table with the world's greatest living musician!' Asquith said when he returned.

'Really?' asked Gregor.

'My boy, did you not hear him tonight? I couldn't get enough. Benny here was daring. Big band music—with no big band! How perfect for these times. I admit I run the risk of sounding pretentious. Your concert was an expression of life at home in 1944.'

Asquith pushed across the table a piece of paper that bore his letterhead, including his address in Elizabeth Bay. 'Valia, are you interested in attending one of those parties I mentioned? It's a salon.'

'I'm not interested, no,' said Valia.

'My word,' replied Asquith. 'That's honest.'

With a sour smile, and without saying any words of farewell, Asquith stood and Lucky got up as well. The two men shook hands as Valia pulled on her hair to stop from laughing. She expected she'd never meet Asquith again. He left behind a cosy-shaped silence. Lucky folded up the paper he'd left behind. The manager brought two room keys, on the house for Benny Goodman and his manager.

From his hotel room Gregor heard the locomotives at Central Station hush and hiss and impatiently grind. Street cats began making bitter sounds. They galloped about and sang with terrible strength and Gregor closed his eyes and wished for them to stop. Twenty-three days from now he'd deliver flowers to Maeve Doyle, manager of the Herbert Arms Hotel, who had found the clarinet for Lucky, the uniforms for them both. They would (briefly) kiss in the hotel garden. Walking home that night, Gregor would be hit and killed by a supply truck a mile or so from Bankstown Airport.

Down the hall, Valia and Lucky sat at the foot of his hotel bed. Their bodies made an A-shape when they kissed. They would make love another time, said Valia. There would be enough time for all that. Lucky asked, What are we to each other? Soon we will find out, Valia said. The new couple, who would marry within the year, spent their first night together in a room booked under a false name.

1971

1.

EMILY PLAYED ALONE in a backyard briny with morning light. The wind suspended strands of her hair while she danced about, dressed in bright new clothes, as if she were soon to attend a party. She held a blue balloon. Her birthday was three days ago but it still felt like a time of celebration. Emily wasn't six anymore, she was seven. The balloon string wrapped around her leg when she whirled like a spinning top—stopping before the motion grew unpleasant—and the corpulent balloon then swung back and forth behind her as she strode across the small yard in long and comical steps, laughing. The wind made her nose run and her eyes water and she didn't bother to wipe away the tears and gunk running down her face. Older girls on bicycles tore up and down the lane behind the house and Emily, caught up in play, responded to their shouts with little hoots of her own.

Emily's mother called her inside: a visitor had come from London. In the laundry, inside the back door, Emily wiped her own face with a tissue and pulled up her socks, retied her laces, straightened her clothes. She didn't want her mother fussing over these things: she liked the feeling of looking after herself. The visitor, as expected, was her birth father, Ian Asquith. Emily could hear his voice in the living room, speaking too loudly and with too much seriousness. He hadn't slept a bit the night before, he said, because his mind had been buzzing like an old machine. Don't worry, he told Emily's mother, he had a ticket for the afternoon train.

Emily gave her father a hug while her mother stood by the kitchen table, and Asquith, flopping on the couch, remarked to his daughter that on the train trip he'd thought about how much he missed spending time with her when she was two years old, how he regretted the loss of her infant babble, her nonsensical speech; he treasured being a part of those dialogues, freed of meaning.

'I'm seven this week,' said Emily.

'Now you are entirely confined in language,' said Asquith, touching her hair. 'Trapped in logos.'

'For Christ's sake, Ian,' said Emily's mother. 'You come up with some rubbish.'

'Where is your husband today?'

'Working in the garage. He's right on the other side of this wall here.'

'There are never any books in this house!' Ian observed. 'I should have brought some. For when she gets older.'

Emily's stepfather was born in Ipswich: his parents were both from Suffolk, as were his maternal grandparents, his great-grandparents and his great-great-grandparents—a cousin had looked into the matter. Emily called her stepfather Rick, short for Derek, a name he'd long ago abandoned rather than share it with his school bully. Rick, who couldn't have children, was endlessly amused by his stepdaughter's habit of addressing him by name. He preferred not to be in the same room as Asquith and made himself scarce whenever visits were scheduled—Rick couldn't stand the sight of the guy. A definite madman, said Rick. Insufferable but not dangerous, said Emily's mother.

How did Ian and Heidi end up together? They'd met at a pub in Hammersmith eight years earlier, when Heidi was twenty-two and newly arrived in England, intending the move to be permanent. She'd grown up in central New South Wales, in a small town heretofore unknown to the people of Ipswich: a place called Nevertire, population 400. It pleased Heidi when the name of her home town drew a blank on the face of a new acquaintance. The absence of recognition expressed how far from her parents she'd settled. Even with close friends, Heidi didn't like to talk about the family she'd left behind in New South Wales, just as she disliked explaining her brief marriage to Asquith. Once they'd heard an anecdote about Ian, and almost any detail would do, friends needed to know: why on earth did she ever marry him?

He was educated. He was handsome. He was native. She fell pregnant in the first month. Like a chore they *did* the marriage, and they did it badly, because it was an awful match—Ian being Ian, Heidi being Heidi—and the impossible couple separated when Emily was about two-and-a-half years old.

After Heidi met Rick and fell in love, mother and daughter and stepdad moved from the noise of London to quiet Ipswich. They tried to conceive a sibling for Emily. They bought a terrace house in a street where all the houses were identical, and which looked much like the home in which Rick was raised. Heidi said it was the best decision they ever made. She did not miss London. In Ipswich she did not miss anyone or anywhere.

Emily folded her legs on the lounge room floor and removed the headband she'd worn while dancing outside, and she took off a beaded bracelet: all part of a costume she'd pulled together that morning. Through the lounge room window she saw the balloon toss about in the backyard.

Asquith spoke to her: 'I have a birthday present for you, but I didn't bring it with me.'

'You forgot Emily's present?' said Heidi.

'It's drying at home,' said Asquith. 'It's a painting. I took a class at the library.'

'She's seven years old. What does she want with a painting?'

'Fair play,' said Asquith, examining his hands. 'Perhaps I'm a bad father.'

'Don't feel sorry for yourself,' said Heidi.

'Daddy, I had a dream about you last night,' said Emily. 'We went to a shop and ate chips. We bought toys.'

'I have a great deal of regret,' Asquith told Heidi. 'You have no idea.'

Heidi said: 'What do you mean?'

'I'm a bad person.'

'Go on.'

'I mean to say,' said Asquith. 'No, rather, let's forget what I said. I'm being melodramatic. You know what it's like when I don't sleep. I'm terribly keyed up. Pour me a cup of tea and then we might all go for a walk. How does that sound?'

'I'm going to get Rick,' said Heidi, who wasn't appeased. 'I'll be back in a minute, Em, all right?'

While Emily heard everything her parents had said, the discourse of grown-ups was a landscape in which she often couldn't get her bearings. Her father was a bad person? But he didn't seem like a baddie. Or he felt sad in his heart? It was probably a grown-up's idea of a joke.

As soon as Heidi left the room, Asquith asked his daughter: 'Would you like your present? We can fetch it.'

'Yes please,' she said.

He rose from the couch and together they went out into the backyard, and from there into the lane behind the house and down to the street. When it started to rain he opened an umbrella and they took shelter underneath it; they did not stop walking until they were sitting on a train to London. Their seats were covered in a red candy-stripe moquette, the lines slightly curved from wear. The air whistle screaked long and loud and the train bobbed away into the west. 'Perhaps you'd like to look out the window,' suggested Asquith. He closed his eyes, and Emily stared at the solemn green countryside and majestic churches sunk deep in the panorama. Her father remained quiet; he barely spoke; he sat with his arms folded. In this way they went on. They went all the way to London, to the indifferent Londoners, who walked past little Emily without seeing her, or so she imagined. And she thought, so this was where he came from, this place could tell me something about him, my real dad, if only I stayed here long enough. She might well have been invisible to everybody except Ian Asquith, who did not hold her hand but who had brought her here, wanted her with him, who guided her along the streets to his home near Acton Town station. For a long time he'd worked in the administrative offices of the Borough of Ealing and lived in this same ground-floor flat.

Four, five, six—Emily counted seven bookcases inside his small home. The flat smelled of cigarettes and cleaning products and did not, to Emily, feel like a place anyone except her father could stay for long. 'Sit down, please,' said Asquith, and he gave her a glass of water into which he'd squeezed lemon juice. The late afternoon sun shone through the trees and rooftops and spotlighted books on the wall, and the ashtray on the arm of a vacant chair, and Asquith's head of grey hair.

'You're still tremendously young,' he said. 'If I go away, if I'm gone, you won't lose much, if one presumes to say that you'd lost anything.'

'I don't understand, Daddy.'

'I've thought about going away. I even made some preparations. But look. Here.'

He handed her the birthday gift: a gaudy painting of a restaurant. The restaurant was in Australia, he said, and he'd copied the picture from a black-and-white postcard. He'd thrown out the postcard, he added, though in hindsight he should have held on to it. Asquith told his daughter he lived in consuming thoughts about decisions he'd made yesterday, last week, decades ago. It was difficult to surrender the past!

Emily asked if that's where he was going, to Australia, when he spoke about travelling somewhere.

'Not at all, too far away. Do you like your painting?'

'I love it, Daddy.'

Asquith cast around the room for something, settling at last on his bookshelf. 'Would you like me to read to you?' he asked.

Emily said yes, she would, and he took down *The Iliad* and read aloud from the beginning, before deciding no, this wouldn't do for a child, and he turned to *Middlemarch* and read her chapters one and two, about Miss Brooke, and next his favourite Waterloo scenes from *The Charterhouse of Parma*, after the performance of which there was a knock on the door.

Asquith put the novel back on the shelf and in a hushed voice told Emily she must take the painting home with her. 'Please don't forget. It's your birthday present. And don't touch the paint.'

Two Metropolitan Police constables announced themselves through the door, then knocked with amplified force. Asquith raised a finger to his mouth: quiet, not a sound. Emily thought: Am I in trouble? Her father closed his eyes and gently nodded his head, as if someone spoke into his ear.

When the knocking stopped and the police seemed to have left, Asquith took her hand and opened the door, tightening up his face against the noise of the hinges. Emily thought: are we sneaking up on someone?

'What are we doing, Daddy?'

'We're making a getaway,' said Asquith.

Looking neither left nor right, they stepped out in the direction of the station, moving swiftly, Asquith carrying the picture of a Lucky's restaurant. On the footpath boys played with shiny marbles and coins. In a building across the street a window flew open and a stream of piano melody burst out, beaming onto the road.

They made it to the station. Asquith gave Emily the painting, which she gripped with both hands. She asked her father if they were going home to Ipswich now, and how long it would take, but he wasn't listening. His eyes had stalled on the station clock.

'What did those men at the door want?' Emily asked. 'Does Mum know them?'

Asquith looked confused by the clock, by the strange aspect of time. Two policemen came towards them on the station platform.

'This is not how I wanted to do it,' Asquith said to Emily. He didn't say another word nor look again at his daughter after he turned and made his way to the platform behind them. Emily had time to think: Wait, he's about to hop on a train going the wrong way. He's leaving without me. Asquith bent down and tumbled forwards onto the tracks and Emily, still holding the picture, saw the excruciations, watched his body broken up by the oncoming train.

2002

1.

CERTAIN FORMER GAMBLING addicts, including Lucky, still possessed the ability to see an intuitive or logical sequence of steps between, for example, the amounts of fifty dollars and fifty thousand. When the idea came to him, when one morning he gave in—after watching a comically topsy-turvy episode of *Wheel of Fortune*—he ironed his best shirt and rolled up the long white sleeves until they reached to his elbow, snug and sock-like. He filled his pockets, folded a newspaper under his arm. With little adjustments he fitted his environment to him. Lucky walked to Marrickville Road, entering the pub with his head bowed, because guilt weighed on his mind. Also: a little hope. Today felt like a holiday.

On this day gambling could be permitted. He went straight past the bar to a small room filled with twelve gaming machines, where he sat before a console called the Golden Pyramid. On the wall behind him hung a poster-sized black-and-white illustration of a bowl of prawns that imitated the sails of the Sydney Opera House; the CBD skyline comprised beer and champagne glasses; the Harbour Bridge a slice of watermelon balanced on a pyramid of donuts. The hedonism and stupidity of this city. The audacity to hang such a picture inside a pub gaming room. The blue light glowing from the machine covered one side of Lucky's body and gave him a feeling of comfort, a warm buzz of recognition, as if here he was known; this place was made for his senses; his chemistry had been taken into account. For this feeling he inserted two twenty-dollar notes.

He set the credits and pay lines and leaned on the button. The screen spun and spun down to $21, until he hit a free-spin feature and the machine produced a stern *ker-ching* sound, then an electronic whistle. Lucky, slumped on his stool, let his head fall into his hands. Those fifteen free spins took him up to $76. He hit the button three more times: another feature, and another, and the accumulation paid $315—a sign to quit the gaming machines.

That morning his mood had shifted, and he couldn't recover it, and he felt for the first time uneasy about his plan to win money on *Wheel of Fortune* and start a restaurant and leave something behind for anyone who still loved him. The *Wheel* audition had been simple. In Lucky the show's producers and casting director had seen what they called the 'human interest factor'. That is, the fact he had founded and lost a restaurant franchise.

In a few days' time he would be taping the first episode. But that morning he woke up and saw the hopelessness of his goal: he wasn't about to win that TV show jackpot. He wouldn't get the money together. Banks wouldn't lend to him, or at least not enough to start a small business. They considered him unreliable, too old, his name devalued, his fire gone to puff. Maybe gambling was a medium through which Lucky and Money could still speak to each other. With a good bet he could briefly overcome his ill fortune, his bad decisions. Through gambling he'd once addressed his self-loathing, his overwhelming sense of failure, which was compounded by the inevitable losses he experienced when betting. Today Lucky told himself he'd been good. He hadn't gambled in almost two years. He deserved a celebration.

In the bar outside the gaming room he drank soda water and played his lucky numbers in Keno. The numbers were old artefacts: birthdays, addresses, and figures with power that he couldn't explain. He couldn't get away from these numbers any more than he could run from his nickname. And he didn't want to leave them behind. He played them. He lost and kept playing them—small wagers. To use other numbers would make him feel separated from the bet, like he was pretending to be someone else.

2.

A month ago, Lucky Mallios, running late, suppressing nerves, auditioned for *Wheel of Fortune*. He'd stood in the network's foyer, where he watched people in summer clothes leave the building for the fiery day. Technicians carried broadcast lights inside, their T-shirts mashed with sweat. The air that circulated through the building was cool and perfumed, velvety and sweet. Lucky closed his eyes, diverting himself from perceptions: the air passed rapidly through his lungs; it metabolised in his brain. Then came a *Wheel of Fortune* production assistant with a handshake, a name tag for Lucky. They moved to a large conference room thick with auditioning contestants, all seated. A producer glared at Lucky before starting a rollcall. The candidates were advised to act naturally but pretend the cameras were on them. This was basically a memory game, said Dan the producer. Who here has a long memory?

In groups of three, auditioning contestants came to the front of the room, taking turns to spin a raffle wheel and solve a mock *Wheel of Fortune* puzzle projected onto a whiteboard. Producers and other show staff sat in the front row. Gameshow workers judged your personality, your story, they discussed whether you were interesting. You were at the mercy of their sympathies. Lucky was among the second group called to the floor.

Before he could spin the wheel, Dan asked: 'What do you do for a crust?'

'I'm retired at this time.'

'What did you do before retirement?'

'I founded the Lucky's restaurant franchise.'

'You're *the* Lucky?' said Dan. 'I used to love those places when I was a kid. What will you do with money from *Wheel of Fortune*?'

'I plan to start a new restaurant,' said Lucky. 'Truth is, I'm busted.'

'Perfect! That means there's a lot riding on this. Are you prepared to talk on TV about the Third of April?'

'If it's not sensationalised.'

'Ladies and gentlemen, *that* is how you successfully audition for a gameshow.'

3.

From Marrickville Road he hailed a taxi to the casino and thought he could literally do this forever, hopping from place to place amid the traffic of the world, laying bets. Once, on runs like these, it was customary for Lucky to play roulette when he entered, to first put down a decent sum on black. And today black came up. 'What're you gonna buy with that?' a man at the table asked Lucky. He said: 'I'll put it towards a new restaurant. I'm going to start again.' The croupier said: 'Good for you, champ! Let me know when you start taking reservations.'

At the roulette table he played the same five lucky numbers, three chips stacked on each square. Five, because that was the number of letters in his name; five numbers and three chips, because that's how he used to play, how it used to work, how he lost respect for reality and moved through rituals towards the climactic moment, how his mind survived among hope and shame and the voices that told him he'd lose again. Other players leaned rigidly against the roulette table, the casino floor like one big messy board game.

As the croupier dragged away his chips, Lucky considered the changes that occurred when his marriage to Valia ended. He associated their separation with the beginning of his interest in gambling, of new friends, of card rooms above fruit shops. Friends was a strong word. Perhaps friendship hadn't been important in his life: most of those men didn't matter to Lucky. After his marriage ended he stopped paying full and pure attention to what was happening to him—his mind divided, back then, into two asymmetries, into the life he experienced every day and an unlived life in which he was still married. One life criticised the other.

After a while the spinning wheel sounded like a long snore. After an hour the game put Lucky into a sort of fugue state and he stopped watching the roulette wheel; he listened for the croupier to call the numbers. The pattern in the carpet began to look like stains. Then he did, the croupier, call Lucky's number, and the table exploded into congratulations, all these strangers thrown into goodwill for the old bloke. 'You won!' said a young woman. 'You massively won!'

The final station: a blackjack table. Lucky stacked his chips, his expectations tenacious and accelerating. If he'd had friends with him, kind Lucky-watchers, they would have advised him to safeguard himself, to go home with the

$4000 or so he now carried in his pocket. By this stage of the night he was no longer aware of cautionary thoughts. Yesterday he'd worried over Emily and her questions about her father; now Lucky looked forward to seeing her again. She was the missing part of the story. She wanted to write about the franchise's legacy but did not realise she was part of that legacy, that Ian Asquith's seed money was the hard truth at the bottom of the business. Which didn't mean Emily should know what her father had done.

In Sydney the blackjack dealers placed the cut card two decks from the end of the shoe, which meant that counting was pointless, and anyway Lucky didn't think he possessed the ability to count. You had to count on a regular basis, you needed time to practise at home, and time at the table, and supposedly he'd quit gambling, he didn't have that kind of time. He needed to get his franchise restarted. The dealer kept staying on soft seventeen. Lucky's long hands moved like the feelers of an insect edging up the wall. At $17,000, a waiter asked if he required a complimentary drink. The dealer asked if he'd like to take a break. The player next to him asked Lucky his name. Lucky said his name was Vasilis because he didn't want any lame jokes about luck around the table. He nodded a lot, his tongue tied like a person who needed to keep eating. The dealer changed. The new dealer called him Darling, called him Hon, called him Mister. She blew her first hand and Lucky reached a total of $31,200. Not a restaurant yet but part of a restaurant. Which part?

Then the dealer killed him. When he fell to $9000 or so, he heard someone behind him say, 'Old mate's lost it'.

The dealer took all his money in six hands. Now she called him Sir. Spectators, a handful, fled in terror towards the roulette tables. A waiter asked if Lucky required a complimentary taxi home.

At home he went to the bedside drawer and took out his address book, found the number and dialled, as he'd promised to do on bad nights like this. He closed his eyes, his flat dark except for the kitchen light, and he pressed the receiver to his ear. To Lucky, the ringtone sounded gravely expressive, already a type of message, a distress signal of someone stranded in an idea. His Gambling Anonymous sponsor was Thanh Truong, a forty-three-year-old building manager in Alexandria. Thanh wouldn't answer, because he never picked up the phone after 9.30 pm, but Lucky left a message saying he'd call again tomorrow, it wasn't urgent, nothing to worry about. Calling the number was his way of saying, I've stopped. This is the last of last times.

1945–1946

1.

IN SEPTEMBER, LUCKY was declared non-essential to the needs of the United States Army Air Force and discharged from the service through a separation centre in Chicago. He stayed with his parents for a fortnight or so, and Lucky's strongest memory of that time returned him to an image of his mother drinking sage tea at a stool near the oven, in a shirtwaister from which she'd removed the belt. His father, at the table, rubbed methylated spirits into his arms (a Mallios remedy for sore muscles and joints). Mother spoke about the letters that came from Greece concerning the people she knew as a child in Pontus, the families who fled to Piraeus and stayed there and died in the famine of 1941–1942.

'Panos went insane watching members of his family die,' she said. 'One after the other in the room they all shared in a shack.'

'No surprise, huh, Pontians the first to die,' said Lucky's father.

'The first to die were the women going without food for their children, like my cousin Maria,' said Lucky's mother. 'And you know what they did with her body?'

'What?' said Lucky.

'Dumped like garbage in the cemetery at night,' she said. 'No decent burial. So they could keep her ration card. They took her food even when she was dead!'

Why this particular memory, these ghastly details? He supposed the memory stuck because it made plain that his parents still thought about people far away, people they remembered from childhood and would never see again—and Lucky hoped this would be the way they'd speak about him, with real emotion, once he left town again. John the Terrible, naturally, did not visit the family home that fortnight. He's busy always, Lucky's father would say.

Lucky travelled back to Australia with a Dutch-owned shipping company, on a German-made steamer given to the Netherlands as war reparations. The signage everywhere remained in German: DAMEN; HERREN; RAUCHEN VERBOTEN. His dark berth smelled of old shoes and had the green metal atmosphere of an office bin. The tempo on board was domestic; some passengers made friends, swapped stories, played songs and crooned together in the lounge. Lucky did not enter into the ship's everyday life. He shared a cabin with two chatty Scotsmen and each day couldn't wait for the hour they left, somewhat reluctantly, to spend time with their families.

The ship passed tiny islands in the distance, as anonymous as clouds. During the three-week journey, Lucky felt as if he moved inside a huge diorama of the world. He often fell asleep by thinking about the pleasing scenarios that awaited: his wedding to Valia. Watching Valia step into a steaming bath. He and Valia on a beach in Sydney sharing a bottle of wine. From his cabin, inside of which swung his coats and shirts, he felt able to picture her at any time of the day, working or eating or sitting in the closed cafe at night, her hand flicking up to distance a fly. In Australia, things would be simple, things were arranged: they'd marry in December and afterwards, for a few months, Lucky would work with Valia's father. Then the couple might see about starting their own business. If the economy improved. On the boat he had two gold rings hidden inside a flap he'd cut into the lining of his suitcase.

Circular Quay came into view, heavy with activity, the harbour's northern shore in repose. Little homes lay as if stamped over the bays. Lucky came down the steamship ramp into the frame of a camera shooting for a newsreel. He smiled, waved, and stepped onto the docks. Crates of imported goods, unloaded from another ship, all appeared cheap and humbled, as if their real value did not yet apply. Lucky walked down the branch, his hair recently cut by the ship's barber, his suit wide in the shoulders, narrow in the hip, brown shoes shining; he walked along the quay's avenue of turpentine, merbau, marble, grain, leather, rubber, cambric from Bengal. Crates stamped ANDIROBA. Valia waited on the south side of Customs House and Lucky came to her in long strides.

'We have—' said Valia, kissing him fast '—much to do.'

He'd kept all her letters since the week they met at the Collins Hotel, and Valia, too, had held on to his correspondence, hiding the notes underneath a set of drawers, since she didn't want her sister or father reading long pornographic stories. It was naked, their writing, like another world on the other side of a mirror, where the future could be planned, where they climbed out of the day's structure and consumed each other.

2.

Early each morning the first to rise was Lucky and, careful to move about quietly, he first lit the wood stove, nudging the Cafe Achillion from its stone sleep. Next he peeled and chipped potatoes. The air in this part of the cafe was soon steamy from the warming stovetop, and the smell of coffee boiled in a briki. For breakfast he mashed a soft-boiled egg into a small bowl with crumbled bread, rigani and ground pepper. If the household were ever woken abruptly in the mornings, it had nothing to do with Lucky's kitchen routine: Penelope's nightmares, which caused her to shout, were the likely cause.

Penelope Asproyerakas was seventeen, the favourite daughter, and quietly aflame with ambition, curiosity and dissatisfaction. Achilles proposed that the following year, when Penny had finished high school, she would start working in the Cafe Achillion, serving customers on the floor like her sister. Whenever he referred to such plans, Penny kept her eyes downcast and heard him out, out of either well-concealed amusement or acceptance—as if she had no choice but to do as her father wished. Her father had his plans, which he made clear, and Penelope had hers, which she kept utterly secret. This delayed their inevitable conflict. Everyone knew it was coming.

By seven o'clock the others joined Lucky in the kitchen. Achilles wandered in carrying the olive-wood club he kept under his bed at night for protection. During the war he cut a branch from the olive tree in the Achillion's backyard, identifying a weapon in the thick shaft of wood. Nobody found the fruit edible; the olives were incurable, at least by Asproyerakas hands. But the tree might serve other purposes. Achilles leaned the heavy club against the wall in the corner of the kitchen. If someone came to rob the place, if there was any kind of trouble, a fight, an abusive customer, he could knock the crooks to the ground without much work, without injuring his hands. Before he carved the olive club, his options were narrow with regard to the drunken and offensive customers of the cafe. Achilles tended to punch them; he went around for weeks afterwards with bandages on his hands and needed help in the kitchen cutting and turning meat. With a busted wrist he couldn't properly use a wooden spoon. Then he made himself a wooden weapon.

The shop opened by eight. Valia worked the counter. She and Lucky took breaks together; sometimes they had sex quickly in their bedroom, or they'd sit knee to knee in a booth and talk. The cafe—which Lucky still called a 'diner' sometimes—closed at 9.30 pm. Then the family swept and mopped the floor, wiped the tables and prepared their own dinner, always including a few Greek plates: youvarlakia, yemista, stifado, a soup. There were no Greek dishes on the cafe's menu; Achilles said Anglo people would never eat the stuff, because the nation was culinarily, racially, ethnically limited. He claimed not a single Greek-Australian cafe served a single Greek dish. Think about that, he would say, think of what was lost!

Until the winter of 1946 Achilles remained polite to anyone who arrived a few minutes after closing time, lingering on the entrance step, some with their faces pressed close to the glass, hoping the Asproyerakas family would offer them a table. Whenever customers knocked on the door outside business hours Achilles told them he was sorry, and his big stone face expanded to smile, but the shop had to shut at some time. Not open all day, not allowed by law. Already the Achillion operated ninety hours a week. He gave late arrivals a sandwich or piece of fruit instead. But one cold day he stopped offering snacks, without exception and without explanation, to any customers who did not observe Achillion time. He couldn't be softened anymore. And there came the night when he heard a loud knock on the locked cafe door and Achilles picked up his olive-wood club, threatening to kill the two men on the other side of the glass who said they were looking for steak and soup.

'We are closed!' said Achilles. 'Get going or I smash your head bloody!'

'We can't buy a loaf of bread?' said one of the men from outside. 'Not much to ask, mate.'

'Maybe I kill you, mate! What do you think? Then I put your body through a machine in the abattoir. And you're never heard from again.'

'Achilles, you can't talk to people like that!' Lucky said. Until a few moments ago, he'd been mopping the cafe floor in a contented trance.

'No, I'm going to deal with these fucking lazies!' said Achilles.

The two prospective customers backed away from the window.

Pointing at them, Achilles said: 'I'll kill you!'

'Hey, how do you know they're not off-duty police?' Lucky asked his father-in-law. 'All the men look like cops around here.'

'If they're cops, they turn up wearing uniform because I give an official discount,' replied Achilles.

'This is some display,' said Valia, coming out to the cafe floor in a change of clothes. 'Give me the big stick.'

Achilles, in the middle of the cafe, swept the air with the olive-wood club as if practising for a violent contest, as if cutting away the features of an invisible monster. The customers outside watched him, interested in the eccentric display of fury. Then Penelope came out to see what was going on. The family, all in the same room for the first time that day, were arranged around the restaurant like figures in a tapestry, woven into representative positions: Achilles in the midst of a rage; Lucky and Valia turning to each other for reference; Penelope at a distance, composed, hands in the pockets of her dress.

'Penny,' said Valia, 'tell our father to put down the stick.'

'You tell him,' Penny said.

Valia told Achilles: 'Your outbursts of anger are only getting worse. The customers hear you screaming murder when you cut your finger in the kitchen, when you can't find a good onion. You walk around angry for hours at a time and no one knows the reason.'

'I wouldn't be surprised if he murdered someone one day,' said Penelope. 'There is no point confronting irrational men.'

'Thanks for your help,' said Valia. 'Thanks for nothing.'

'Penelope, you ought to be part of this conversation,' said Lucky.

'You've been in this family for what? Ten minutes? And you're telling me what to do?' said Penny.

'Penelope, don't make smart comments,' said Achilles. 'We're lucky to have, well, Lucky in the family.'

'You'll ruin this business if you assault someone with a club like that,' Valia told her father. 'You'll maim someone.'

'Be good to people,' said Lucky.

'Thou shouldst be nice,' said Penny.

'Tonight, I let them go,' Achilles said.

At dinner, for the first few minutes at least, the only voice at the dinner table was Achilles'—he began with some story about the ration card system, how restaurants like theirs were at a disadvantage. Then he asked the family to spare a thought for Greece, which was now at war with itself. Next, glasses and plates and bowls and jars of oil and vinegar were passed around and the sounds of fork-work, of sighs and remarks on the food, the yemista, savoro, and silverbeet cooked like horta. As usual, Lucky made sure he was the last member of the family to begin eating.

When Achilles finished he slung one arm over the back of his chair and lit a cigarette. As soon as possible Penny excused herself from the table. The table was dead and she was alive.

'You don't like smoking?' said Achilles to Penelope as she departed. 'No saying of thanks? For you, we do all this cooking? Authentic Greek food not possible to find better anywhere in Sydney?'

'Good cooking, everyone,' said Penny. 'Goodnight.'

'We oughta talk about this olive-wood club of yours,' said Lucky.

'I must have it to keep customers in line,' said Achilles. 'Look at how they come to the door after closing time. You and I cook with our right and left hands all day and they turn up when they like and expect us to offer hot food? No thanks, mister! During the war we were too nice to everyone. No more of that bullshit.'

'You should give us the club,' said Valia. 'We'll keep it under our bed. In future, Lucky can handle anyone who comes in late or drunk or acts rude. Everyone loves Lucky already.'

'Except for Penny,' said Lucky.

'She'll come around,' said Valia.

Achilles said: 'I made that club! Made from our own tree! It's a special thing.'

'Let's not fight about this,' said Lucky.

'Compromise then. In future the club stays on the verandah,' said Valia. 'You don't bring it to the kitchen every morning.'

'I promise to you,' said Achilles. 'The club stays on the verandah except in an emergency.'

In her bedroom, Penelope put away the book she was reading and turned off her lamp. The book was *Two Lives: Marie and Pierre Curie* by Thomas Morton, on loan from the school library. In the dark she thought of radium glowing, a cool blue flicker, and of electrical coiling, vats of chemicals; she saw Marie and Pierre together in a laboratory pouring liquids from flask to flask, their souls filling up. At night they discussed experiments, results, possibilities. Here was what Penny wanted from a partner: constant stimulation, partnership in work, and a never-ending passage of conversation about the most important subjects to them both. Why shouldn't she want these things? If that life was possible for a Polish woman in Paris, why not a somewhat Greek girl in Sydney?

Might it be a problem that Walter Schüller, a dark-haired German, a builder, wasn't much like Pierre Curie; wasn't a scientist, wasn't well educated, wasn't sublime? It was a problem, Penny supposed, that could be overcome, with kindness, with passion, perhaps. Always polite, at times overly so, Walter never failed to say hello to Penny when he saw her on the street—he laid new gutters and road railings around Bardwell Park—and they easily fell into conversation. She answered his inexhaustible questions about her science classes, her family. Walter said he wanted to study at university, but he said this in a way that gave Penny the impression it was already too late for him. He was big-bodied and long-necked and possessed perfect teeth, swelling green eyes. Blades of hair fell over his forehead. Penny told Walter about the letter she'd written to the University of Sydney expressing an interest in science degrees, requesting an interview for the women's college. The letter, sent months ago, had included references from her school's headmaster and science teacher. Walter remembered to ask, each time they met, whether she'd heard from the university. In some sense he'd become part of her endeavour. No, Penelope had still not heard. It had been eight, nine, and then ten weeks since she wrote to the faculty of science.

That night, each member of the family reposed in different rooms: Achilles Asproyerakas sat on his verandah bed and made minor alterations to the olive-wood club. As he shaved the wood with a carving knife, it became easier to imagine another group of customers coming to the door after closing time, tomorrow or the next day, rudely demanding dinner, even breaking the shop window in protest. In return Achilles would give those pigs the olive wood. It offered him a shot of relief to see the city cast in that way, as comprising heroes and villains and acts of violence that settled the matter. It was entertaining, the supposition of good and evil. Achilles didn't go to films, but he imagined this justice fantasy was the attraction, the sense of order, the purpose of narrative.

Penny, who resembled her mother to a degree that disconcerted Achilles, appeared to have interests that excluded the cafe. The other day in the kitchen, out of nowhere, in the middle of lunch service, she asked Achilles if he knew what radium was, and if he'd ever heard of Marie Curie. How would he know these things? What was he, a schoolteacher, a marker of exams? When Achilles answered in these terms she smiled briefly, as if his response confirmed something. Her teeth were yoghurt-white like her mother's; she looked as thin as a salt shaker beside her sister, who possessed the bodily dimensions that Achilles associated with Greekness, with his own mother, with his aunts, with Ithakans. But if asked (and this query was never presented to him, rather a question he posed only to himself), Achilles would have said Penelope was the fairer daughter, because of that certain resemblance. His connection to Eleftheria had been bad from the start. Probably his fault. Then his relationship with Penelope should be better, he thought. It could be a way to make amends for his marriage. Maybe Penny would change her mind about working in the cafe, maybe she'd come to enjoy Achillion life, like Lucky. There was love going on here, Achilles told himself.

He finished with the club and studied his hands. His fingernails were grainy and dark yellow like stained pine. He picked up a one-page letter from the university, which had arrived that day. A stranger, a professor of chemistry, invited Penelope Asproyerakas to meet with him and discuss a possible course of study. Achilles read the letter, and read it again, until it no longer upset him, then he folded the paper, slid it back into the envelope and carried it out of the room, into the kitchen.

A sleepy Valia, after brushing her teeth with powder, picked up the stack of magazines she'd been setting aside. With cigarette papers she'd tabbed the articles that might interest Penny—about Australian women at teachers' college; women who were midwives and doctors; or who were writers; or who worked in the Foreign Service. Over several weeks Valia had compiled stories that described a range of professions possible in 1946. None of these articles mentioned working in a family-run restaurant; just as well, since it was now plain as a cafe plate that Penny wasn't meant for the Achillion. Valia hoped her sister might read these stories and see, in some electric moment, a line of work to pursue. Maybe Penny already possessed secret life plans; or maybe she'd view Valia's best intentions, her maternal effort, as another kind of interference? You couldn't tell how Penny would respond. Valia went down the hall and knocked on her sister's door, the magazines under one arm, then she turned the doorknob and called her sister's name into the obscurity of the dark room. Penny's legs moved in the bed.

Valia put the magazines on a stool and said she'd come across some information about the modern workforce. 'Maybe not all that interesting. But you might want to take a look.'

In the dark Penny told her sister: 'I want to study science at the University of Sydney.'

'Good!' Valia stopped, not sure what to say. 'I think that would suit you.'

'Don't say a word to our father. I'm expecting a letter from the university any day. Then I'll tell him.'

Achilles' posture that night, when he entered the kitchen, was that of a man about to steal something. Crouching down at the stove, he massaged his temples with one hand and with the other fed the letter from the university into the furnace. And now that, he thought, would be the end of the matter; no more study for Penelope. He had made the cafe. He had made the family.

'What are you burning there?' asked Lucky, who'd been sitting at the booth nearest the kitchen entrance.

'A letter from someone asking for money, big surprise,' said Achilles. 'So I put them into the fucking fire.'

'Say, is there anything you want to talk about? You seem unhappy. It's obvious. It's all over you.'

'I am a happy person deep inside,' said Achilles. 'I have two good daughters. We have a beautiful business and when I wake up I say to myself I'm satisfied to live in this place and give my daughters a path in life. And you too. You get the path as well. I like you. You're a bit Greek. You're a bit American. What are you? I don't know. You work hard.'

'When was the last time you left the cafe? How about we go for a drink one afternoon? We should go to the pub on a weekly basis—Thursday, I think. Talk to some people. We might learn something from them.'

'We don't go in pubs,' said Achilles. 'We don't need to. We've got the cafe. Everything is here!'

3.

Valia's undiminishing desire to get out more—to see more of the city than the interior of the Achillion, to have sex with her husband in a building that wasn't also occupied by her father and sister, and to have loud sex—coincided with the visit to Sydney of the actual Benny Goodman and band, whose concert tour was brought to Valia's attention one morning by a newspaper. She read the paper in bed, sucking on sugared almonds they sold in the cafe. Lucky tramped in from the kitchen and changed his shirt, which had torn from armpit to waist as he reached over the stove to save the briki from boiling over.

'We must see Benny Goodman,' she said. 'It's perfect.'

'I'd like that,' said Lucky.

'We'll get a hotel that night. Look into it, Lucky.'

'We'll pay top dollar. We'll splash out.'

'We can stay the whole weekend.'

'Maybe three days?'

'The first day we'll go to the concert. The second day we spend in bed. The third: we'll visit the stores and buy you a clarinet. I like the thought of you playing music again.'

'I don't know, sweetheart. What I'm good at is kitchen work.'

'Let's open a restaurant in the city near the harbour.'

'A place where people go before the theatre. Steaks and chicken and seafood. With a main dining room downstairs and more private eating rooms upstairs.'

'And we'll live on the third floor of the building.'

'Parquet floors and columns and red tablecloths. Like the places I knew in Chicago.'

'We'll have two children.'

Lucky said: 'What do you think of having three or four?'

The night of the Benny Goodman concert, Lucky and Valia checked into a hotel in Paddington, and once inside the room they soon jumped on each other and made love and came to rest not entirely unclothed on the floor of their room, the boiling orange bedclothes undisturbed. They dressed for the concert: Valia loaded her hair into a bun and tied it with white ribbon; out of the bag came a black blouse and a long striped skirt. Lucky wore a Norfolk jacket, a brown bow tie and duck canvas trousers—he appeared thrown together. They took a tram to Park Street and waited a long time to cross George Street; then inside the theatre and up a dark staircase. Red portraits of colonial figures hung on the high, white walls. Lucky and Valia walked along the hallway and down a second staircase of wrought iron, and up another set of stairs and kept walking until they could hear no voices. Circular rugs lay on the marble floor. Valia rose up another set of stairs with a coil of anticipation around her spine. They were lost. Valia was angry; she felt ridiculous, walking one direction when she could have walked down another corridor, and they hadn't seen another person, no one, and couldn't ask the way. The implication that came to mind, that she didn't belong in this place, that she was only a cafe girl, brought her nerves right up to the surface, and her skirt started to irritate her—the cloth too stiff. At this point Valia slipped a few metres ahead of Lucky, moving fast, as she did in the cafe, as if about to break into a run. She heard voices, and as she turned a corner she saw them, a crowd of maybe three dozen people in black jackets, Benny Goodman surely among them.

Americans were standing everywhere, smoking, drinking beer or water, eating sandwiches; some had instrument cases at their feet. Lucky felt an odd, simple relief hearing their accents. He and Valia followed a waiter into the room until they reached the centre, both of them recognising that childish thrill of going unnoticed, and while they stood together, before anyone realised they were not supposed to be there, a man in a large blazer came towards them, his shiny lapels like a brassy badge of rank. He wore a stiff shirt and loafers with a waxy, beetle-shell shine. Benny Goodman broke seamlessly into the huddle of Lucky and Valia. They introduced themselves.

Goodman said without smiling: 'I noticed some unfamiliar faces in the room and thought, "What is their story? How do they fit in?" And, of course, "Are they married?"'

'We don't fit in here,' said Valia.

'We are married,' said Lucky.

'You're a damn lucky man, Mr Lucky. And you sound American,' Goodman noted. 'How did you meet?'

'During the war,' said Valia. 'We met a few blocks from here.'

'There's gotta be more to that story,' said Goodman.

Valia said: 'That question is posed of couples all the time—how did you meet? But it's more interesting why a couple stays together.'

'Oh, gosh no. Everyone gets the meet-cute question and no exceptions, I'm afraid,' said Goodman. 'Let's hear it. I've travelled a hell of a long way to be here and I'm never coming back to Sydney, I assure you, so humour me.'

Valia looked at her husband and her expression said: All right, you tell the story.

Lucky said: 'I was a mess steward, and I was miserable, and a messmate convinced me to play a concert in Sydney. I can play the clarinet.'

'You don't say! I'm down a clarinet man right now. This morning I told him he was in the wrong line of work. He was slow, out of step, asleep on his feet. Men like that waste my time, everyone's time.'

'People said I looked like you,' Lucky went on, 'and, the fact is, I pretended to be you, to be Benny Goodman on a USO tour.'

'What the hell! And you got away with this? I don't see any kind of resemblance. No offence to you.'

'The night of the concert, yes, I got away with it.'

'Everyone believed he was you,' said Valia. 'And that's how we met.'

'I oughta call the police this second,' said Goodman, leaning back slightly. He touched his own collar, his hair. 'Were you any good?'

'I was real good,' said Lucky.

'Are you two making fun of me?' Benny Goodman said. 'That's gotta be the craziest thing I ever heard in all the places I been.'

'It did happen,' said Valia. 'He was great.'

Goodman sniffed smugly and checked his watch. Valia could not look at Lucky in case she laughed.

'How about we see if you can play?' said Goodman. 'Let's find an empty room in this dump and if you show me the goods, you can join the band, only for today.'

'I don't want to play anymore,' said Lucky. 'I got my life settled now.'

'You don't want to prove yourself? Plenty of folks would kill for a shot with me. This is the best band in the world, there's none other like it. Such an opportunity will never come again.'

'I'd embarrass myself, I'm certain of it,' said Lucky. 'We came for the show, Mr Goodman.'

'Then you're in the wrong room. The hall is downstairs. And I still have a half a mind to call the police and have you removed.'

4.

Penelope tried on one of her mother's old dresses and before the garment made her cry she tore the thing from the neck down and fed it to the incinerator outside.

Sitting under the vines in a bathrobe, a puzzle of shade fell in segments around her, concocting an arboreal, out-of-hours light. The incinerator made no sound. Smoke stabbed up through the chimney, blown into the foliage of the olive tree, now five metres high. The family's olive tree kept growing up and up as if made of magic leftover from childhood.

When they were both children, both sitting in the tree, Valia had told to Penny stories from their family history, including a few words on how matters might have stood three or four thousand years ago. Their parents came from the island of Ithaka—a place Valia had never been. Penelope said the towns of Australia were islands of a kind. No, Valia told her, these towns were built on land stolen from civilisations that were older than anything Hellenic. Ithaka (natively known as *Ithaki*) was an island. It was a destination in poetry books, better known as a symbol for home than a real place where people lived, though some actually did, some of whom were aunts, uncles, cousins and more distant kin. Valia's tales were purposed to be a disclosure of their family's world-historic importance, since such standing wasn't apparent in an unremarkable suburb of Sydney. The Asproyerakas family, she said, was the oldest on Ithaka, and since the families that go back a long way on the island were interrelated, there was a chance that their ancestors were on the island during the reign of Odysseus and were almost certainly allied by marriage to King Odysseus or his offspring. And they existed, these heroes, the ancients didn't make up names; there was usually some original you could pin the deed on, a man who thought he could fly, the woman who killed her children to spite her husband.

'I don't believe you,' said Penelope.

'But I know more than you,' said Valia.

'You're more bossy, that's what.'

While telling these stories, Valia would cut slivers from the branches of the olive tree, and she and Penelope ran their fingers along the sapwood, along the opalescent green bone Valia would recall many years later, whenever she opened an avocado, and touched the flesh still stuck to the avocado stone.

Now it was September 1946: Valia Asproyerakas, twenty years old, married for five months, her hair done, apron tied, taking a break from the Achillion counter, pushed open the back door with her foot and went outside, where Penelope sat under the red vines, her mother's dress burning in the incinerator behind her. Valia asked for a smoke, and she caught the single cigarette with one hand, a box of matches with the other. Like workmates, like teammates, they often threw things to each other.

Penny said: 'I can hear you and Lucky at night.'

'And what you do hear?'

'I don't need to spell it out.'

'Yes you do. Tell me what you're talking about.'

'Valia, the tone in your voice is aggressive.'

Penny's words were issued in a faraway voice.

Valia said: 'If anyone is hostile in this family—apart from Achilles—it's you. You are aloof. Aloofly hostile.'

'Sorry, sister, but *aloofly* is not a word.'

'Some days you're all shrugs and never minds and you don't care what's going on around you, and that's just another kind of hostility that puts me at some distance from you. I understand you're young and young people can be difficult.'

'You want me to be more friendly?'

'That would be nice.'

'I can hear you and Lucky in the middle of the night making love, or whatever it is you're doing. It sounds like shoddy carpentry going on.'

'You'd like us to be quiet?'

'We all share this space, sister.'

'I'm married, Penny. I sleep with my husband. We fuck.'

'I see, that's what sex sounds like when you're married.'

Penelope, finished with this conversation, stood up to leave. In the kitchen she told Achilles: 'I'm going out for a few hours.'

'Why for? It's a no-school day.'

'I have a friend to meet.'

'Who's the friend?'

'Someone you don't know.'

Achilles said: 'Your friends know where you are. They'll come to the cafe. Bring them here. They won't have to pay full price, unless they insist on paying. And it's good manners for them to insist.'

He cleaned the stovetop with a paint scraper. Sweat beaded on his forearms and this pleased him because it meant that the stove was hot, the customers were ordering full meals, and he was exercised. He understood that his attempts to control other people were futile, that despite him they would go on doing and getting what they wished, and this tormenting knowledge allowed Achilles to continue his controlling behaviour without much reflection, further assisted by his family's tendency to avoid confrontation with him. They put up with Achilles' moods: they paid the small price as though it were a toll that one generation paid to another, rarely putting him in his place (apart from the night of the olive-wood club). And Achilles believed his life, in relation to theirs, was a monotonous succession of unspeakable yet small humiliations, his unhappiness relieved only by moments of delusional hope, when he believed one day others would listen to him, confide in him, and call him wise.

Lucky was the first family member to discover Penny's relationship with Walter Schüller. They had already met, Walter and Lucky, outside the Taylor Street branch of the Colonial Bank, while both men waited for the doors to open. In retrospect, Lucky accepted that he had clumsily inflicted small talk on a reluctant Walter, who was even more indisposed to a handshake. Walter sucked in his cheeks severely when he smoked, as if with disappointment, and his large frame made the cigarettes look undersized, the habit ill-suited to him.

'You're from Baden Baden?' Lucky had asked him. 'I've heard of it.'

'Maybe one day you saw a map.'

'Did you come here before the war, or after?'

'Before. I was interned.'

'Do you get asked that a lot?'

'All the time. It's why I hate questions from strangers.'

A few weeks later, through one of the cafe windows, Lucky saw the German for the last time. Penny and Walter were on a street corner, standing close to each other, clearly composed as a pair on a new footpath that Walter had recently laid down for a price the council found irresistible. Lucky pushed the Benny Goodman glasses back into place. Penny and Walter's bodies were squared. Quickly her hand touched his. Then they looked down at the ground between them, in some kind of embarrassment of intimacy. Lucky could see what they meant to each other.

That afternoon, at a discreet moment, he told Penny: 'I think you should be more careful. That's all I want to say.'

'What are you talking about?'

'You know what.'

'Do I look like the bloody oracle to you?'

'I'm talking about your charming German friend, Walter. I saw you two together on the goddamn street.'

'He asked me how I was and I felt sorry for him. He thinks everyone hates him.'

'In my experience he's not pleasant in conversation.'

'My advice to you, Lucky: don't grow into the wretched life my father has planned for everyone.'

'I suggest you don't spend time with Walter in public. Your father is like a crazy man at the moment.'

'I rarely see Walter in public,' said Penny, smiling voraciously. 'Mostly I visit his house.'

'If Achilles finds out, what's he going to do to Walter? Your father hates Germans.'

'My father is a fool. And you should hear what he says about Americans behind your back.'

'I didn't think you'd be this difficult. For a young person, you have a lot of edges, Penny.'

'Thanks for this little talk. You've never been more impressive.'

If the Asproyerakas family were a plane, Penny was jumping out. If Penny were an open parachute, the family was row upon row of razor-sharp trees.

5.

For dinner, Achilles flattened keftedes into meat patties, hoping to surprise and impress his American son-in-law with a cheeseburger, or what Achilles believed was an improvement on the cheeseburger, a sandwich he'd heard about and further investigated while sitting on the back-yard toilet, flicking through magazines that Valia bought and Penelope didn't appear to ever read. Instead of buns Achilles used the ends of bread loaves.

Valia made a mess of her burger. She said: 'This cannot go on the menu.'

'We could call it the Achillion Burger,' said Achilles.

'I like it,' said Lucky. 'I like it a whole lot.'

'I don't,' said Penny. 'It's a complete failure.'

'That comes as no surprise,' said Achilles.

'I'm helping you make good business decisions,' Penny said. 'Take my advice or don't.'

Achilles said: 'Let's forget about the burger. There's more

to tell you. I am getting what they call a pastime. At fairs and rodeos they hold boxing matches, and in future I will take part. I will become a boxer.'

'That's bare-knuckle boxing!' said Valia. 'That's not a hobby, that's dangerous. You'll die. A man with ability will kill you.'

'You may be in a difficult weight class,' said Lucky. 'Some people simply aren't the right-sized human for boxing.'

'I think I'm a perfect weight,' said Achilles. 'I have this energy building and building. What, you think I should play chess at the beach?'

'It might be good for you to knock some sense into people,' said Penny. 'Or vice versa.'

Achilles did not know what vice versa meant. He said: 'Next big decision to make: we need to fix up the cafe. This is a dialogue we're having here. We're in a philosophical mood. We need to give the cafe a stronger theme. Lucky, how well do you know this city?'

'I'm learning all the time.'

Achilles said: 'On Pitt Street there's a cafe called the California. I saw a picture in one of those magazines. The word California is spelled in tiles on the cafe floor. Big letters, you know, C-A-L-I-F-O-R-N-I-A. Those bastards have American everything, sundaes and soda fountains and the full milk bar experience. But they don't have a real American. Do you understand what a theme is?'

'Yes,' said Lucky. 'I understand.'

'You are our real American.'

Valia wanted to know: 'Where is this going?'

Achilles: 'I want our customers to have a genuine Australian-American-Greek milk bar-cafe education. Lemon and pineapple drinks, that's the next favourite thing. A soda fountain, sundaes, shakes of milk. People will eat it up. Maybe a US sign for display, big like CALIFORNIA. We want an American theme. Name some other states in America.'

'Illinois? That's where I was born.'

'I can't see it in my mind. Name me some more.'

<h2 style="text-align:center">6.</h2>

After a busy lunch service, Penny informed her father she was more than friends with Walter (she used his real name, Waltraud). She said they had no plans yet to become what she described as 'matrimonially established' (this term she took from *Great Expectations*). She sought to be honest with her father. The news she presented to Achilles had been written down, memorised, and had rested patiently in her pocket for a whole week, the speech practised many times in private. Penny hoped she could tell her father the things she might have told her mother. Walter, a builder, had expressed a wish to eventually study science, and this pleased her, Penny told her father, because next year she hoped to attend the University of Sydney. She was waiting for a letter from the faculty.

The scene was played out in Penny's room. Achilles stood and she sat at her desk, surplus classroom furniture, with four books before her: uppermost in the pile was *A Girl of the Limberlost*, which Penny had read twice. After she finished speaking, Achilles asked his daughter to stretch out her arms in front. This she did. He'd said nothing about Walter. She imagined her father was looking for marks or bruises, worried that Walter might have hurt her. She blithely said, 'Here,' and turned over her forearms, hardly thicker than her wrists. Her palms faced upwards, both hands rested on the books, and she waited for her father to acknowledge that there were no marks on her body. Achilles Asproyerakas left the room then returned with his olive-wood club and he brought the cudgel down across her arms, breaking bone and fracturing the wooden desktop with a splintery shattering crack. The moment he heard Penny's cries—the worst sound Achilles ever heard—he was no longer angry with his daughter.

Achilles needed to be somewhere else, to get out of the room and leave the cafe, to follow the lines of this shattering. Valia would arrive soon, and she'd be in a position to provide whatever care was necessary.

'Lucky!' Achilles barked as he entered the kitchen, motioning with his head, removing his apron.

'What the hell did you do?' asked Lucky, watching warily.

'Come with me. We are going to find this Nazi bastard. If you're my family, you will come.'

'I'm staying here, Achilles.'

It was so hot the day was over for the suburb. Walter would probably be at home. Achilles knew what to look for; a few times Walter had come in for beef sandwiches and baked beans. The German's vehicle: a Ford Popular. Achilles, in no state to drive, climbed behind the wheel of his utility, which the family always referred to as the Cafe Truck.

~

Two customers, a married couple, took Penny to the hospital in their sedan, with Valia riding next to her in the back seat. Lucky stayed behind, suddenly not at home in the Achillion, the site itself depleted and felled, but he did his commercial duty: other customers were still in the cafe eating. They'd sat and whispered through the screams that came out from behind the kitchen. When he was alone, Lucky wiped down the stovetop with a wet cloth and the plate gave off cooking smells, the wet streaks crackling like spices over fire.

Achilles drove around looking for Walter and after a few hours he stopped his car to walk the streets, fist clenched, saturated with himself, and in his mind he set up a confrontation that was two blows long and conclusive, a full stop. There, the grammar of Achilles, shepherd of his people. Soon it was too dark for him to see, and he couldn't read street signs, or the numbers on houses, or his own watch.

'I don't want to see police,' Penny told the nurse at Canterbury Hospital. She had said the same thing to Valia, and to the doctor who applied a plaster cast to her arm. Then Penelope held her breath; this was what she did when she wanted to stop thinking about something.

Valia vowed she and Lucky would leave the Achillion that same day and she left the room before the orderlies brought in two new patients, both injured in the same car accident. After them arrived the traffic of nurses and doctors. Penelope, from her bed, watched a blue bee come in through one window and fly out another. Walter arrived and kissed her on the forehead, his glance rapid and hot, and he looked around and under the bed and in the cupboard for anything that belonged to her or might be useful to them. He found nothing. He suggested they move to Canberra, temporarily, and Penny instantly agreed—that was how the best decisions were arrived at, she thought; they should be made without hesitation. Walter heard there was work going in the capital city laying footpaths and roads, pouring foundations. Construction's bread-and-butters. Walter knew two Austrian men, brothers, who lived down there. They had a spare room. Penny didn't care where she lived. In the hospital she decided she didn't live anywhere, yet. Home was a place in the future. Walter's limbs shook as he picked her up from the bed.

'The cast feels heavy,' she said. 'Am I heavy?'

'The same as before,' he said.

As Penny was put down in the car's back seat, on a make-shift bed of pillows and blankets, and as she and Walter drove south, Penelope had the sick feeling she was being twisted against her will, beyond her control, and that other people could do something to you and this might change you forever, and because of these wounds and the defences you set up thereafter, you might become someone you never intended to be. Unless—unless what?

Without saying a word to Achilles, who sat out on the back verandah smoking cigarette after cigarette, Valia and Lucky packed two suitcases and left the Achillion. They found a train to Central Station and a tram that passed through

Paddington. Once inside a hotel, Valia lay down on the bed looking up at the ceiling rosette. She'd stayed in this building before: the weekend they saw Benny Goodman perform, the night they bumped into him. Now they stayed in the cheapest room available. The rosette's plaster was mouldy. Valia's head turned and grazed the room's dull sights: a patch in the wall still to be painted, a broom fallen from behind the door, a new cobweb. These disappointments seemed of a piece with Achilles' crime. Lucky unpacked and the stark sound of banging cupboards and drawers was caught up in Valia's sense of despair.

'Achilles should be the one leaving the cafe, not us,' she said. 'Penny should not be leaving home. It's all wrong. We must get her back.'

'I figure this is the stage where you and I do our own thing.'

Valia fell into a foul mood for weeks, disappointed, angry, scowling: Achilles had ruined the Asproyerakas family— and they hadn't been a great clan to begin with. When she and Lucky went for walks down along the bay, she preferred not to speak about what happened at the Achillion. A sunset glow sputtered from the long thin clouds suspended over the harbour, and the cliffs of the northern shore, vividly outlined, were revealed as from the fists of a giant.

7.

Business disappeared at the cafe. The booths were empty. Achilles was disgraced. Only one customer the morning after Penny and Valia and Lucky left. There were few sounds gloomier, to Achilles, than the echo of a dry cough in an empty shop. He used his free time to cook his favourite dishes for himself: savoro, and beef stifado bulked up with prunes, and in the morning he made patsas, which he scrupulously prepared, removing every speck of waste from the tripe. People said you couldn't taste the shit, even if a little went into the soup, but Achilles always could.

He was both superstitious and religious but observed the rituals and dogma of superstition more frequently than he did religion. The basis of any particular superstition, in his case, could be highly idiosyncratic, incongruent with any Greek canon of irrational beliefs: he believed that monkeys brought bad luck, for example, and that even to lay eyes on a picture of this animal might result in bad fortune or illness to you or someone in your home. With vivid enthusiasm, his mother once told him that monkeys were unlucky and he found this wisdom as portable as a recipe. He couldn't leave his mother's notion behind in Ithaka, where no one shared the opinion. He wasn't surprised to learn that King Alexander of Greece died of a macaque bite in 1920.

Superstition haunted you like the dead, and as a natural part of this discourse the monkey became extra-animal, supernatural, spectral, powerful, familial. Superstition was the dead talking to you.

No customers, again, in the Achillion. The people walking past didn't even slow down. Maybe there had been a council meeting about him. Maybe he was cursed. In a booth, Achilles flipped his worry beads over his wrist like a whip, and the amber clacked with a bright metallic sound. When would his daughters return? How does a person exit a family? Walk away and never speak to their kin again, he supposed. The years would go by. Then he'd fall mortally ill and Penny and Valia would visit him in his final days to bear witness, their hands over their eyes, and listen to his little voice say goodbye, and sorry—at last a final apology. They'd forgive him, he imagined, because everything ends, including anger and hatred and revenge. At last they'd love him again. But to be loved at the precipice of death! Not a reunion a father could look forward to.

For the first time in the history of the Cafe Achillion, he wrote a note to hang in the window: *Back soon in 10 minutes flat.* It injured him to close the shop. But what else could he do? If he stayed in the cafe he might start thinking he was the last person in Bardwell Park; he'd go mad. Achilles put the takings from the previous month into a bag and rushed down to the bank in a grey cardigan and an apron. And by God there it was, his curse animal, on a poster advertising the Los Dios Circus: an illustration featuring a conceited monkey in a bandleader costume and an elephant, in the background, wearing a crown. Achilles put up his hands to block out the image. Without setting foot inside the bank, he turned around and went back to the cafe. If something bad should happen today, he asked God, don't make me wait! Achilles locked the doors, sat down in the booth and didn't get up—didn't dare do another thing on this unlucky day—until about 5 pm, when someone knocked on the closed cafe doors and peered inside, into the immaterial gloom of the unlit cafe. It was Lucky, or one of the Furies in the disguise of a son-in-law.

Achilles unlatched the door and said: 'What do you want? You want money, is that it? You want to attack me?'

'I need to pick up a few of our things.'

'Today is not a good time. Come back again and bring Valia,' Achilles said, shutting the door on his son-in-law.

Next day, at dinner, two customers. Two men sat in separate booths, waiting for their meal: two men who, by coincidence, both ordered the mixed grill, the Achillion's most popular dish. Achilles set their meat on the stove, from left to right: bacon, sausage, mutton chop, ox tongue, tomato (grills came with half a fried tomato on the side). While they were waiting, the customers started arguing with each other—Achilles, watching through the peephole between the kitchen and cafe, didn't understand what they were quarrelling about. Something about a person known to them both, someone who'd 'had enough of that man', which could refer to any number of people, which also vaguely described the present condition of the Asproyerakas family, and in a stinging moment of second-hand shame Achilles turned away from the peephole and his gaze fell inadvertently on the olive-wood club propped up in the corner of the room.

By the time he'd pushed through the door into the cafe, the two customers had left their booths and were brawling on the floor, rolling around in such entanglement that Achilles had difficulty telling one guy from the other.

He stood over the nearest man and struck him in the shoulder with the olive-wood club. The blow glanced across and cut open this fellow's high forehead. The other man, receiving blows to the ribs, screamed, 'Don't!', and out of a pity reflex Achilles turned back to the first man, who was dazed and trying to sit up, blood from the head wound skittering over his face. Out of an acutely buried impulse, and surprising even himself, Achilles uttered the word 'Youvarlakia' (meatballs in lemon sauce), as he brought the weapon down on the man's knee, making the sound of a stick across a ball. It was the other man's turn again. He took the club around his middle. 'Youvarlakia!' Achilles said again. A marvellous dish he couldn't place on the menu because Australians wouldn't order it. And he dragged the two brawlers out onto the footpath and closed the cafe, cleaned up the blood, extinguished the stove, and drank one glass of whiskey—no more (he felt like more). He expected the men to come back with guns or knives.

That night Achilles stood at the front window and looked out, waiting for a person, or a gang, to return seeking revenge. Why didn't they come back?

He bought a gun the next day. The city was oversupplied with black market ex-army service guns, a customer had said months ago. At the Bardwell Newsagency, a business that also sold firearms and which everyone referred to as the 'paper shop', Achilles asked the owner to show him the new rifles in store. Nodding, his eyes unfocused, not much interested in the overview of stock, Achilles waited to ask whether there might be any 'second-hand rifles' for sale. As a matter of fact, said the owner, there was a .303 ex-military gun available. He asked if Achilles was an anarchist, or if he were planning to shoot anyone. Achilles said he wanted a weapon for the cafe, in case of emergency. He had no plans to ever use the thing. Other people possessed guns. He required one too.

Then Achilles began to pray: at times to God, at times to his deceased wife, Eleftheria. *Please bring back my daughters and my customers. If you do I promise to be kind to all men.* For a week he said this prayer when he got into bed and when he woke up, and each night he slept poorly, had to medicate himself with drink or excessive amounts of food. In the second week of prayer he called in a Greek Orthodox community priest, Father Nektarios, a tall and pale man whose cheekbones were accentuated by red filigreed veins. The priest asked for payment (Achilles provided) and then they sat together and prayed in a booth of the cafe. They prayed, specifically, for customers to return. Achilles didn't tell Father Nektarios about the outrage committed against Penelope, but the priest, though he socialised little, had heard the gossip about the cafe owner, Mad Achilles, and his daughters. Nektarios didn't ask about the assault—wanting to spare himself a difficult conversation—but he vaguely asked after Achilles' family, and Achilles said his daughters were at school. Like that, done: the two patriarchs' dance of denial and avoidance. On the table between them lay an icon of St Georgios, patron of the Hellenic army. For thirty minutes, Achilles estimated, he and Nektarios prayed hard for people to return to the cafe.

'And will this curse end?' asked Achilles, after paying Nektarios.

'It will end,' said the priest. 'In one month!'

A new customer, stewbum drunk, arrived two days later. He rode a grey, malnourished horse, bridle but no saddle, into the Cafe Achillion and gave a tug on the reins when he reached the counter. The cafe doors were tall, they pushed inwards, and the poor horse was indoors before any objection could be raised. Achilles came out from the kitchen and pointed to a small sign stationed above the cigarette stand:

NO DOGS NO CATS OR OTHER ANIMALS AT ANY TIME
—THE OWNER ACHILLES

While the horse moved about sideways with a tiddly click-clack, the rider bellowed his order of a T-bone steak, cooked medium, with gravy and egg on the side. Without a word, Achilles went back into the kitchen, loaded his gun, and he crossed himself as he walked down the cafe floor, stopping in front of the horse. He aimed at a spot in front of the ear and shot the animal, sprinkling the floor with blood, toppling it. The head of Achilles, shaken by a gust of horror, gave a jerk, and his eyes darted from the twitching animal to the unsteady rider who got to his feet and ran out the door.

Achilles checked his apron for blood spatter: there was none, not a stain on his clothes. He put the rifle behind the counter and let his body go loose, go completely weak. It took some time before he could bring himself to look at the horse's body and the blood running from its nose to the table at booth four. He needed another pair of hands. But who cared enough to help him? Achilles went outside and waved down a car.

'I have a problem in my shop,' he told the driver.

'What sorta problem?'

'A horse died in there.'

'What's a dead horse doing in a cafe, mate?'

'It's not my horse. Someone rode in there, caused trouble, and took off. I don't know how to explain.'

With the driver's assistance, he moved the animal's body from the shop floor to the tray of the Cafe Truck, and then Achilles drove the corpse to the council tip, where he set the remains alight, offering a prayer cobbled together from his memories of the few funerals he'd attended. Over the horse, in English, he said:

Sleep forever
Pardon all our iniquities
Wash us and make us whiter than snow

2002

1.

THE MURDERER HENRY Matfield died on the bank of a river that crossed into the Deua National Park where he'd been in hiding since the Third of April. Matfield had shot himself in the head with his rifle, using his thumb to pull the trigger: the bullet exited the rear of his skull and little damage was done to his face. The bushwalkers who found Henry recognised him from images they'd seen on television, and his mother identified the body at the state coroner's complex back in Sydney.

Emily wanted to speak with Henry's parents, who had never, to her knowledge, given a media interview. Already she'd checked the online telephone directory for the Matfields' number (news stories referred to Henry as a 'Petersham man'), she'd looked through old White Pages at the Surry Hills library, and she called the Matfields' former lawyer-spokesman and asked his assistant to forward a message. Emily didn't expect much to come of that particular call. Help from other peoples' lawyers? She checked the voter roll with the electoral commission, but the Matfields had either dropped off the register or requested their details be kept private. An ex-colleague, a reporter at *The Independent*, had once told Emily that chasing a person for an interview was like opening a CD case but finding the wrong CD inside, and then opening another case and finding nothing inside, and so on and so forth through the pile until, at last, you found what you were looking for. Back then Emily considered this metaphor clunky and juvenile. Now she felt a little clunky herself. In London she'd read reports from the coroner, from the inquest, and the inquiry into the police handling of the case, but still she felt like she hadn't prepared enough. She hadn't anticipated a problem with contacting the Matfields. She hadn't done this kind of work in years! Instead, for almost a decade, she'd fixed sentences such as: *The shark attack occurred at lunchtime.* And: *The man was found dead suffering from an unknown medical condition.*

Perhaps all newspaper reporters—and for a moment she saw them as a force, a clique with knowledge she didn't possess—owed Emily for her years of mostly thankless copyediting. She called in the debt; she got in touch with journalists who covered the shooting at Lucky's to ask if they'd be prepared to pass on the phone number of Henry's parents. The case was eight years old and no longer front-of-the-book news. They ought to share! thought Emily.

First she dialled the switchboard of *The Australian* and asked for Rebecca Sturt, who'd reported the Third of April. Rebecca, now chief-of-staff, told her: 'The family have disappeared.'

'What do you mean by disappeared?'

'I tried to find them a few years ago for a story about the fifth anniversary of the massacre but I couldn't get hold of them. There you go: they disappeared. I got the yarn up anyway.'

Next Emily contacted a court reporter at the *Sydney Morning Herald*. The journalist—her voice was throaty and hurried—said Adam Matfield, Henry's father, had died a few years earlier. Joanna Matfield was residing somewhere in the Blue Mountains. 'But I don't pass on numbers to other journos,' the reporter said. 'And anyway, seriously, Joanna will never talk to the media.'

Emily called Peter Popescu, not knowing what else to do, determined this time to prise the number out of him. He said he was fine, thank you, about to take a lunch break. Emily promised him she wouldn't mess up an interview with Joanna, would not misrepresent her experience or views, would not write about the Third of April without acquiring meaningful consent. Would not pursue the article at all if enough people refused to speak to her. Emily said she herself had witnessed a traumatic event as a child and it made her want to write *well* about violence and grief and trauma, to narrativise an event with honesty.

'Look—don't say where you got the number,' said Popescu, relenting. 'Hang on, wait: that would be dishonest. If Joanna asks, yes, tell her I gave it to you. No question she suffered in her own way. But don't quote me on that. And also give her my best?'

Emily found cold phone calls difficult—all that needy, intrusive and mercenary interaction. She went for a walk up and down the hotel hallway and when she returned to her room it seemed more possible, likely even, that Joanna would be ready to talk, finally ready to talk at length about her son, the catastrophe of her only child. Henry was born to someone; he was a boy once, a toddler, a kid who knew nothing about guns or murder, and then something had happened, something had failed in his environment or family or his mental process. Henry's mother, if anyone, understood this full tragedy. There must be a surge of words waiting in Joanna Matfield. In the hallway Emily walked these thoughts into her blood.

She picked up the phone and called Joanna, who said with anger: 'I will never talk to you. Please do not call again.'

Still feeling jolted and shamed by these words, Emily followed one impossible call with another: George Lee, father of Chris, a chef killed at Lucky's cafe. In a *Herald* story from 1994, which Emily kept in a folder of clippings, George was described as an employee at a shoe repair store in Marrickville. On the phone with the only such store in that area, Emily asked for George Lee, and when he came to the phone she heard him exhale loudly, like he'd had this conversation before. Emily explained why she was calling.

'Can we meet? Whenever might be convenient for you? It can be for as brief a period of time as you wish.'

'You want a picture of Chris—something to use in the article, right?'

'No, I'm not asking for a picture.'

'I never talk about the person who did it. In our family, we don't talk about him. We believe no one should talk about him.'

Emily said: 'Often in the media we ask bereaved people to speak about their grief when it's still recent, when it's almost never appropriate. In that early period of mourning, a loss can be hard to apprehend—it should be a private time. If you're willing, I want to discuss how you've coped with this loss over time, over almost eight years.'

'What I have to say is that I cope by knowing that I should be here for the rest of my family. I remind myself that I should keep living. That I can't go to a clifftop on the harbour and do myself in. Because I have other children. I'm a grandfather.'

When George raised the subject of suicide, Emily felt an urge to say her father took his own life. That she watched him do it. That one of her earliest feelings of permanence was the wish he'd stayed alive. But she and George weren't comrades in grief; Emily didn't want him to think she'd claim that status.

George continued: 'Fact is, I don't understand how the grief has changed, or how it's changed me. I understand what you want. But I can't give it to you.'

It was Emily's fourth day in Sydney. Sometimes she thought she was too heartbroken and unskilled to do this part of the job, to ask strangers about murder; the death and grief might be too moving and terrible and inscrutable for her to address, and she could only linger in front of the event, the Third of April rising like a monument, and then leave. Her self-doubt was made worse when people were unwilling to talk to her. And it could be made worse by an old part of Emily saying: *whatever it is you're doing, you're doing it wrong. Don't trust yourself.*

She called Sophia, the survivor. A boy answered the phone, said, 'Speaking, please?', before passing the phone to his mother.

Emily said: 'I'm writing an article about the Lucky's franchise for the *New Yorker* magazine. I've been talking to Lucky Mallios and I'd love to ask you some questions, if you—'

'No, oh fuck no. I've done this before, and I'm not going through it again.'

'The piece will be more of an essay than straight reporting.'

'What's the difference?'

'This would be more like, well, narrative non-fiction.'

'I don't need any essays at the moment. I've got a lot going on myself.'

At this point Emily's mother appeared in her mind. Her mum's voice seemed to come from the empty corner of the hotel room.

'Emmy, what's gone wrong now?' said the representation of Emily's mother.

'Some people don't want to speak to me,' Emily replied.

'It's your tone, isn't it? Your questions are too nosey. Have you forgotten your manners?'

'If you actually have manners, you don't forget them.'

'Is that directed at me? Are you saying I'm rude?'

'I don't know how else to tell you.'

Keep making calls, Emily advised herself. She rang Lucky to arrange another interview. He answered and it sounded as if he dropped the receiver, then picked it up and placed it under his chin, his voice faint.

'Let's meet the day after tomorrow,' he said. 'There's something important I want to show you. It will work beautifully in your story, I guarantee.'

'Lucky, there's something else. I have this feeling that you *did* know my father. I need to know more about him. It's of real personal importance to me.'

'My memory is good,' Lucky said, and stopped there.

'And?'

'And I can't remember him. I don't believe I ever met the guy. If I could help you, no question about it, I would. I like you. How's the article going?'

He was clearly lying about her father. How long would he keep this up? However long, she could wait for the lie to be exhausted.

'George Lee and Joanna Matfield and Sophia don't want to participate.'

'Let me talk to Sophia. I should call her anyway. It's been too long. The others, I can't help you. Could be, you know, there's nothing new to say about the shooting.'

2.

Emily left her room to go outside for a cigarette. Her mobile phone buzzed and rang in the back pocket of her jeans as she walked towards the lift quick and busy. She cleared her throat and jabbed at the answer button. Whoever was calling, she thought, even Michael, they were a good kind of interruption, more important than tobacco, which she'd quit almost three years ago. Such a discipline had required enormous effort. It engaged her imagination: in order to stop herself from buying Marlboro Lights on bad days Emily had, at different times, envisaged a doctor giving her a four-month prognosis, then imagined telling her hypo-thetical child about her terminal illness, and saying last goodbyes to mother and stepfather and Liam and husband. She'd pictured her funeral. Michael's eulogy was inaccurate on several points.

'It's me,' said Michael. 'Where are you?'

'About to smoke a cigarette.'

'But you quit!'

'A lot has changed in the past week. I'm starting life from scratch.'

'I didn't sleep much last night.'

'Because you were up late with Therese.'

'No, I spent the night by myself because I had a terrible day.'

'Terrible? That is terrible.'

'And your parents called again, your mum. I didn't mention, you know, what's been happening, because that's for you to explain. It's not my place. I take it you haven't told them, since your mother didn't mention . . . it.'

'It?' Emily snorted. 'I'll get in touch with them soon.'

'I'm not sure I want to be with Therese. That's what I want to tell you. There are no guarantees with that relationship, if you'd call it a relationship. This is a confusing time and I'm sorry I'm dragging you into my confusion.'

'Michael, you're now making this worse than it already is.'

'I'm not doing it on purpose. I don't know what I'm doing.'

'I can tell that,' said Emily. 'If I could help you, I still wouldn't.'

She passed the time between her conversation with Michael and the call she made to her mother in Ipswich by consecutively smoking two cigarettes outside, a few doors down from the hotel, amid the chuckle-speak of people leaving bars, before she disposed of the packet in a bin on the street. She understood what was happening: marriages ended; people were suddenly alone; people retreated into behaviours that reminded them of their past self. You had to give yourself a break! But she couldn't exalt in her failures anymore—at least not right now. 'Fuck you, again,' she said, wedging the Marlboro packet into the overstuffed bin. She went upstairs and sat on the floor, stiffly stretching before folding her legs and calling Ipswich.

'What's wrong with your voice?' her mother asked. 'You sound nasal.'

Smoking made Emily sound like she had a cold. 'I picked up a bug on the flight. The usual thing.'

'We went shopping today,' her mother said. 'Here, Rick wants to talk to you.'

Emily's stepfather, Rick, got on the phone and said: 'Right. We saw some overcoats in town, good tweed ones. Made in Donegal, on sale, all sizes, men's and women's. Would you like me to buy one for you? I'm going back tomorrow. You'd be a small, I'd say. The clothes are true to size.'

'No, thank you.'

'All right. Okay. Anyway, the price was reasonable and the colours were tremendous. Send me an email if you change your mind. I'll put your mother back on.'

For a long time, during Emily's teenage years, the spontaneously kind Rick had managed to disappoint his bookish stepdaughter because he had not the slightest interest in literature, not even the newspaper, and would plainly state, *I've never read a book in my life*, and say so proudly at times, the way some people boast of not having a single filling in their mouth. When Emily grew up and went off to university in London, she'd cruelly convey her stepfather's claim to friends, in part because it was an odd thing for a person to say, and in part because it spoke to the distance between his life and hers. Later, she came to see that what she'd once taken for disappointment, and betrayal even, in the worst fevers of adolescent contempt, was partly something else: she wanted Rick to be a little more like Ian. But without the catastrophe.

'Rick's not enjoying the long winter this year,' said Heidi. 'But how's Mr Michael? He must be missing you.'

'Let's not call him Mr Michael. He's fine, we spoke a few

minutes ago,' said Emily. She wasn't ready to tell her parents about Therese. 'Mum, I know that Dad—Ian, I mean—lived in Sydney for a few years during the war. What do you know about his life here? He must have said something about that time. Do you know where he lived?'

'Oh, God. Who knows? He never talked about the place. The man was a mystery.'

'He must have mentioned Sydney to you,' Emily persisted.

A pause over the phone. 'Maybe there *is* a little detail I may not have mentioned.'

Emily opened her notebook. Please Mum, she thought, give me something of substance. Tell me where I come from.

'Once, he said he'd published some writing, a poem or a play, in a little magazine. I think it was after university. It might have been during his posting in Australia. Ian wouldn't show me the play or poem, or whatever it was: said he didn't have a copy—that's how much he thought of the thing. He said he wrote under his initials, I.W. Asquith.'

'You've never told me this! Why didn't you mention that he'd written something? Can you understand why it's meaningful for me to know that my father was a writer?'

'He wasn't a real writer. It's not important. I'd forgotten.'

Heidi used avoidance and silence to cope with Ian Asquith's suicide. She believed that repression could heal the mind. All her life Emily had tried to convey that her own brain did not work that way, did not forget by command.

Emily said: 'It is important! You shouldn't forget such stuff. Writing was something he did in his life and it's something I do in mine.'

'Oh, Ian was a disturbed man. It was probably just a nothing poem. You wrote poems for the school magazine, remember? And Rick is your proper father. Rick is good-natured and clever and good-looking. We're lucky to have him. Anyway, I never asked Ian about his writing.'

'Why not?'

'Because, Emily, I don't interrogate people. I accept what they say, and let them decide the limits of what to tell me. That's how I am.'

'What do you mean by that?'

'I'm not always trying to squeeze information out of people. I'm no journalist.'

'Mum, I care about stories. My whole career has been devoted to storytelling in one way or another.'

'You used to be a proofreader, darling.'

After the call, Emily turned on the television (a news bulletin) and pulled down the heavy bedspread, leaving it furrowed on the floor like a drawn-back curtain. She turned off her phone, she ran a hand over the bleached pillowcases, the cool and soft sheets. She wanted to scream. She slept.

3.

It rained early the next morning, bringing out the sickbitter smells of road oils and ozone. Emily entered the University of Sydney campus, her sneakers squeaking on the wet footpath. Summer school was over, autumn semester yet to commence: a few solitary students in the library foyer.

The air-conditioning sank into Emily's damp hair. She took the stairs to one of the lower-ground levels and walked through a cubist sequence of rooms. Along one brick wall was a series of concave brass plates, which brought to mind the inside of a clarinet. Mortuary light in the basement. As soon as search engines had become available Emily looked up her father's name; even in Sydney she Googled his first name plus surname, finding nothing. But she had never once Googled his initials. Who string searches a name using that person's full initials? Ian's middle name was Wesley. She found a computer, opened an arts and humanities database, and typed I.W. Asquith in the search bar.

1938-1945

1.

THE OLD NOTEBOOK was a gift from his father, a banker, arriving by post a few months after Ian Asquith entered university. With luck, his father explained, the gift would interest one of the professors of Greek at the University of Edinburgh, or some other high-up who could assist Ian's candid ambition to finish his undergraduate career as a medallist. One of his father's clients, an antiquarian and an investor in British consols, had passed on this pocket journal as part of the informal currency traded between people in business. Like his father, Asquith had no real friends; like his mother, the young man wore glasses, and further impaired his sight by late reading in bad light. At night he burned oily rags in the fireplace of his student apartment—rags he acquired without charge from a townsman, a train mechanic. This fuel burned intensely and sent up a thick, irregular smoke from the chimney. The bookshelves in young Asquith's apartment were sunk into and formed part of the wall.

This notebook had originally belonged to the classical scholar Christoph Ziegler (1814–1888), and was half filled with transcriptions of Greek texts and Ziegler's own notes in German. Ian's copy of *The Biographical Encyclopaedia of Classical Scholars* listed the two chief accomplishments of this Ziegler, a philologist and schoolmaster in Stuttgart, as, first, his long essay on satyr plays and tragic tetralogies, and second, the three volumes of *Greek Bucolic Poets*, which best represented Ziegler's scholarly tastes and presented all his discoveries in the Ambrosian Library. In his will, Ziegler left instructions for the sale of his private library and papers to fund stipends for students from Stuttgart and Ulm.

After a series of unprofitable transactions on the antiquarian market, the notebook came into Ian's possession. Asquith wrote a letter of thanks to his father's business associate, and this man replied with further details of the gift. Ziegler's journal, a combination of diary, transcription and commentary, had had a single purpose and was used during a few weeks in 1863: it concerned Ziegler's visit to the city of Smyrna, where he expected to find an undiscovered play by an ancient Greek bucolic poet known as Bion. Word had reached Ziegler that a comedy—on paper, with parchment scraps of a previous copy—was kept at someone's home as an heirloom, and he went to Smyrna hoping this comedy would place Bion in the ranks of Aristophanes or Theocritus. The play's subject was the myth of Polydeuces and Kastor, the twins who feuded with their twin cousins.

Bion was born in Asia Minor and died by poisoning in Sicily. There was little information to settle his date: a common estimate being the second century BC. He wrote the line:

We waste our lives on gainful work and yearning for wealth.

After a Tuesday morning lecture, Ian Asquith, now a university student of about eighteen months, took his notebook to the professor he considered most approachable and, in full supplicating-student mode, explained that he, Ian, had no idea what to do with the thing. Ian said he'd tried to read the opening pages, but his Greek and German weren't up to the task. And even if his languages had been sufficient, he'd still appreciate a superior opinion on what exactly Ziegler found in Smyrna. The professor asked to borrow the notebook for one night, and the next day they met again in his L-shaped office.

Perhaps advancement was as simple as Father made it seem: find shared ground, offer gifts, pronounce your humility. The notebook was working as intended.

The next day in the office Ian squirmed about, imagining the bookshelves were about to topple over him. The professor said Ziegler hadn't found what he was looking for in Turkey. The Smyrna writings were not by Bion, nor one of his imitators, and they could be dated to the early fourteenth century. What Ziegler had found, the professor explained, were a number of rather worthless trimeter dialogues concerning Polydeuces and Kastor, which somehow started the rumour it was a complete play—scholars craved examples of the Greek New Comedy in the nineteenth century.

The professor now asked what Ian thought to do with his life, since the young man had the privilege of many options. Initially, Ian took this remark to mean that he was bright enough to enter any number of professions, instead of recognising the observation for what it was: a reference to Ian Asquith's family wealth. Ian responded that he'd like to be a scholar, that the advancement of classical studies would be the joy and glory of his life. It was all he wanted: to be a good scholar.

The professor had a way of leaning far back in his chair, which made it clear he was at ease and that others ought to be so too. He told Ian he didn't think such a career path were possible. Unfortunately, Ian, about halfway through his degree, would almost certainly never in his lifetime possess the skills required to make an impression on the study of classical literature. The professor—who before going up to Edinburgh had held the Regius Professorship of Greek at Cambridge—said he liked Ian, and these matter-of-fact discussions with students were the least pleasant part of academic work.

Worst of all, said the professor (suspended on the chair's back legs like a duke), Ian's understanding of literature might be described as asinine. Ian was much too concerned with finding personal guidance in the work under examination and expressing some sense of having imbibed a worthwhile moral lesson. This was absolutely not what one should look for in poetry, said the professor, without saying what he himself sought, without explaining the function of literature.

For the first time in his life, Ian could see that the things he most wanted would always be out of reach. He belonged elsewhere? All this striving with Greek cases and plurals and tense stems was a false direction? Ian said he sometimes thought about a career in the Foreign Service. The civil service was a fine idea, said the professor.

2.

The significance of the Ziegler notebook changed as Asquith grew older. At first it was an embarrassing object, a reminder of failure—at the same time, it was a sly thing he couldn't throw away. He thought about sending the notebook to the British Library, or perhaps the Pontian Society of Britain, where it might have value as a remnant of Hellenic Smyrna. Instead he held on to the journal, and read a little further in the field of bucolic scholarship, and found himself admiring the odd lyrics that Ziegler had found. The professor at Edinburgh, that pompous old prick, was wrong; the Smyrna writings were bloody good.

Came the day that Asquith began to write in the notebook itself. He needed to prove a point about his classical learning. From the notebook, he tore out the pages in which Ziegler announced the visit to Smyrna had been a failure, then Asquith began to write on the empty pages. He wrote a play, a comedy called *The Twins* (Δίδυμος). Ziegler's Greek script was angular and inconsistent with the character of

149

his drizzly Latin and German handwriting. Ziegler's plain Greek script might have been written by anyone, Asquith told himself as he copied the great scholar's hand. He had 187 blank pages to work with; he wrote with a Swiss dip pen. If anyone asked to see the notebook, he could hand it over as proof of the source.

Asquith wrote the play in English first. Then came the Greek, written straight into Ziegler's notebook; he would claim the original copy had been destroyed in the Great Fire of Smyrna. All this siphoning became a daily routine. He came to his desk at the same time each evening. When he looked at the stars he had the feeling he was looking into the past. There were dictionaries, there was the notebook, and his books of poetry and drama spread like a phalanx across the desk. All these objects came together to allow him to finally make something good. He had the sense of being inside a device of his own invention, a machine with esoteric contours and secret compartments; he switched the device on and off and it did not break. The contraption produced a piece of writing set in iambic trimeter. The result was nothing like him, and more like art. And whenever Asquith got stuck he pinched a few words from the genuine Bion of Smyrna, thinking that most writers steal, a little, from their earlier work.

The Twins was composed between October 1945 and January 1946 in Sydney, and at the guesthouse of a sheep station near Goulburn, New South Wales—a property that belonged to a friend of the family, and which Asquith visited from time to time, leaving a few pounds to show gratitude and ensure he'd be welcome again. He could afford these displays. In the evening, the window of the Goulburn property's guesthouse offered Asquith a perfect picture of a bucolic sort of sunset, providing him with an image for the comedy's beginning, a dusk scene that introduced Polydeuces and Kastor, as the twins hurried through a field with stolen cattle.

Asquith's fake—which he presented as a translation of a manuscript that could be attributed to Bion of Smyrna, written about 1000 BC, and transcribed by the late scholar Christoph Ziegler—was first tested on a colleague at the British Consulate, an unprofessional reader of ancient Greek. Under secretive terms ('Do come, it's important, I'll explain later'), Asquith invited this man to his Sydney flat, lightly furnished in the expatriate style. He waited until after they'd finished the small meal he'd prepared—small because he didn't want to drag the moment out—before producing the notebook in which he'd written his comic play. Or, as he said, Bion of Smyrna's play. Asquith also served up a pile of folio papers, these being the English translation of the fabricated comedy. He'd made an interesting discovery, he said, as regards to the beginnings of Western literature: a lost Greek play, a great comedy, something of a jackpot, overlooked by a dead German scholar.

'I had no idea you had such a mind!' said Asquith's colleague after reading the translation. 'And the notebook came to you when you were a student? It's a wonder you didn't stick with the classics. Perhaps you might reconsider that career move.'

'Your opinion of the play? Did you follow the Greek?'

'The translation reads beautifully. Look here, I had no idea, Ian—none of us at the consulate had any idea you were at work on this. We thought you were nothing but another windbag.'

For several weeks Asquith told no one else about the play, and instead he worried incessantly about the project. His anxiety concerned the quality of the fabrication, not fear of his fraud being exposed, and he suspected his colleague had been insincere in his praise for the play. Asquith was of the belief that other people traded in insincerity more readily than the time of day.

Then, one night, he met an American embassy officer at an agricultural trade conference dinner. It was one of those nights when the diplomatic bureaucracy felt, to Asquith, like a mock feudal world in which nothing important could ever be accomplished. Hierarchies could be preserved. The world could not be saved. Their conversation turned to their social life during the war, and Asquith said he'd once had the honour of meeting Benny Goodman at the Collins Club as part of a USO tour.

He couldn't have met him, the American said. Benny Goodman had never visited Australia.

'But he performed as Benny Goodman,' Asquith insisted.

'Then he must have been a fake.'

'You sure?'

'Sure as shit I am.'

A sudden flash of mortification in Asquith, before he realised the imposter could be useful. The fake 'Goodman' showed him what was possible: he demonstrated the lengths to which you might go. His fraud suggested Asquith should go further with the Bion project rather than, as he'd been thinking lately, destroying the notebook and manuscript and trying to fare better at his consulate job.

Soon Asquith was reading from the play at his classical-themed book club in Elizabeth Bay. He announced to the book club members that Ziegler—who preferred Theokritos among bucolics and thought Bion was trivial—had probably failed to see merit in *The Twins* and thus, while he took notes of the Greek text in 1863, he had never adequately translated it and had failed to alert the scholarly community. An excerpt from *The Twins* was published in a new literary journal, the *Meanjin Papers*. Next, the *Weekly Times* wanted to run an extract. The journalistic angle was Amateur Scholar Finds Treasure of Antiquity Ignored by Dead German Expert. Also, the *Southern Review* published six pages of Greek trimeter verse by 'Bion' alongside Asquith's translation, flanked by a background article on the right-page strip, which gave an account of how Asquith had found the notebook. He published under the name I.W. Asquith. He was becoming a new person in his new country. He wanted to be loved and admired for an ability that no one had acknowledged or even suspected.

3.

One day in October, Ian Asquith took the morning train to Canberra, where he'd arranged to stay at the quarters of the British High Commission. The rooms overlooked a paddock and rubbish tip on a grim plain that would soon be flooded to create a lake, according to long-delayed town plans. Such a body of water would be ideal for the mosquito population. These insects knew Asquith well. As second secretary at the British consulate in Sydney, one of Asquith's tasks was to visit the national capital and keep the high commissioner up to the letter on whatever he wished to know about business in Sydney. Asquith regarded most of his duties as a waste of time. He did not work hard. He had other interests. In consequence, a stern letter had arrived from Canberra. It said Asquith was not fulfilling his responsibilities, his position was in question, and a complaint regarding incompetency had been made. In response, he boarded a train to the capital, bringing with him excerpts of the Bion translation to show the commissioner, who himself was strong on Euripides and Pindar.

In the main dining room of Artie's Restaurant, before the commissioner could raise the subject of the complaint, Asquith began their conversation with a summary of the Bion play. He handed over a published excerpt and asked for an honest opinion on *The Twins*.

Once reprieved, once praised, Asquith enjoyed dinner with his superior. They failed to discuss in detail the complaint of incompetency, because the commissioner said he didn't want to bother much with tedious talk, although he advised Asquith to keep at least one eye on his paperwork. Instead they discussed Moschus and Bion and Theokritos, they spoke about literature as if it were a vice they kept from colleagues.

Three times during the meal he asked the commissioner if he'd enjoyed the Bion translation.

'Please, speak honestly,' Asquith urged him.

'I would say,' the commissioner said finally, 'that this Bion of Smyrna was probably a genius.'

The next day another excerpt of *The Twins* appeared in the *Sydney Morning Herald*. I.W. Asquith sent the newspaper what he believed was the best sequence of his play: the part in which Kastor and Polydeuces dispatch their rival cousins, Idas and Lynceus, with assistance from Zeus. The front page of that same edition carried a story, which Asquith skimmed, about radiation sickness in Nagasaki and Hiroshima.

2002

1.

LUCKY WAITED AT the entrance to Victoria Park, squinting vaguely through the tinted spectacles that made him look, thought Emily, like an old-timey racketeer. They greeted each other by lightly squeezing hands and walked in the direction of Glebe Point Road. The sounds of traffic streamed like heavy colours into the park: the compression brakes, the bumpy rumble of trucks and buses. The dried-out grass, planted too late in August, blew away in dead tufts down towards a central pond. Uphill in the park stood a boy and girl flying kites, remote as statues, while the kites too looked frozen in the air.

'Let's begin with a mild scolding,' Emily said playfully.

'I can take it,' Lucky said. 'Don't spare me.'

'You weren't truthful about the nature of your money problems after the shooting. You told me you made poor business decisions, but I know you developed a gambling problem.'

'It's true. For some time I had a serious problem. How did you find out?'

If Lucky held back information, then Emily felt she should, too. Her reply was instantly equivalent: 'I'd rather not say.'

'Hey, doesn't matter. The gambling is behind me. I'm out!'

'It's bad for both of us if you lie. I have a lot riding on this job. A commission for the *New Yorker* is a big thing for someone like me. I have nothing else going on, career-wise. And you want your story told, don't you? If you lie, the story might be killed during the fact-checking process.'

'No, but I want you to make me look good, or make me look not terrible. People think gamblers are arseholes. The worst kind of addict.'

'Don't embellish your life. You don't need to. You've accomplished a great deal already,' said Emily.

'I'm not so sure. If you write about the gambling, make sure you state I had a gambling problem only *after* the shooting. I probably burned through six hundred thousand dollars. I was a bad case. Out of my mind.'

'How does someone lose that kind of money?'

'You use your savings. Then you take out loans. Then credit cards. Then you borrow money from people you were in business with. That's how you lose your house. I knew other gamblers like me. Totally possessed. There was this couple, we met when the temporary casino opened, we always said hello. She liked machines and he liked cards.

When he had a heart attack at the poker table the casino staff came to inform her but she refused to leave the machine, said she'd go to the hospital later, okay, when she finished playing. I heard that conversation, I was a few machines down. I knew another guy who used to wear an adult diaper to the casino so he could keep playing blackjack—the only time he went to the toilet was to cut his wrists. I don't claim to be better than them. We had the same addiction. Some died of it.'

'What did you bet on?'

'Football games. Boxing matches. Cards. Roulette. Poker machines.'

'So, everything then.'

'Except horses and dogs. I didn't bet on animals. For a long time I gambled a little, without it being an issue. Twenty dollars here and there. After '94, I had a big problem on my hands. There was something wrong with me after the shooting. I felt like my life was over.'

They walked through the dried-out park, Emily holding the voice recorder between them like a little torch. She'd never gambled, never cared for it. No: once, when she was fifteen, her stepfather Rick had placed bets on two horses in the Grand National, intending the race to be a father–daughter bonding activity, an afternoon at home in front of the television. They each chose ponies whose names had some appeal. Rick was not a regular punter himself. But neither horse finished the race; neither survived the day, both shot at the track. Let's *never ever* do this again, Emily told her stepfather.

'What was good about gambling?' she asked Lucky. 'There must have been pleasure in it.'

'Sure, it affects your dopamine receptors. I got a hit when I won.'

'Could you still get that thrill from gambling?'

'Yes. No. I don't want to find out. When I was betting, I got in a state of mind in which I thought I could make up for the past—for the mistakes, for the terrible things that happened—with a big win. It's hard to explain. It's shameful and I don't forgive myself for losing that money.'

'I'm interested in how the gambling was connected to the Third of April.'

'If I talk about my addiction I'll look ridiculous in your article. Am I worthy of sympathy?'

'Yes, you are. A lot of people have this problem.'

Emily let the silence stretch, until Lucky was ready to say: 'After the Third of April I felt swallowed up, I felt fury, futility, defeat. Everyone in my restaurant, except Sophia, dead in a pool of blood while I was at home watching *Wheel of Fortune*. It undid me. The chaos in the world got to me and left me unhinged and the gambling was the result of that sadness and self-loathing. Gambling was a final investment in life—a preparation for death. I thought that when I got to the end of my money, that would be the end of my story and the end of my unhappiness. I realise this sounds crazy. I could have done other things with that money rather than waste it, self-harm with it. I could have given the money to someone in need.'

'Who would you give the money to now, if you could?'

'I should nominate millions of people, billions. But among the people I know, it would be Sophia. She's important, she and her kid. They're part of my story, but I don't see them much. Sophia was in a bad way after the Third of April and now she's out of work, and she and her son are leaving their rental and moving in with a friend. They're waiting for public housing. I called and gave her your number, like I promised. She might contact you.'

'Thank you.'

'Then again, she might not call you.'

'I don't want to coerce anyone into speaking. I want full consent. She was traumatised; I wasn't. If she's not comfortable, I'm not comfortable.'

'I told Sophia I trusted you completely.'

'How long was gambling a problem?'

'Five years, maybe, before I got help. In that time I spent the money from the restaurant sale. Then I used my house as collateral. There were days when I told myself the truth: if I kept going I'd eventually lose everything. And I told myself that when I was finally broke I'd go home and swallow something and die. That's one solution to a gambling problem. But when I was finally broke I decided I didn't want to kill myself. Instead I want to resurrect the franchise: I'm still in the game. My head is still in the restaurant world. Haven't got the money together yet.'

'I want to ask you about Henry. You saw him on the Third of April.'

'You know the facts of it.'

'He came to your house that day. Before he went to the restaurant.'

'I don't know why he didn't kill me. No one can answer that question.'

'What did he say when he knocked on your door?'

'We've talked about gambling. Let's stick to one disaster per day.'

'Then we'll talk about Henry when you're ready,' said Emily. There was an urge to ignore his deflection, to let him know that she was not entirely in his power. Emily decided not to press him. He was talking. What he said was heartfelt. That was something. There would be tomorrow. She'd get what she wanted.

They came to the edge of the park, to a pedestrian crossing. Across the gridlocked swim of Parramatta Road the shopfronts were dirty with soot and dingy in the shade. When the lights changed, Lucky and Emily crossed amid a crowd of prams and shoppers, and students killing time between classes, couples steering each other towards a cafe, while two wasted young men rushed the other way into the windblown park, which sloped and deepened like a scene painting. Lucky told Emily he wanted to show her something.

2.

Yesterday, in the basement of the university library, Emily had read her father's play, or his translations of a play by Bion, the constituent parts thereof: those excerpts published under the name I.W. Asquith in magazines or newspapers between 1945 and 1946. Put together, these extracts gave a strong sense of the narrative, which dramatised the myth of inseparable twins Kastor and Polydeuces, known as the Dioscuri or the Gemini. In Ian Asquith's play, the Dioscuri enter into a long blood feud with their cousins and this dispute ends in a brawl that only Polydeuces survives. Taking pity on the twins, now separated by mortality, Zeus allows them to be reunited, providing they share their fates and move back and forth between the Place of the Dead and the Mountains of the Gods, spending one day in Hades and the next on Olympus. Emily found the translation, in verse, fairly readable:

CHORUS:
Once, all mortals had two lives: the first for woes,
the second for joy.
We were content this way, after misery to find
happiness at last.
Then the gods grew bored, and assigned mortals
one life instead.

She discovered a scholarly article from 1977, 'Frauds and fabrications in post-war Australian literature', published in *Commonwealth Literary Studies*, which gave an account of several frauds and hoaxes, most of them perpetrated on short-lived literary magazines. Emily tabbed the article, and the fragments of Asquith's play, and carried the journals over to a photocopier, feeding twenty-cent pieces into the machine, carefully squaring up each page on the copier plate, I.W. Asquith's name on the yellow pages like an heir-loom. She'd never thought she would find him on the page in a library, let alone like this, in disgrace.

The appendix to 'Frauds and fabrications in post-war Australian literature' included this letter to the editor in the *Sydney Morning Herald*, 7 March 1946, written by the Dean of Classics at the University of Sydney:

Dear editor,

Regarding Mr I.W. Asquith's astonishing find, I am puzzled that the many editors who promoted his translations neglected to seek a second opinion from the Classics Department at this university. I am afraid the poems are not Bion's. According to a profile writer at one of your competitor newspapers, Mr Asquith claims the work comes from a notebook by the classical scholar Christoph Ziegler, and that Ziegler misattributed the poems to a poet other than Bion. I am aware of Ziegler's work. Had he turned up a lost epic by Bion—a writer he knew better than any scholar living or dead—I doubt he would have overlooked or made an error in identification. Indeed, it would have been one of the most significant finds in the history of literary archaeology.

Regardless, Mr Asquith makes a grave mistake in his supposed translations. Another journal, the *Southern Review*, has printed some of the original Greek that Mr Asquith claims to have discovered. But the Greek he puts in Bion's mouth lapses occasionally into late medieval. Bion wrote in the second century BC. Perhaps Mr Asquith thought that when Greek is involved, any old Greek will do. I suspected, I feared, and now I assert that the poems are fakes.

Howard Mathison

Dean of Classics

University of Sydney

Emily went to the newspaper room and verified the letter on microfiche: she pulled on the wheel and the machine whirred down long tracks of news columns until it shuddered and stopped on Howard Mathison's letter. Then she went back to the 1977 article (written by Markus Fish) and reread the essay: Fish claimed that Asquith, after being exposed as a fraud, 'did not publish again—at least, not under the name I.W. Asquith.'

Reading about the fabrication was an unbearably personal experience for Emily. His life was a tragedy, she knew that. But what exactly, she'd wondered, did his life look like? What was lost? And now, after decades, it felt like an intrusion to see her father's secret laid out like this. Was the fabrication a response to some disappointment? What did disgrace do to him? Ian's rogue writing, once exposed, must have crushed him. His civil service career was over. People likely avoided him. Embarrassment, isolation. Here, too, was Emily's secret side: a strand of kinship between them. Asquith was a fraud, and Emily felt like an imposter herself, first in her family (about whom Michael used to say: *You fell from a different tree, didn't you?*) and then in her marriage. As a writer, from her earliest articles, she felt like an imposter in typical ways: that an idea for an article or short story was fraudulent, or unimportant or, if it were important, that she wasn't the writer for the job. Her ambition to write about Lucky's for the Great Magazine was, in truth, born out of Emily's old sorrow, not purely an ambition to tell the story of the rise and fall of these restaurants.

Emily sat for a while at a carrel desk in the basement. Her mind didn't strain to summon up an image of her father's body. Emily saw that painting of Lucky's restaurant. Saw herself as a young woman, before a New Year's Eve party, fixing her hair in the mirror. You're not an imposter, Emily told herself now. Your marriage didn't work out the way you hoped, that's all. And many writers feel like frauds, a little. How can they not? They're transforming amorphous life into black-and-white lines and curls. She told her anxious mind the following: You worry about me failing, you want to avoid disappointment, but you're making me feel like I've failed when I've barely started a task. And what is more fucking fraudulent than that?

3.

On Glebe Point Road, as Lucky slowed down to peer inside a hotpot restaurant, Emily told him she had spent yesterday at the university library. She read about her father.

'You keep mentioning him,' said Lucky. 'I'm curious about the guy.'

'At the end of the war, Dad fabricated an ancient Greek play. The fraud was exposed and he lost his job in Sydney.'

'Funny thing to do. Must have been a mad philhellene.'

'He must have had some point to prove,' Emily said.

'Maybe he felt he could only succeed if he became someone else. How do you think the fraud, getting caught, affected your father?'

'I don't know how it changed him—if it changed him at all. He took his own life when I was a girl.'

Emily looked at Lucky to see how he received the news about her father's suicide. If it were news.

'My God. Did he leave a note?'

'No note,' said Emily. The question landed oddly. No one had ever asked about the existence of a note that soon after learning of Asquith's suicide. Emily wanted to tell him that she'd seen her father jump under the train; that the real shit of life was behind her questions, behind her need to know something more about Asquith. Then Lucky stopped on the footpath.

'My friend, this is it—this is what I want to show you,' Lucky said, pointing to the vacant shop in front of him. 'It's genuine deco. It's got to be deco.'

The empty shop had two glass display windows on either side of the doorway. A blue-and-white FOR SALE sign consumed one of the windows. The doors were old and heavy and wooden, with iron rail handles and glass panels frosted with a pendant design. Inside, the walls were bright white and there were black drop sheets on the floor.

Emily understood from her preparatory reading that

Lucky's had been a cosy and informal business culture, substantially different from the martial style of late-twentieth century franchising. Lucky's, in its early days, comprised a network of family operations: the franchisees and their families, most of them migrants, lived in rooms attached to the cafe itself. While running a Lucky's restaurant in the city or outer suburbs or country towns, it was typical for franchisees to save money for their own business, to use Lucky as a stepping stone. Emily imagined him keeping in touch with the progress of outlets through a stream of bank statements, phone calls, walk-in gossip, letters, card games. She doubted he ever wrote a single memo.

Emily asked: 'This used to be one of your cafes?'

'Not used to be. Going to be. This is where I am meant to start again. Bury me here. Under this entrance step!'

'Where are you going to get the money?'

'Still need a few things to go my way.'

'You're gambling again?'

'Emily, tell me: how do I look, generally speaking? I hardly look in the mirror anymore. A glance is more than enough these days.'

Emily said: 'You look . . . good.'

'I have the body of an old man.'

'But the innate force of someone half my age.'

'Good enough to appear on television?'

'Oh please, *are* you appearing on television?'

'Next Tuesday I'll be wearing this same suit at a taping of *Wheel of Fortune*. All going well, I'll reach the jackpot episode by the next day's taping. If I win the jackpot, I'll have money for a restaurant. And I tell you, *Wheel* is the easiest game show on television. The phrases are all too common. Find yourself in trouble? Buy a vowel. And look at the foot traffic on this street! This is my chance right here. You know, I used to visit an illegal gaming room on this street.'

'This is just more gambling, I think,' said Emily.

He said: 'I'd like you to be my plus one at the taping. It will be good for your story. You'll get some nice detail.'

She couldn't bring herself to accept that his TV appearance and her Sydney visit had coincided by chance. He must have told the producers he was available only this week or next, and they gave him what he wanted. What he wanted was the glorious ending of his story to be dramatised in the *New Yorker*. His final investment in life. He saw himself as her collaborator. His shrewdness, his energy, his unlikely plans. Emily had to respect his talent for hope. She said: 'There must be better ways of getting the money together.'

'I'm old. Who's going to lend me a couple hundred grand?'

'A bank. Or you could find investors, people with money and experience.'

'I saw a bank manager and he said he'd loan me the money if I put up my house. Then I had to tell him I rent. I saw other loan officers. Next I went to see an old business friend of mine, Michael Ventouras (he's Greek, he changed his first name but didn't bother with surname). Michael used to be the state manager of Streets Ice Creams, and he made a packet because of people like me; we sold the Streets range in Lucky's for thirty years. When I asked him for a loan, Michael said, *I can't do it. I've got grandkids.*'

'Starting a small business is stressful and you're not young.'

'This is my last chance to do something.'

'I'd like to know why you don't have pride in what you've accomplished. What am I missing? What aren't you telling me?'

'I'm broke as hell and that's enough to suck the pride out of you. I'm not exactly going out first class. I have three reasons to go on *Wheel*. One: I could sure do with the money. Two: the franchise ended in a horrific tragedy. Everyone in this city knows that. Everyone knows about the Third of April, but people don't know the good things about Lucky's, or maybe they forgot, maybe they're too young. There's always chitchat on the show between the host and contestants and that's a chance for me to remind people that Lucky's was once an important place: a second home. Three, and most important, I need to leave behind something useful. I want Sophia to manage Lucky's. She can take a salary and profits, and she can have the joint when I'm gone. I want to leave something behind for the people who are important to me.'

'Have you told Sophia about this plan?'

'No, I'm afraid that she'll say she's not interested. You'll come to the taping?'

'I'll come,' said Emily. She stepped away from the vacant shopfront and Lucky followed, beaming, ready now for the rest of the interview, which Emily said should deal with the history and structure of the franchise. Let's cover all that, said Lucky, there's much to say. On St Johns Road they sat down at a new bar, an airy place of chrome and wood and interior graffiti that Emily felt tried too hard. She drank wine; he had soda water. For two hours Lucky described the lifespan of his franchise, rapidly shovelling details, speaking as if he'd forgotten himself, yet saying not one word about the fire at the Cafe Achillion. Or how Ian Asquith was involved in the death of Penelope.

1946

1.

NO LIGHTS VISIBLE behind the shopfront, no smoke from the chimney. Lucky knocked gently on a segment of glass. After waiting and waiting, he banged on the door's wooden mid-rail and peered once more into the Achillion gloom, his hands cupped around his eyes. His first thought: Achilles, consumed by shame, had fled the city and abandoned his palace.

Then Asproyerakas emerged from the shadows and unlatched and opened the door, leading his son-in-law wordlessly through the cafe, past the kitchen, its smells of cold fat and bad tomatoes, along a dark hallway. They came to the living room, narrowly lit by the woozy hum of a single dangling lightbulb. Achilles' eyelids were dark and droopy, his nostrils flared like suction cups. The table was covered with a white lace tablecloth crumbed with cigarette ash.

'Do you have a new job?' Achilles asked.

Lucky, who did not have a new job, suspected by now that his unsuccessful search for restaurant and hotel work in the past three weeks might have something to do with the fact he was American, or because he was ethnically Greek—or probably both. Or maybe employers didn't like something else about him. There had occurred a change in status. Americans looked out of place in postwar Australia. The previous year, hundreds of thousands of GIs and air force and navy men were resident in the state capitals, omnipresent and exotic, but virtually no one returned after the war. Australian wives moved to the United States. There were days when Lucky suspected he was the only American living in Sydney.

'Come back to the cafe,' said Achilles. 'That's where you belong.'

'We can't do that. We can't forgive you. And it's gonna be that way for a long time. I'm here because I need to pack up some things.'

'Take what you want. Take some cigarettes. I'll keep out of your way.'

Lucky and Valia's former bedroom lay closest to the cafe's gargling generator, which once produced what Lucky had found to be accommodating noises that invited him to the heavy sleep of a happy life. Achilles was the one problem with the Achillion. He wrecked their home. He made the cafe squalid. He paced the lounge room, shifting chairs around. Lucky packed the clothes Valia had left behind, those she requested, including a few things he never liked—a Little Bo Peep-style hat, a purple cardigan

172

she wore some nights after closing time. For her part, Valia disliked Lucky's shoes, said they needed replacing, but his feet were bony and his Haglund's heel bled easily and he wasn't willing to wear in new boots. Without a proper home, without much money, Lucky took comfort in petty thoughts, in the normal, superficial spite between husband and wife, in the one or two things he never liked, and which revealed the measure of their good marriage. He could hear someone fiddling with the back gate.

The sounds of the yard were familiar to Lucky. The components of the back gate were a sheet of compacted iron riveted to a frame, a chain, a lock, hinges, and these parts made distinctive noises when touched.

He checked the verandah: 'You there, Achilles?'

Lucky went through the yard, out the gate, and down the lane. He called out his father-in-law's name. Who was the old man meeting? Since when did Achilles have a friend? The lane ended in a large pothole. The street looked as dark and still as a back road in a small town, the cold night air loaded with pressure. He chose a direction. Two blocks away, he found Achilles in front of the fruit store, pouring gasoline onto the windows and steps.

'What are you, a fucking nutcase?' Lucky hissed.

Achilles' plan was to lure business back to his cafe by destroying the Bardwell Fruit and Vegetable Shop. Without this source of food, according to the plot, the locals might once again dine out at the Achillion and Mr Asproyerakas would forgive them for abandoning him. No one lived behind the fruit and vegetable shop. Achilles could raze the whole building and not kill anyone. He could not let the world be. Not the way it was.

'You helping me set this fire or not?' Achilles asked.

Lucky picked up the can of fuel and, with a shuck of his head, motioned to leave. Achilles squinted at him. Petrol ran down the footpath and around Achilles' feet; the fuel dripped off the window ledges and tiled entrance step. Lucky grabbed his father-in-law around the shoulders to walk him away from the fruit shop. When Achilles attempted to twist out of his hold, Lucky squeezed his hand around the old man's neck, bending Achilles forwards, staggering down the lane.

'I'm trying to get rid of a curse!' said Achilles, once they were back in the kitchen at the cafe. 'That fruit shop is our problem, a competitor.'

'A problem is when you express your frustrations with violence. A solution is when I come along and stop you screwing up again. Do you understand I left America to marry into this family?'

'Yes, you left your big country—but you get to marry Valia, who is much better looking than you. Listen to me: tonight I went out there trying to do something for all of us. If I burned down the fruit shop while you were here, packing bags, then I'd have what they call an alibi, you understand? Do you think I'm stupid? I saw my chance and went for it.'

'I think you've lost your mind, Achilles.'

'I'm trying to protect my family's business! I'm doing everything in my power to improve our position. That can of petrol was our answer. And where is the can?'

'I think,' said Lucky, 'we left it outside the shop.' For a few moments he'd felt entirely sensible and capable. Now he did not.

'I'm going back,' said Achilles.

'You're not going back and I'm not either. Someone might see us. Go to bed, mister. You look goddamn terrible.'

'I do?'

Late in the night, when Achilles was asleep, Lucky borrowed the Cafe Truck and returned to the hotel in Paddington. There, he woke up Valia and described the scene outside the Bardwell Fruit and Vegetable Shop.

'We must get rid of my father,' she said. 'This is our chance to take the cafe from him. It's perfect. This is our chance to get Penelope back.'

'It is?'

'I want my father to suffer for what he did to Penny. We need to separate him from his cafe. That's what he loves best and that's what we'll take from him. We'll send him away.'

'How the hell do we do that?' Lucky asked.

'I know exactly how.'

'And we end up running the cafe?'

'We'll give it a year,' said Valia.

'I can live with that.'

'We'll return to the Achillion in the morning and go back to work as usual: I'll be at the counter and you take the kitchen. We'll invite the police for lunch, on the house. Are you listening?'

~

The next morning at the cafe, Valia told Achilles—who in a quiet moment gave thanks to Father Nektarios and God himself for bringing her home—that he was restricted to the rooms behind the kitchen in case someone had seen him last night outside the fruit shop and called the police. She reminded Achilles that he'd made a great mistake by leaving the petrol can behind. Close the curtains in the back rooms, she advised him. Don't make any noise.

At midday she found Achilles in the backyard, admiring his olive tree, and urged him to hide because the police had arrived, and one of them had asked to use the toilet, probably wanting to look around the place. To see if the owner was present. Peering out from behind the dry goods shed, Achilles waited and watched, feeling as if something were piercing his spine, as the constable entered and exited the outhouse, stopping under the grapevines to tie his boot-laces on the way back into the cafe.

Sometime later Valia came out to see Achilles, who sat against the shed, the sun on his face, his eyes closed. There was, she thought, something helpless about him. He suffered. He was routed. She could reach down and snatch out his soul.

'What did you say to the police?' he asked. 'Do they know I beat up some drunks the other week?'

'Lucky got rid of them.'

'He's good, that Lucky.'

'They said last night someone doused the fruit shop with petrol. Apparently you can still smell it down there. They found a can.'

'The smell will be gone soon. Nothing to worry about.'

A few hours later, Valia rushed out to the back verandah where Achilles lay on his mattress, inspecting his worry beads. He looked disappointed by them. They looked cheap. 'The police came back after dinner,' she told him.

'Again! What do they know? What did they say?'

'This time they asked for you. I told them you were in Queensland.'

'Good job.'

'You have to leave,' Valia said. 'We have money for a train ticket—here.' Valia dropped an envelope into her father's lap. 'You have to go tonight. I'll help you pack. Bill Papadamatis is in Brisbane—he'll give you work.'

'Too far away! And this is my home. This is the Achillion.'

'It's obvious the police suspect you tried to burn down that store. What if they come back with a warrant to search the place?'

'Police in this city probably don't go to such lengths. And what exactly is a warrant?'

'You have to leave,' Valia repeated. 'Do you want to kill this business completely?'

Achilles refused a final meal at the cafe and, instead, he demanded a few words with Lucky. He spoke as if he were handing over the property forever, as if Lucky were his younger self and Achilles wanted that younger self to have the benefit of some experience. Maybe Lucky should spend his military severance pay? The cafe needed a soda fountain— this gimmick would bring customers by the hundreds. He told Lucky he should donate money to the local Anglican and Catholic churches, equal amounts. Do what you can for the Orthodox. You don't have to go to mass; give the money to the priests, and in person. But never to the local Marist brothers, who are dishonest. Ask the priests about weddings and funerals on their calendar and remind them we offer catering for big events, said Achilles. We did such work before the war and it will come back in time. Don't be afraid to write letters to the families. Sometimes the bride's family pays for the banquet, sometimes not. Maybe ask the priest who will pay. And we need dogs to protect the yard. We never had dogs because I don't like animals. Here is my gun. Find a jukebox.

Achilles said: 'If I go to Brisbane, will it make things better with Penny and Valia?'

'I honestly don't know,' Lucky said.

Achilles walked around his home for what would be the last time. When his head itched, he scratched it with the end of a pencil. He wanted to give Lucky additional advice: drink more; go to the pub after lunch; make friends. I failed in those ways. The laneway out the back is where you go after you learn your wife is dead. You never know what comes next in life. You never know what you are going to do yourself. The olive tree is strong enough to hold a hanging man. The American theme of the cafe is most important: on the menu we need hamburgers, sundaes and other American items. There was something he didn't mention to Lucky: Achilles had his doubts about whether the police were looking for him—but he recognised his downfall; he accepted that a period of exile might be necessary for his daughters to forgive him.

'I come back in nine months?' said Achilles.

'A year, to be safe,' Lucky suggested.

Achilles said to Lucky: 'You're a practical man, but also a dreamer. I don't understand how a person could be both. And I have a request: I want to stay one more day. I'll go to Brisbane tomorrow.'

'You're leaving tonight,' Lucky insisted. 'You don't appreciate what's at stake here. The police might come back to search the cafe.'

'Also, you have permission to change the name of the business. Maybe the name is cursed? Call it *Lucky's* if you like, or *Valia's*. Or *Penelope's*—yes, that is a good name.'

On the way to Central Station, Achilles sat in the Cafe Truck with his head between his knees, out of sight, as instructed.

2.

'Done,' said Lucky when Achilles had gone.

'Defeated,' said Valia. 'Now we are going to run this place the way we like.'

But it was the same old story with custom. People stayed away. Lucky rose before dawn to light the stove. He burned the olive-wood and his father-in-law's clothes. Achilles' ghost was made of a gassy, auxiliary substance that seeped out onto the street.

That old man is gone! Valia called out in her mind when she opened the cafe doors.

Lucky bought new awnings with his separation pay;

orange and white stripes. On a timber board he painted a sign to hang in the window: UNDER NEW MANAGEMENT.

One week this happened: the customers came back.

On the footpath each morning two or three labourers waited for the doors to open. After school, children stood and ferociously swallowed Achillion sandwiches. Traffic collected, a hundred patrons before lunchtime: from among these customers came a rumour that Mad Achilles had been sent to a mental asylum. There was talk of a feud among the Asproyerakas clan, a good faction and a bad—and the good side had triumphed. The cafe was restored.

Children came in to study Lucky Mallios. Pale youngsters stood at the kitchen door and asked questions while he scraped the stove and cleaned the surface with a wet rag tied to a broom handle. His voice sounded flat when he was busy.

Q. What did you do during the war?

A. I was a cook.

Q. If America is so great, why aren't you living there?

A. My wife was born in Sydney. This is her home.

Q. Why do migrants come to this country?

A. Migrants come for a new life. They're changed by their new home and in turn they alter that country.

Q. Will your people drop another atomic bomb?

A. I hope not. I fear they will.

Q. Who in the whole world do you admire most?

A. Valia, my wife.

Each day Lucky resembled more and more the person he needed to be, if he must build a franchise. With the father-in-law gone, he gave free rein to his instinct for organisation. He put Achilles' papers into filing cabinets, paid tax debts, negotiated improved terms with distributors. The local council, persuaded by Lucky's argument, planted maples in the middle of the footpath. In front of the cafe it almost felt like a promenade. At Valia's urging, Lucky bought a mechanised potato peeler. You turned on the motor, fed potatoes into a spout at the top, and in seconds they tumbled out, peeled, glistening like eggs. The peaceable Achillion sparkled.

Except Penelope was missing. Valia didn't have an address, didn't know if she was still in Sydney. The school hadn't seen her in months. If she could, Valia would have written to her sister: *You must come home. You and Lucky are all I have. You must continue your studies.*

'We need a soda fountain,' said Valia from the bath one day. She and Lucky had developed the habit of discussing work while one of them lay in the bath. They took turns: one in the bath, one on a little stool next to the tub. Lucky took the stool first. There were breadcrumbs on his nose and chin. He'd made potato keftedes for dinner.

'What does a soda fountain cost?' he asked.

'We'll make it back.'

'What if your father returns?'

Valia rolled over in the bath. Lucky swallowed awkwardly, coughed.

'We'll dismantle the fountain and take it with us when we go.'

~

They bought a soda fountain, and its two polished steel handles, rising from behind the counter, became their favourite objects in the cafe. The swell of one handle was stamped LUCKY'S, the other VALIA'S.

'It looks like a bird in flight,' said Lucky.

'It's the most beautiful thing we own,' said Valia.

She bought a jukebox, which was delivered and installed late on a Friday night. Exhausted, they had time for one song before bed. 'Moonlight Serenade' by Glenn Miller. Valia had specified: no Benny Goodman records. The man was gifted but unpleasant.

A letter from Achilles arrived: his return address was the Brisbane cafe that housed and employed him. *This place is a real shit*, he wrote. *Every day in Brisbane it rains. It rains like the legs of chairs are falling from the sky.*

Valia read the note from her father without great interest, without judgement. Achilles scolded her for not writing to him, but assumed that her failure to write meant the cafe business had improved. He asked—and the whole purpose of the letter appeared to be a single question—he asked if they'd hired someone to replace him. Achilles Asproyerakas wrote: *There is no one who has taken my role?*

He signed off with:

Please say you are not angry, and the black cat that crossed our path has evaporated.

True,

Achilles

3.

Penny walked back into the Achillion with a suitcase in one hand and her handbag slung over her shoulder, rolling her neck in weariness. A week ago she'd learned that Achilles had moved to Brisbane. A Region Transport truck driver, Walter's friend and an Earlwood resident, delivered the news in Canberra one afternoon, and he did so in a tentative voice, probably suspecting what Penelope might do when she learned her father was in exile.

She told Walter they were not a suitable couple. To stay any longer in Canberra would be to stay in limbo.

She let go of her suitcase, which hit the cafe floor with a thud. The Achillion belonged to Penny again. She banged on the counter bell. Valia came out from the kitchen with plates and quickly conveyed them to the booths before rushing to embrace Penelope, to stamp kisses on both cheeks. They weren't normally so touchy, the Achillion sisters.

'You're staying, I hope,' Valia said. The cafe was full. Valia wiped her hands on her apron in a gesture of accomplishment—the Achillion was liberated, her sister home—then hoisted Penny's suitcase containing books, shoes, a Canberra coat. Lucky said hello but didn't try to hug the girl—he had a T-bone steak in each hand, blood down to his wrists. He laid the steaks on the hottest part of the stove.

'Where's Walter?' Valia asked when they arrived at Penny's room.

'Walter and I are finished,' said Penny.

'What happened?'

'I don't want to talk about it. He's a good man. It's just—you wouldn't understand.'

'Why wouldn't I understand?'

'Your love story is simple. It's complete. You met Lucky and that's that. Things are different for me.'

'All right. But we can talk about anything,' said Valia. 'About Walter or father or school or university. And if you want money, ask us.'

'I will need money.'

Penny lay down on her bed. Altogether, she'd been away for two insensate months. The first month had fallen during school holidays, the second during term time. The school year must be reclaimed, said Valia. Some textbooks must be reread, said Penelope.

'I'll go back to school next week,' said Penny. 'Until then I want to sleep.'

Valia turned off the light on her way out, and Penny rested for a while, then slept, and in the morning she drafted a follow-up letter to the University of Sydney. She enquired whether they'd received the previous correspondence and references from her headmaster and the head science teacher at her high school. Might there still be time for an interview? There must be a fine art to these letters, thought Penny: some code, some formula that other Australians understood. There must be something she didn't get right in that first correspondence, and that was why the university hadn't responded. In her new letter, Penelope Asproyerakas used many words to, in essence, say the following in code: she rejected her father's expectations and dreamed of being a scientist.

4.

On a Wednesday in July, the *Sydney Morning Herald* exposed I.W. Asquith's fraud: he had falsely claimed to have discovered a play from the Hellenistic Period. He lost his British consulate job that Friday. He was guilty of misconduct. The high commissioner, doing the proper thing, came to Sydney and met with Ian at the office.

'It's a bloody embarrassment,' the commissioner said. 'Turns out this daft play is all your work.'

'I'm profoundly sorry, sir,' said Asquith.

'We can't have it.'

'Yes, and I'm ashamed,' said Asquith. 'And I understand that diplomats can't be seen to behave in such ways.'

'I suppose, yes, in a broad sense you were a diplomat.'

In failure, Asquith confronted certain facts he'd managed to ignore during the lifespan of his fraud: the fabricated play was the product of a wound left by his university education, by his inability to become a scholar of classical literature. That he'd now ruined his civil service career and turned his life into the consequence of common and ineludible disappointments of early adulthood—dissatisfaction with his teachers, frustration with his talent, with the outcome of his education—which were all hurts he should have relinquished but couldn't, well, this made him feel ever more pathetic. He had allowed himself to be disfigured by the experience of failure. In response Ian Asquith, fond of alcohol, began to drink heavily.

~

By 3 pm the following Friday, there were eleven bottles on Asquith's table at the Pilkington Arms in Chippendale, three with beer still inside. He reached out and, by mistake, knocked over a glass, which rolled back into his palm. This rolling action interested Asquith and he moved the glass back and forth under his hand, only stopping when it occurred to him how this might appear to the bartender, who didn't like him. He'd introduced himself, and tried to explain that he'd written a play in trimeter and, well, it was a long story. The sound of his accent somehow kept provoking the bartender into repeating his words, in mockery. Asquith lost track of what he had said, and what was being said to him. The clock above the door was hard to read and many things were quickly becoming difficult to comprehend. Asquith wiped his lips with a handkerchief. He almost never finished a sentence when he was thoroughly drunk: as soon as he himself got the gist of what he was saying, he stopped right there.

'You are . . .' he said.

The bartender walked over. She said: 'We've seen a few fancy drunks in here.'

She poured the remains of his other bottles into a glass and took away the empties. When Asquith had drained the glass he rolled the damn thing along the table and let it fall to the floor, where it did not break. Looked under the table and near the door but it was nowhere, and there was hardly any light inside the pub.

'I've wasted so much time!' he yelled in the direction of the bar.

People talked about him.

'I do feel poorly,' Asquith said.

In the pub toilets, he slid into the nearest stall and the latch clicked across like a mean kiss.

The actual shit, of humans, was deposited everywhere, as if sprayed, as if thrown from a height: on the floor around the bowl, the lip, the walls, in solid and diarrheic form, the result of several bowel movements. Unsteady, Asquith put down a hand when he leaned over to vomit into the bowl. The vomit fell mostly where intended. He covered his nose while gasping. Wept quietly, so no one would bother him. He squatted on his toes. His balance was all wrong and impossible to sustain—crouched down over the bowl like that, but not too close, because the porcelain was covered in shit. One of his hands was in the stuff, steadying him for another minute or so. His shoulder now rested on the dirty wall. His jacket must be soiled. No one came into the toilets, because maybe perhaps they knew, out in the bar, probably they had done this to him. Maybe it had been prepared for him. Sitting on the floor now, more terrified than he'd ever been; he stayed like this for half an hour or so. Then he began to vomit again, into the bowl, onto the floor. Asquith couldn't leave until he'd emptied his stomach, which took some time.

Suddenly up and moving, leaving his good grey blazer behind. The bartender called out to him. Asquith was sure he heard the word 'Ian' as he tumbled in the street. In total there were three taxi rides: the first tossed him out within a hundred metres, after smelling him; then he found another driver, who caught a whiff around William Street and promptly ejected him. By persistent means he got home. The only fare he paid was to the last cab driver, who threw him out on Greenknowe Avenue, not far from his flat in Elizabeth Bay.

Asquith's clothes and shoes went straight from his body into the unlit fireplace. There was shit on his cheek and something moving, it seemed, under his collar. Then he removed his clothes from the fireplace and threw them down into the street, ashamed, terrified, certain that someone was in the flat with him.

Next, Asquith took up the keys and went out, entirely naked, to fetch his leather shoes, a bottle of sherry in his hand; the bottle corked and raised in case someone attacked him. He rescued his shoes, but left the rest of his clothes outside.

Before sleep he removed all his books from the bookcase and laid them in piles on the floor next to his bed. (It was difficult, the next day, to remember why he went through with such an exercise.) From this into unconsciousness and then Asquith woke up, without his painful body registering the rest. He had little recollection of getting home—just flashes of still images—or what happened afterwards, but this information was of little interest to him; that he'd somehow found his way back and into bed was enough. The toilet incident was like a fall from a horse. 'Everyone should fall from their horse now and then,' Asquith said to himself in the bath. Every day a little fall. More people, he thought, should go through what I am going through.

When crossing the road on his way to pick up the morning newspapers, he averted his eyes, because to look directly at his best clothes covered with shit in the gutter might have been enough to make him scream. Pollen floated around him like supernatural molecules.

At the newsagent, Asquith bought several suburban papers: he no longer read the *Herald*, but didn't intend to give up his habit of reading all news just because he had been exposed as a fraud.

An exhausted Asquith returned to his flat and sat in the front room, next to a five-tier whatnot displaying clapsticks on the top shelf and porcelain frivolities below. Vents laced the ceilings. Fruit flies came through the window. In the tabloid *The Truth*, which he considered grotty but essential, he came across an article about a three-pound fine imposed on Mr Stratis Simos, 'owner of a dago eating house', for not having kept clean a soda fountain. Asquith did not approve of the bigoted language, nor steep fines for restaurant drink fountains when the city's pubs were in a deplorable state. Sydney would be dead without cafes. The article prompted him to think of a woman he met during the war, Valia Asproyerakas. He was unsure whether Asproyerakas meant 'white hawk' or 'white old man'.

Maybe Valia knew what had happened to the Benny Goodman imposter, he thought. Maybe the fake Benny Goodman had been ruined too. That would only be fair.

5.

The forename 'Ian' came from Asquith's one-armed grandfather, whose portrait hung prominently in the family's

Buckinghamshire house, a property he'd bought in retirement. Grandfather Ian was a vast man with a long, jagged beard that not one descendent replicated; he was a soldier before he became a stockbroker for a London firm, selling consols to Austrians and Frenchmen. Asquith's own father was involved in consols, and, before the revolution, in the trade of Russian Three Per Cents. Since the year dot Asquith had zero interest in the stock exchange.

Asquith's elder brother Philip, a banker, inherited the grandfatherly house near the town of Gerrards Cross. Pines, apple trees and a small meadow formed the greater part of the family estate. Dry-stone walls bordered both sides of the permanently damp lane that connected roadway to home. In front of the house was a small close, planted with alders and berries. Behind the building were kitchen gardens, the Asquith family graveyard beyond. Ian, second son, received a large sum of money when he found work with the Foreign Service. His younger sister, Jennifer, was advised from an early age that she would never receive much in the way of an inheritance and instead was encouraged to marry or otherwise obtain wealth. Jennifer became a nurse.

By December 1946, Asquith expected that people in London, and perhaps everyone he knew, would eventually discover how he'd lost his job. He feared his old friends, who hadn't seen him since the war began, would consider him a fool. Probably they always had. Now, in Sydney, it was beyond doubt. Out of sadness and loneliness and shame—for his fraud—Ian Asquith would have killed himself right there in his Elizabeth Bay flat, but he did not, at that time, want the banner of suicide swaying over the family graveyard. Not that he considered the act of suicide shameful. But others did. Other people interfered in his life, even when he wanted to leave it.

Forget your hopes. Was that the line from Dante? *Your old hopes are what brought you here.*

But there remained a blessing or two, Asquith thought. He could afford to stay in Sydney. He could draw on the savings in his bank account. He had something more to prove.

His destination: a luminous and overflowing ship of a building. The store windows were full of fruit and toys and tobacco products. Two little girls walked out hand in hand, each with a paper bag of sweets. The Cafe Achillion. A jewelled cavern inside—wooden panels, mirrors, brass, deco pendants. Sunlight came in like a breath through the swinging saloon doors.

Asquith sat down in a booth and fidgeted with the salt shaker, a sleek thing that reminded him of a stick of chalk. The cafe was near full and noisy over a Glenn Miller waltz playing on the jukebox. In the next booth a mischievous mother was teaching her daughters to sing 'The Internationale'. Then out from the kitchen came Valia, tall, smooth, smiling in a spotless black shop dress. She put down a glass and poured him a pineapple drink. A courtesy, she explained.

'I believe we've met before,' he said.

'Maybe you have the wrong person.'

'During the war, one night in the city. You must remember. Isn't your name Asproyerakas?'

'It's Valia Mallios now.'

'My word, I like this pineapple drink. You don't recall when we met?'

'No, sir. Would you like to order something?'

'I'll need more time to decide.'

'Sing out when you know,' said Valia, then she moved on to check on the next table.

Asquith thought, Do I make such a small impression on other people? Has my appearance changed that much?

He stood and conferred in the mirror above the booth, and as usual his eyes fixed on his hair, a combed-back mingling of black and waxy grey. All Asquiths, men and women, went grey in their twenties. He sat down, not the least bit hungry. Then Lucky appeared on the floor of the Achillion, leaving the kitchen with a plate of sausages. Asquith stared, his mind adjusting to the sight of the American. Lucky had cut himself shaving and wore a black sticking plaster on his neck. Had Valia been a part of the Benny Goodman fraud, too? Had they once thought of Asquith as some kind of mark? Affronted, Ian followed the imposter back to the kitchen.

'Excuse this intrusion, but no doubt you remember me,' Asquith said.

'Sure I do,' said Lucky, his back to the stove. 'The Benny Goodman night.'

'You had me absolutely fooled that evening. A few months later I discovered that Benny Goodman had never visited Australia during the war.'

'I should apologise for all that nonsense. I wanted to be someone else for a while. It's hard to explain.'

'No, it's easy to understand.'

'My name's Lucky. My real name is Vasilis Mallios, but call me Lucky. That night, the Benny Goodman thing, it was the night I met my wife. It was an important night. It changed everything.'

'Then the fraud turned out incredibly well for you. Not many people get away with something like that. But are you still a musician?'

'Haven't played since that day.'

'Just like that, you stopped being an artist?'

'I wasn't much of an artist.'

'I thought you had some talent. Do you feel like a failure, though?'

'Maybe I failed at music, but not some other things. Anyhow, failure is a reaction. It's a response to an event. Failure, success: these aren't always determined by other people. Least, I hope that's how it works.'

'This is interesting, Lucky, this idea that you had to become someone else in order to make your art. It's something I understand.'

'How are you doing yourself, sir?'

'I'm going through a rough patch. No need to bore you with details. I must admit I'm envious of your situation.'

Penny yawned herself through the kitchen, a book held up to her face, on her way to the family booth in the cafe.

'Have you eaten?' Lucky asked Asquith.

'I'm not terribly hungry.'

'Why don't you come back tomorrow night and I'll do something special for you. A roast. Do you like kleftiko? Come tomorrow at about six.'

Valia came to the entrance of the kitchen, ready to give Lucky an order. The whistle blast of a kettle went off. Asquith's head was hot.

'Honey, this is Ian—remember? From the Benny Goodman night, during the war?'

'Oh, *now* I see it!' said Valia. But Asquith had the sense she'd recognised him from the start, that she understood he hadn't come to their cafe by chance.

'Tomorrow night we're doing a special dish for Ian,' said Lucky.

Valia said: 'But the whole cafe is booked for the Kogarah Girls Sports Club function.'

'Right, it is,' said Lucky. 'Ian, how about the night after next?'

Before Asquith could answer, Valia said: 'We're catering for the Bradbury wedding. Mr Bradbury's sister is Penny's math teacher and we have to go the extra mile because Penelope's missed so much school. It will be a long night.'

'How about I drop by another time? said Asquith. 'In a few weeks?'

Tree shadows slipped over the bonnet of Ian Asquith's car and fell flat on the road behind. He'd need to do something about the Ford before leaving for London. Maybe he could give it away to someone on the street—simply hand over the keys. He wouldn't drive out this way again, wouldn't revisit the Achillion, because of the unflattering comparisons that might be intensified in his mind, because his life, in relation to Lucky's, already seemed a special sort of fiasco. The American had got away with everything.

Asquith drove through a five-point intersection, his car shaking as it rolled over recently buried tramlines, as barely concealed resentments made themselves felt. Asquith blamed his father for being a philistine—a businessman and not a scholar. He blamed his teachers at university; they hadn't taught him anything, really. He blamed all classicists and philologists for the conditions of their clique. And he blamed himself. Bion of Smyrna was a bad idea. In his mind there played a cinema reel of a naked Lucky and Valia thudding up against each other in the cafe kitchen. If only Lucky would stumble, Asquith thought, if only something bad happened to him, then everyone would see what must become of frauds. It felt manifestly unjust that Lucky could marry Valia, that his artistic ambitions could dissipate and no longer trouble him, and that he lived happily ever after in a popular restaurant, while Asquith's life unravelled.

6.

At the establishment that he'd now come to think of as the Shit Pub, after his Sadean bathroom experience, Asquith sat alone near the door and slyly observed the patrons who entered. As the hour passed these drab men all appeared much the same, all weary, all scrawny. For assistance, he went to the bar and ordered two drinks from the same woman who—he strongly suspected—had served him that day of the toilet incident.

'Excuse me,' said Asquith. 'Who is the toughest chap in here, the meanest?'

'Are you a policeman?' asked the bartender.

'Definitely not.'

'That bloke over there is the worst kind,' she said, nodding towards a bearded man who stood at a high table, a cigarette dangling from his lips while he rolled another smoke, pulling tobacco from a pouch inside his jacket pocket.

'But you be careful about him,' the woman said. 'Don't get yourself harmed.'

Asquith went straight up to the bearded man and put down a glass of beer, an offering.

'What might you do for a living, sir?'

'Why you want to know?'

'I may have a business proposal,' said Asquith.

'I'm sort of a debt collector,' the man said. 'Got an outstanding debtor?'

'In a certain sense, I do.'

'Keep talking then.'

'It's a small job, but easy work, if not entirely legal.'

'Work that's not legal is extra,' said the man, leaning back.

'Never mind collecting any debt. I'd like you to smash a few windows in a cafe. Nothing too severe. Make a mess and then be on your way. And be sure no one sees you. I'll pay you five pounds for your services.'

'Five? Six I'd say. Where's this cafe?'

'Here's the address.' And Asquith handed the man a folded piece of paper. 'Make a mess. We want to teach him a lesson.'

'Is this cafe run by grease-balls?'

'They are of Greek heritage.'

'I hate the Greeks in this city. If their country is a mess they should stay and fix it, I reckon.'

'You'll take the job?'

'I'll enjoy doing this. For a bob extra I'll burn the whole place down.'

'No. Don't burn anything down. Break a few windows. Inconvenience them. The man who runs the cafe got away with something he shouldn't have. We're squaring the ledger. You're enacting a kind of justice.'

'Fair enough. Give me the money now, and I don't take coins.'

The rain fell while they spoke: a shower that quickly turned to drizzle and finished. Good, Asquith intended to leave right away.

'To be clear,' he said, 'I'm not asking you to burn down the cafe.'

'If I want to burn a place to the ground, that's what bloody happens. You understand?'

'Understood. Just make a mess, please, nothing more.'

He pushed the money across to the man—whose name he didn't care to know—and the notes were snatched away. On the dark sheesham table, Asquith's long hand looked like a daub of white, enriched by a plain ring on his index finger.

7.

Lucky woke up to the sound of picture frames falling in the cafe. He rose coughing, the room smoky, and didn't bother with clothes, was naked when he opened the bedroom door and slammed it shut again when he saw, at the end of the hallway, the kitchen door ablaze. He turned to Valia, who cupped her mouth with both hands, and he said the cafe was on fire. Valia emptied the two drawers of their bedside table onto a sheet—the contents being their papers and jewellery—rolled it up and threw the package out of the window before climbing out herself, as Lucky put on pants and a jumper and went to find Penny.

Fire now bounced from wall to wall across the ceiling of the hallway and roved down Penny's bedroom door. Lucky kicked the door, his forearm held protectively in front of his face. Valia crossed the street, a trace of blood in her footprints—a cut from a protruding nailhead in the window frame. She could not feel the graze. The Achillion started shrieking. It was lit up inside, a globe in which a coil burned. Windows popped, incandescent particles blew across the street and landed on Valia's forearm. Inside, a gust of flame knocked Lucky backwards; on the floor he clawed off his burning jumper and on hands and knees he peered into Penny's bedroom. He couldn't see her: all he saw was fire. Some kind of fuel in the kitchen caught alight and whistled up until it popped. The reflection of the fire glowed over Valia's face, her grinding jaw. A bell rang down the street and Lucky, alone, climbed out of the window in his bedroom. Valia went around to the lane behind the cafe, in case Penelope had escaped through the back. Only smoke slipped out from under the gate.

Firemen in brown coats arrived. The burning structure changed shape, drifted upwards. Lucky, shirtless, the hair on his head and chest singed, sat down in the gutter.

At the front of the cafe Valia stood next to the firemen and pointed to her bedroom window.

'What are you doing? Go in there!' she told them. The firemen discussed the electrical wires in the street.

'We can't,' one of them said.

'My sister might be inside! You need to find her!'

'We can't. The fire's too big.'

The Achillion truck, parked in front, burned too. A westerly blew on the cafe. Three policemen walked Valia and Lucky to the end of the street, where they sat down in the park and she smoked each cigarette they offered to her as a form of comfort. Another scalding fire truck siren passed behind them. Valia kept asking if anyone had seen her sister, kept describing Penelope: the same height as me, hair to her shoulders, brown eyes, face like mine but longer. Maybe Penny was wandering around somewhere, confused, she thought. Penelope would have inhaled smoke and she might have passed out in someone's front yard.

At dawn one of the cops said: 'Where's Achilles?'

Lucky said: 'He moved to Brisbane.'

The same policeman said: 'Do you know how the fire started?'

Lucky shook his head. He said he'd put out the stove. The wiring was checked a week ago. He'd been the last to bed. They'd all been asleep for hours.

Valia sat in the back seat of the police car as it cruised past the remains of the Achillion. The sight of the ruined cafe did not fully enter Valia's mind, did not seem quite real. How did *this* happen, and then *that*? How could Penny be gone? Firemen threw buckets of water over a heap of what used to be the window displays. Valia held the door handle tightly as they drew away from the site—perhaps the grip gave courage. It hit her like blindness: she and Lucky were leaving the ashes of the Achillion. Penelope was not.

8.

Two mounds of garbage and the iron stove, still standing, were all that remained of the cafe. Achilles had left Brisbane on a train yesterday, after Lucky informed him of the fire. Asproyerakas wore his shirtsleeves rolled up, and rolled up some more, to the point where these resembled tubes around his arm. He swore at whoever had taken away the cafe's bricks. Some of the bricks he might have reused. The pale gouge of the bulldozer's blade marked a path through the site. Piles of refuse here and there.

Achilles walked down to where the verandah had been. Stood there for a while. He couldn't bear to linger where Penny's room used to be. At the back of the block it looked as though the olive tree had uprooted itself and run away, leaving a hole in the ground like a sunken star. Out in the back lane Achilles trod footprints of black mud. The answer was this: build everything exactly as before. Or perhaps: end his life. How long could he walk around thinking about what Penelope felt, what she saw in the last moments of her life? Would this have happened if he'd been there? Could he have put out the fire? Yes, Achilles thought, or perished.

He persisted with his aggrieved, bloody-minded attitude at the police station that evening. Achilles and a policeman sat in a first-floor room with no door and a sink. Crates of old newspapers along one wall. The policeman asked about the funeral, yet to be held. He enquired about Valia, if Achilles knew where she now resided (he didn't).

'But what you must do is find the person who killed Penelope,' said Achilles. 'What can you tell me?'

'I want to ask you that question, Mr Achilles . . . Your last name is unpronounceable.'

'No, what happens is you do the police work. My daughter is dead. She had a German friend, a man called Walter something. Start there.'

'Canberra police have already questioned Walter Schüller. He was in Bega that night.'

'Where? Suspicious! You go question him.'

'Tell me about your insurance policy,' said the policeman. He gave the impression that he knew when someone was trying to put one over him.

'It's with Scott and Roberts Insurers.'

'What will you do with the money if the company pays

out? They might not like the claim. Are you aware of the term "Greek Lightning"?'

'I don't accept that term.'

'How did the fire start, you reckon?'

'You tell me the answer! What kind of police are you? Do you work here? This is wasting time!' said Achilles.

'We think the fire was deliberately lit. Did you burn down the Achillion?'

'Don't ask me that.'

'Did you pay another person to burn down the cafe? To be clear: I'm not accusing you of murdering your daughter. Perhaps someone you know lit the fire, for insurance purposes, but no one expected anyone to get hurt. Is that right? Mistakes happen, Mr Achilles.'

'A few months ago I threw out some customers. Maybe I got too rough on these men. They might be responsible for burning down the cafe. Almost three months back, it was.'

'That's a long time. But we'll look into it.'

'Maybe they waited. Maybe they let time pass so we wouldn't suspect them. Here, I can describe these men for you.'

'We'll get you some paper.'

'Let me say this: if don't you find who started the fire, I will kill someone,' said Achilles, his voice rising. 'Maybe even a policeman.'

'I think we'd better put you in a cell until you calm down.'

Achilles stood, raised his fists and settled his feet: 'You what? Ella, you son of a bitchy!'

They handcuffed Achilles and pushed him against the room's brick wall, pressing on his chest until he fainted.

The police removed his shoes and wallet and worry beads and put him in a cell for the night. Before falling asleep, he was solely occupied in working out descriptions of those customers he'd attacked months earlier at the Achillion. He dreamed of Penelope walking in Centennial Park, where he took the girls one Christmas Day in wartime.

9.

In the hotel room, weeks later, Valia sat at the small desk and sighed out of her cardigan, sipped her coffee, held her thin body in the correct posture. Her back and stomach were strong. A matter of genes. Introduced to the room, at the end of the bedspread, was a bag of letters that conveyed sympathies—not many of these—and above this bag lay an indentation in the sheets; the outline of a movement, the impression of a solitary person who'd laid down with her legs curled up. She and Achilles didn't speak at the funeral: they put Penny in the ground and Valia came back to the hotel, back into bed, restless. The glass of water on the bedside table was half empty and stale.

She looked up at the bare walls of the room. Couldn't they nail up some pictures? Why couldn't Lucky find a job? Why, Valia wondered, wasn't I kinder to Penny?

Valia asked Lucky: 'Do you remember what I said that night after Penny came back from Canberra?'

'I can't remember,' said Lucky.

'I took her to the bedroom and then I came out to the kitchen and you said: "How is she?" and I said: "Still obstinate", and I felt happy with that description, as if I finally matched my sister with a word.'

'Why are you telling me this?'

'Because I'm ashamed! Why else would I mention it?'

In the afternoon, Lucky heard a light knock on the door, but instead of answering he waited for the knock to come again. If it were important, they'd keep banging. He now sat at the desk; Valia lay on the bed.

'A man named Ian Asquith is downstairs asking to see you,' said a hotel worker through the door.

'I'll come down,' said Lucky.

'Bring me back a glass of something,' said Valia.

The long curtains in the hotel bar were made of thick amber velvet that easily concealed the two hotel cats. In the shadowed corner a piano had been left open for guests. At a table in the bright middle of the room, Asquith stood up, offered his condolences, and they shook hands and sat, both men pale in the uniform black of their clothing.

'How did you find me?' Lucky wanted to know.

'I paid a policeman.'

Asquith continued: 'I'd heard about your loss but did not attend the funeral. Terrible thing. A nightmare come to life.'

'You didn't know Penny. We wouldn't expect you to come.'

Asquith touched an envelope through the fabric of his jacket pocket. Lucky noticed the way the Englishman's legs twitched. Asquith smelled of alcohol.

'Do you know how the fire started?' asked Asquith.

'The police think it was deliberately lit.'

'Good grief.'

'Last I heard from the police, they still suspected Valia's father, who is a maniac in some ways. But he didn't do this.'

Ian sat still and steamed through his suit. He wanted to confess, to say he was sorry, that he'd paid that thug only to smash windows, not burn the place down. The outcomes of violence are unpredictable. But that wasn't what he'd come here to say. 'I have a gift,' said Asquith, reaching for the papers in his jacket.

'Yes.' It was becoming obvious to Lucky there was something more to the visit than common condolences.

'Soon I'll be returning to London, because I no longer have a job. You probably don't wish to hear about my financial position in detail.'

'You have money. You come from money.'

Asquith continued: 'I have a sum I wish to offer you.'

He handed over an envelope. Inside was a single sheet of paper on which he'd written a figure in Australian pounds. Lucky fidgeted with the paper until it was perfectly square with the bar table.

'This is the amount?' Lucky asked. The numbers appeared to be a mistake.

'It's not satisfactory?'

'It's an enormous sum.'

'There are several reasons why I want you to accept the money. Remember the Benny Goodman night, during the war? You pretended to be the man you couldn't be. That's what I find fascinating. I am guilty of a similar fraud. I felt a kinship with you.'

'That's a bizarre thing to say.'

'It must sound peculiar. Yet it makes perfect sense to me.'

'What do you want in return? There's gotta be some catch to money like this.'

'There's not. Use the money as you see fit. This afternoon I will go down to the bank and make the transfer. Do you accept the gift?'

'Yes,' said Lucky. 'Thank you.'

'Wonderful! I'm pleased. I feel relieved.'

'I'm not sure I understand why you're giving me the money.'

'I simply want to do good here. I'm departing from Australia, this part of my life is over, and I want to leave behind something of value.'

Lucky stared at the numbers in front of him. At that moment, in his eyes, before the next cafe, before the franchise, the money was at its most abstract. The sum represented nothing: its meaning hadn't yet taken, it didn't seem connected to goodwill. Money as resource. Money as pure energy. From the first, Lucky knew there was something strange about Ian's benevolence, but he pushed this vague suspicion from his mind—well, people could be strange—while shoots of possibility grew from the five-digit sum, as he came to possess the money, as it became part of his will and capacity.

Asquith wanted to ask right away: What will you do with my gift?

1972

1.

THEY WALKED THROUGH a car rental lot about 10 am, and Emily was touched by the suggestive desolation of the space, which made her think of other people's completed holidays, and the return to normal lives, the photographs and toys these strangers might have brought home. Her stepfather, Rick, took his time and chose a van: a yellow Toyota with a maroon stripe down the centre of the roof. His smile composed and constant, he packed their suitcases into the van and, on the road, explained the route out of Sydney with an enthusiasm that Emily had never seen and which she later realised was his way of working through a spell of nervousness, his increasing dread.

At a set of traffic lights, Emily's mother, Heidi, tuned the radio and after a choppy rasp of static the voice of a radio presenter came through: 'Grab your hat, it's gonna be a scorcher!'

'My favourite station growing up,' said Emily's mother.

The announcer's overexcited voice filled the car like soap bubbles pumped through the window.

Rick deadpanned: 'Grab your hat, it's gonna be a scorcher.'

The family set themselves two aims for the holiday: to visit Emily's grandparents, and to 'get away from things', as Heidi put it. 'Things' being Ian Asquith's suicide the previous year. Emily was having trouble sleeping; every other night she wet the bed; often she didn't remember what had happened earlier in the day, couldn't remember the day of the week, seemed to be excluded from normal temporality.

They drove westwards out of Sydney, Emily yawning, her mother telling stories, her stepfather eating apples with only one hand on the wheel, the van cutting into the hazy distance. By midday, Emily's eyes had adjusted to the bush, and she no longer saw repetition and monotony but a sequence of giant components. The dirt slightly reddened. The land flattened. The immensity of the country, the giant sky, passed into her mind. The vinyl seats burned her legs when she stretched out. Her mother leaned forwards and stared out the windscreen, looking for kangaroos. 'There's one!' she'd say, and her stepfather slowed down and pressed the horn. Whenever the car went over a cattle grid, Rick said: 'Grab your hat, it's gonna be a scorcher!'

Emily took the view that her parents' improvised jokes (which were unfunny) also implicitly excluded her. Perhaps her Australian grandparents might be different (she'd never met them), they might extend themselves, might offer what other children seemed to receive from their grandparents—a kind of conspiratorial relationship, free from the burden of parenting. She wanted to know that delight, whatever it was, and naturally she hoped to be spoiled. Rick's parents were dead. Her paternal grandparents may as well have died with her father.

The van pulled up outside a yellow weatherboard house in the town of Nevertire, and from the front window Emily's grandparents watched the three of them get out, watched them come up to the door, as if they didn't know why the visitors came.

'Would you like to borrow a brush?' Emily's grandmother asked her, once everyone was inside. 'Your hair is knotted.'

Emily said yes, not knowing she could have refused, and inside the door Grandma brushed her granddaughter's hair briskly. The guests removed their shoes.

'What are you doing for work these days?' the grandmother asked Rick.

'I'm an electrician.'

'Is business good? Any employees?'

'It's me for the time being.'

'You could've married an electrician here,' said Emily's grandfather, addressing Heidi.

Emily could feel this comment stab the atmosphere of the lounge room. Heidi led Grandma into an adjoining kitchen, where they spoke with a degree of privacy. The curtains of the west-facing lounge room were drawn, and hung without a fold, and light entered from the doorways. Emily sat on an upholstered stool. The massive body of her grandfather, in his reclining chair, had its back to the light. His head bent forwards, furrowed, perhaps angry. His feet were bare and blackened on the sole, and Emily's attention drifted to the pile of her grandparents' shoes near the door. They were mainly of two kinds: sandals and work boots. Seeded into the carpet were burrs, some of which looked like the thorax of an insect, others like the spiky mouthparts of bugs.

Emily's mother's voice was rising in the next room, a slow gradient. Rick tried to make small talk with Granddad. 'Driving up we saw a few roos,' Rick said. Then, from the kitchen, Emily's grandmother shouted, 'I didn't ask none of you to come!'

Heidi returned to the lounge room and for a moment she and Rick looked at each other, wordlessly deciding what to do next. Then Heidi grabbed Emily's hand and they stuck their feet into shoes and left the house, and the grandparents did not follow.

As they pulled the van doors closed, Emily looked at her stepfather, expecting him to lighten the situation, to say perhaps: 'It's gonna be a scorcher.' But Rick, without a word, pointed the van down the road, turned left and, following his wife's directions, left the village of Nevertire and drove to the next town, Narromine.

Heidi turned to face Emily and said their job, as parents, was to help her overcome what had happened. By coming to Australia—and the doctor in Ipswich had said it was a good idea—they'd wanted to expand Emily's idea of family. Clearly they'd made a mistake coming to Nevertire. They shouldn't bring Emily into contact with people who weren't good for her. Heidi said she herself wasn't a perfect mother, she was sorry, she didn't know what she was doing.

In Narromine, they stopped in front of a Lucky's restaurant, parking the van on an angle. When Emily thought about that day, she remembered the moment they parked the van on the main street, the engine off, and the three of them sat there exhausted, as if catching their breath.

'They're open,' Heidi said. 'They're always open.'

'Is this the same place in that painting?' said Emily, referring to Ian Asquith's picture, which then hung in the cold of their garage. The cafe created the impression of a small object suddenly enlarged and come to life—a merging of Emily's view and her father's vision. The building looked rosier and more golden than the painting.

'The same franchise but a different site,' Heidi said, checking the state of her eyes in the rear-view mirror. 'I went to school with the owner's children.'

The doors of Lucky's opened and almost as one the aproned staff turned to look at Emily's family. There were no other customers in the crepuscular light of the cafe. The dimness suggested a club, a place for residents. We're not welcome here either, Emily thought. She wanted to tell them about the painting. Her dead father. They practically had a right to be there.

'Heidi!' said one of the waitresses. 'You don't visit too often!'

Emily's mother introduced her family to Dina Pylios, a friend from high school. Dina's eyes were dark and soft and gave a look of warm attention. The restaurant closed early on Mondays, she explained. 'But have you eaten?'

'No,' said Heidi, shaking her head.

'Have you been to see your parents?'

'Been and gone,' said Heidi.

Dina nodded; she knew what Heidi's parents were like.

'Then you will have dinner with us,' said Dina.

'We shouldn't,' said Emily's mother.

'You don't have a choice. I'm locking the door now.'

Rick helped to push the tables together and arrange the chairs. Out came a large tablecloth and eight of them took their seats—Dina and her parents, her brother, her cousin, and Emily's family. Glasses of beer and water were poured. At the table arrived cheese and yemista, maroulosalata and sofrito.

Dina said Heidi and her family should stay the night in the house behind the restaurant, in a spare room they kept for visitors. Dina said it would be a shame to come back and act like a foreigner, to sleep in hotels everywhere. And she already made the bed ten minutes ago.

In the spare room, Emily asked to sleep on Rick's coat in case she wet herself again—her tone embarrassed but insistent—and he spread his coat across the mattress and slept on the floor, while Heidi shared the bed with her daughter. In the dark Emily said she was forgetting some details about Ian Asquith, whom she referred to as *my father*. Heidi said loss of memory was normal. It was your mind trying to protect you after a bad event. Your brain was beautifully built, she said to Emily. It was good to forget certain things. Emily said she could recall the way her father had looked at her at the train station, like he'd got them both lost. But still, she wanted to know: what colour were his eyes?

2002

1.

EMILY SAT AT the desk in her hotel, calling ex-franchisees, asking about their careers, their thoughts about Lucky Mallios, seeking anecdotes that she might nest in the background sections of her story. A woman named Evdokia Lukowski said she'd emigrated from Ukraine in 1952, pregnant and single. She was transferred to an Australian displaced persons camp in Benalla, Victoria, where the staff pressured unmarried mothers to offer their infants for adoption because, the punishing administrators claimed, single migrant mothers would face extreme difficulty marrying or finding work, would fail to assimilate, would over-rely on public housing and other forms of social assistance. As a consequence of this attitude, said Evdokia, single women who arrived in Australia pregnant, and who kept their children, could stay for years in this particular displaced persons camp, tasked each day with childcare and make-work chores. These mothers, she said, truly languished. Evdokia didn't intend to raise her daughter in Block 3 Benalla. She wrote a letter to Lucky's office in Sydney, explaining her situation, declaring she'd cooked for her family in Ukraine and now for people in the Australian camp, and she would work harder than any man or woman in the business. If you could maintain and cook on a Ukrainian pich oven you could use any stove. Lucky offered Evdokia a half-share in the Newcastle franchise.

In the afternoon, Emily got up from her desk and went to the cafe across the street from the hotel, sitting near the entrance, where a cat roosted on the windowsill. She heard the close flap of wings above the awning. The spicy smells of spit-roasting meat drifted down the road. At the corner, pink jasmine covered the side wall of a terrace house like flesh. Emily listened to a couple, both Scots, argue until the woman got up from the table and said this had not been any kind of holiday, let's face it, they'd been miserable the entire time, and she'd find somewhere else to stay tonight. Emily viewed the scene with interest, almost satisfaction: here was something important, the truth discovered in a quiet cafe—the couple was not well matched. Better lives were now possible.

From the cafe window, Emily watched her friend Liam, dressed all in navy, wheel a suitcase down the other side of the street and enter her hotel. She knew Liam was in the country—an event at a Melbourne university—but he hadn't given her a date for his arrival in Sydney. For some reason he'd never bothered with that detail. Emily crossed the road and peered into the hotel foyer where he stood at the reception desk. The automatic doors detected her shape and opened.

'Surprise!' said Liam, turning around.

'I knew you'd be arriving soon,' said Emily. She hugged him. She lightly punched him on the arm.

'Maybe I should have called ahead. Is it odd, arriving like this?'

She replied, 'I don't know, is it?', which was often what Emily said whenever Liam asked a question that she thought didn't need asking.

Liam checked in, making small talk with the receptionist, Isabel, about long flights and jetlag. He looked tanned, his face freckled; his hair imperfectly parted. He wore a thick oxford shirt with pearl buttons, and collar buttoned down—preppy style becoming popular again. Liam dressed much better than he did when they were in their twenties. He held his carry-on bag with two hands, thin and heavily veined.

'How's the magazine?' Emily asked as they stepped into the elevator.

'Oh Jesus, I'd prefer to talk about your stuff.'

'We'll get to that. Tell me something about Lorrie Moore. Or maybe John McPhee. Are you writing anything?'

'I'm trying to write a piece about the North-West Passage but the material might be totally beyond me. This morning I removed the terms "silly" and "unseasonably" from the story. Those two words kept appearing in my first draft. I don't know why.'

'Now you have a story that isn't silly or unseasonable.'

'It's been a while since I wrote anything longer than an email. The draft is a right mess. I don't like to think about it.'

'I don't like to think about nuclear bombs. Or my husband.'

'Ha!' said Liam. 'I never think about him.'

Emily followed Liam into his room and watched him unpack his suitcase inside five minutes, setting down papers and pencils and books on the desk. A television hung in one corner; a mirror was mounted high on one of the walls. She imagined men craning their necks to look up at the mirror, brushing their bald spot. Liam's hair had thinned on the crown since she last saw him. He leaned against a desk and Emily stood near the window.

'You realise,' said Liam, 'we've known each other for almost half our lives.'

'Tell me some gossip. Are you seeing anyone?'

'Can I pass?'

'You are seeing someone, but it's not serious.'

'She's in an open relationship with her husband. Her name's Susan.'

'It's not your shrink?' She knew Liam's psychotherapist was named Susan, or Suzanne, or something like that.

'Not my shrink. But Shrink Susan disapproves of the relationship. She also says the Other Susan has a borderline personality disorder. And she said that people with person-ality disorders are excellent in bed. Completely spurious diagnosis.'

'I think you should find a new therapist.'

'That's what the Other Susan told me. But let's talk about your situation: Michael got in touch yesterday—an email.'

'Why did he do that?' said Emily, shaking her head with contempt. 'He must want everyone to hate him.'

'I gather from the email that he's a troubled fellow right now.'

'What did he say? Has he shaved his head or chopped off an ear?'

'It was short and lacking in coherence. I can show it to you later, if you like. In essence, he wanted to tell someone he felt bad and that he still loves you.'

'What am I going to do?'

'You can't stay married to someone that stupid. The man is utterly anodyne. I think it's over. It's impossible.'

'Next subject. I need alcohol to discuss marriage any further.'

'If you need to talk shit about him, I'm up for it. So, your article, what have you got?'

'It's getting there. I have more interviews lined up. Some people didn't want to speak about the shooting. Maybe my approach was off?'

'What about the shooter's family? Any of them still alive?'

'The mother hung up on me.'

'I can help, if you want someone to make phone calls. What about Lucky? Did you tell him about the painting?'

'He's odd and sort of audacious. He sold most of the franchise in the seventies and I'm yet to speak to the second set of owners. It's obvious Lucky is trying to hide something. Any number of things.'

'It's obvious? Good thing. You can unpick bad liars.'

'He's broke but wants to start the franchise again. Lucky intends to win the *Wheel of Fortune* jackpot. The episode is shooting in a few days' time.'

'Now I like him. What he's lying about?'

'There's a weird part. Have you ever heard of a writer called Bion of Smyrna?'

'He was one of the bucolic poets. In Berlin I shared an apartment with a philologist who used to shoot amphetamines into his feet. Nice guy, all the same.'

'My father Ian concocted a play and claimed it was written by this Bion. Dad was supposedly the translator of the text. He got exposed, in the end, and lost his diplomatic job in Sydney. I just discovered this story. I don't know if the Bion thing is connected to the franchise. But maybe it is. I think Lucky knew my father.'

'Or maybe Bion of Smyrna is a separate story. How do you know Lucky was friends with your father? That would explain the painting.'

'I'm not sure they were friends. I asked Lucky if he knew my father and he said no. But he's lying. Sometimes you can tell when a person is not telling the truth. And sometimes you can't. For example, Michael was fucking Therese.'

'Keep asking Lucky about your dad. Why would he lie?'

'Because he's hiding something!' Emily said. It made her furious: her father was behind the locked door in Lucky. 'Why do you keep looking at the bathroom?'

'I need a shower.'

'So do I,' said Emily. 'We could shower together?'

Liam looked at Emily, tilted his head. 'Are you joking?'

They undressed in haste and forgot the shower and she'd hardly taken off her underwear when Liam pressed himself against her, kissing her neck, and she pushed his head down towards her groin. She groaned; he was good at this, better than Michael. Then, without much trouble, he found a condom in his suitcase, while she positioned herself on the bed, while her hand went down between her legs: she was wet. He grabbed her hips, drew her pelvis against his, and they began slamming against each other, his fingers digging into her hair, her grasping handfuls of his arse. At one point he looked at her, as if surprised: yes, this really was Emily.

Afterwards, they lay a little distance apart on the king-size bed, the condom slowly working itself off Liam's softening cock.

He said: 'Let's get dressed. There's something else we need to talk about.'

2.

She had wanted sex. She had wanted escape. To use her body, to make it work again. Something had switched off in Emily, and she wanted it back on.

Before bed the night before, with the overhead lights off, her hotel room dark except for a shimmer beamed from the TV, Emily had watched a documentary about people who trained dogs to find truffles. Some farmers used domestic pigs for the task but, too often, the voiceover explained, these animals would discover the truffles only to eat them. Emily wondered what it might be like to see a pig swallow five thousand dollars worth of fungi. Crazy, what some people valued. Emily had three hundred and fifty pounds left in savings.

The bedside phone rang and she knew, somehow, that it would be Michael.

He said: 'I don't want this conversation to turn into an argument.'

'It's exactly the kind of conversation that ought to turn into a fight.'

'This is difficult for me too.'

'Oh, really? Then how can I make this easier for you?'

'I'm calling from home,' Michael said, his words sounding bruised. 'I haven't moved out yet. I don't know. Hey, maybe when you come home I can meet you at Heathrow? What do you think? Or maybe not. Oh, another thing: I'd like to read a book of non-fiction. Short narratives I can dip in and out of. So is there something like that here in the flat? If not, give me a title and I can go to Foyles.'

'You want a bloody book recommendation?' Emily ended the call, as if discharging a soft valve, all too aware of how her heart was fully exposed to someone in the midst of—not a breakdown, not a mid-life crisis—but an idiot moment. It was simple to be rude to him on the phone, but it was less easy to be angry with him when she was alone, and he was in her head, and she didn't want him to be there.

3.

Liam and Emily sat on the bed. They were dressed again. With his expression suddenly tense and his hands all over his face to cover the stress, he said: 'Now I need to tell you something.'

'Doesn't sound good,' she said.

'I've been thinking about the Ladbroke Grove days. We were single most of that time.'

'The people we knew were terrible. In fact, that's still a problem I'm facing in London.'

'Could it be, I suppose, that we never bothered with anybody else back then because we already got so much from our friendship with each other? We may as well have been a couple.'

Emily realised she was about to discover another fundamental misconception about her life. Yes, she had been wrong about her marriage, had until last week thought all the troubles with Michael were repairable. Was she wrong about her oldest friendship, too? With Liam, she had always avoided misread intentions, perfidies, jealousies, schisms. They could flirt in fun with great ease and without consequence. Minutes ago they had fucked. They'd once done the same years ago. It was never complicated, never difficult.

'What I mean to say, Emily, is that I'm in love with you and it's been that way for a long time.'

'It's okay,' she said. Which was all she could think to say.

'You had no idea I was in love with you?'

'I thought you were my friend. All this time you've been walking around with these feelings, not telling me?'

'It's not like a disease eating away at my brain. And for a considerable period of time you have been married to a moron.'

'You're supposed to be my best friend!'

'We're a little old for best friends, aren't we?'

'We're not too old. Liam, the timing is not good.'

'Nothing is more important to me,' said Liam. 'I have to tell you the truth now. All the same I don't want to rush your decision. If you need time to think, maybe I should go out for a walk. Yes, I'll go and . . . find a large meal.'

4.

Emily and Liam had made love once before, in 1989, when they lived together in Ladbroke Grove. Their rooms shared a wall; they both owned bicycles and parked them in the hallway, propped against each other. Sometimes at night their bikes tumbled to the floor with a jingling noise that woke Liam but never Emily. After Goldsmiths College, Emily worked in a Kilburn pub and wrote short fiction in her spare time—each of these stories, all set in Suffolk, were about cruelty of various kinds. Stories about artists, restaurants, pubs, suicides. A story about the plague. She couldn't get her stuff published. Liam encouraged her to try journalism, and one day she sent letters to the daily newspapers in London, asking for any kind of job in the newsroom. A chief subeditor at the *Evening Standard* called and offered her three shifts a week, casual employment.

One Sunday afternoon Emily and Liam came in from the pub and sat with mugs of tea on the couch, and at some point their feet touched, and then their legs, and arms, and lips, and they staggered to the nearest bedroom (his), where they stripped naked and rotated through several sexual positions, as if engaged in a routine.

'What next?' Emily said, at one stage, over her shoulder.

'We can do whatever you like?' said Liam, in the manner of a question.

Afterwards, as they lay together, Emily told him about her childhood holiday in Australia, and her aborted meeting with her grandparents, and how they'd stayed the night at the back of a cafe in a small town. And how this was a period in which she had regressed to wetting the bed, at the age of eight, traumatised by seeing her father throw himself under a train the previous year. Every night during that holiday in Australia—they visited Sydney and the Central Coast—she slept on her stepfather's lined coat, which stayed dry until the night before they flew back to England.

'I don't know why I told you that,' said Emily.

'No, I'm happy we can talk about these things. About anything.'

'This shouldn't happen again, should it?' said Emily.

'It shouldn't,' said Liam. 'But it was a great deal of fun.'

'We're silly,' Emily said, getting dressed. She left Liam naked in his bed, and they never spoke again about the afternoon they had sex. It was, Emily imagined, the sort of thing that happened in most other share apartments occupied by young people in London.

5.

Liam did not, in the end, go out for a large meal. In his hotel room Emily moved from the bed to the desk. On the desk, already unpacked, was a thin stack of papers: someone's story for the magazine, which Liam had edited with blue pencil. Emily loved his handwriting, its loops and billows: it was both pretty and difficult to read. He appeared to find it hard to look at her. Some people don't know what they mean to you. For years, when no one was around, Emily found herself saying Liam's name out loud, idly, as if they were in the same room. She didn't have many friends, not true friends. She loved Liam, yes, it was a kind of love, but if they began a romantic relationship she was certain it would not last long, that it would be a performed kind of intimacy, and performed badly, and she'd lose him entirely in the end. He was like family. Emily was an only child. Some people don't know how important they are to you.

'I can't be with you,' Emily said.

'All right.'

'It's because—'

'I'm fine with not knowing why,' Liam said.

'But I don't intend to walk away from this friendship.'

'On second thought, I'd like to know why we can't be together.'

'Because we're friends. That's what we are. *Friends*. That's what we've always been. It's meaningful to me because it's a friendship. You can't be anything other than a friend.'

'You're saying the word "friend" a lot.'

'I don't have a lot of them.'

'I think you're the love of my life.'

'That life is not the one we're having.'

'You don't find me physically attractive.'

'You're attractive. Jesus.'

'Maybe I can change my flight and go home today.'

'Is this commission a quid pro quo thing?'

'No! The *New Yorker* doesn't do quid pro quo, and I would never do that to you. I like the story idea. I like your writing. The commission is genuine. We're really doing this.'

'Tell me now if you're not going to honour the commission, and I'll go home.'

'File the story as normal. Do you remember that day we slept together, a hundred years ago? Had sex.'

'Okay. Yes.'

'Afterwards you left the room and we never acknowledged that it happened.'

'You'd like me to pretend this conversation never happened?'

'That would be ideal.'

'But I'll see you before you go?'

'Probably not,' said Liam.

The way back to her room—the walk down the hall, the lift down four floors—imprinted itself on her brain; it was the kind of moment, the kind of feeling, that she feared she'd remember even as she experienced it. Her husband, her friend Liam, the commission: would they all be taken away from her? In her absence (Emily left her phone in her room, because she wasn't yet in the habit of taking it every-where) messages had been left by Sophia, the survivor of the Third of April, and Shirley Gibson, who with her husband Sam had taken over the Lucky's franchise. Both Sophia and Shirley said they would be happy to be interviewed. Sophia said: 'I have spare time. But you gotta come to me. I don't have a working car right now.' Shirley said: 'Let's do the interview somewhere nice. I know a gorgeous place in Drummoyne.'

Before returning their calls, Emily wanted to ring her early-rising mother, who said yes she could talk, was not busy, had put on a leg of gammon for lunch. The meat was simmering in dry apple cider.

Emily said: 'Michael told me he's having an affair.'

'Michael's been having an affair?' her mother repeated, before repeating it twice more and hereby notifying Rick of the development. 'My God. Who with? A woman? A man?'

'I know next to nothing about her and I want it to stay that way.'

'Look, you two can sort it out, can't you? No point in getting divorced. When you come back to England you'll sit down and fix things, won't you?'

'I'm not sure that's possible.'

''Course it's possible. Anything's possible in a marriage. Gosh, he had a little affair; he made a terrible mistake. No doubt he's sorry. I know Michael. That man will be on his knees ready to beg forgiveness by the time you come back.'

'I doubt it will matter, Mum.'

'Rick wants to have a word. Hang on.'

Emily's stepfather said: 'The bastard's got himself a girl-friend, does he?'

'I wanted to let you and Mum know what's going on.'

'To be honest, Em, I never thought you and Michael would stay together. Said this to your mum a while back. Maybe it was a good marriage for a while, but it wasn't forever. Sorry to say, I knew something like this would happen.'

'You called it, Rick.'

6.

After high school, Emily left her parents' home in Suffolk and spent her first year of university living alone in a Childs Hill studio apartment that belonged to a friend of the family. She believed Londoners could immediately tell that nothing of a permanent nature would come of her stay. To pay bills and cover expenses, Emily spent her savings and worked in pubs—anywhere that would hire her. She was poor. The apartment's owner, who had moved to Dublin, left behind an elderly cat to care for and eventually put down. Above the bed she hung Ian Asquith's painting. In the bathtub Emily tried to improve her French, reading *Au Pays de la Magie* by Henri Michaux. Then she picked up Duras's *La Vie Matérielle*. The plumbing leaked in so many places you couldn't get to them all. A family of squirrels appeared at the courtyard window, and a group of Goldsmiths students took her into their circle. Emily's early Big City experiences were typical, and often she was aware of this fact. The good moments she stored up like gold. By October it seemed London had accepted her. And maybe she would stay for good.

Now Emily dreaded the idea of going home. Late that night she sent an email to Michael. *I want you to move out today or tomorrow*, she wrote. *I don't want to think another second about you and another person in my home.*

1957

1.

VALIA LEFT LUCKY twice before she ended the marriage in 1957, declaring their problems unchanged and intolerable. The first instance she left him might serve as a sample of their final years together, the time they ground through as labour.

That morning Lucky woke early in a country hotel, jolted out of sleep by the fluid, merged shrieks of chickens in a nearby yard, the day still dark like a vacuum. The room contained a bed, an armchair, and a rocking horse for guests with children. Cowra treasured its new Lucky's restaurant to the extent that the franchisee requested larger premises at a new location on the main street. Some days there was a queue for dinner. Country people don't like to queue. Time to expand, agreed Lucky. He drove to Cowra and looked at the real estate available in town—in February it was all rusting lawns and dusty cars—and said he'd need a week to think about things. As a matter of professional practice, he gave himself one week to decide on any purchase more costly than a soda fountain. He'd reach an answer eventually, often at home in Sydney, during dinner or breakfast, in the midst of conversation with Valia, or while trying to fall asleep.

Sleep-fuddled Lucky breathed shallowly and wavered outside before getting into the car, as if he were stepping onto a tiny boat. He didn't bother with breakfast. He was consumed by the franchise. He was a sacrifice, and he accepted the cost: it indicated that the restaurants were prevailing, that he'd done the right thing with Asquith's gift.

With Ian's money, he initially bought three properties in Sydney and built identical restaurants. He could have set up more outlets, but he started with a trio and waited to see what would happen, to see if the rain came, if the soil was alkaline, if there was sabotage from Greek-Australian cafes already established. (In the 1940s, a joke circulated among Anglo Sydneysiders. Q: Why was there no Greek mafia? A: Every Greek who ran a cafe thought he was a mob boss.) Some families used the franchises as intermediate arrangements. They paid Lucky his monthly fee—there was no payroll system—they paid most overheads and saved for their own cafe. The Lucky's business, to most franchisees, screamed of safety, stopgap, trampoline. The earliest franchisees cashed out in the early 1950s. They proved that progress could be made.

Lucky ran a joint in Stanmore, Antony Glavas and his brother Jim worked a restaurant in Castlereagh Street in the city, and Peter Niforis and his wife Roslyn, a Ngiyampaa woman, introduced Lucky's to the suburb of Marrickville. Peter could cook (he made a perfect boutridia) but Roslyn captained their franchise, turning over tables, calling the customers *sweetheart*, calling the suppliers *matey* when they tried to game her. At their first meeting, responding to an advertisement for franchisees, Roslyn was all stratagem and honesty and unmoving confidence and said her plan was to work like a team of twenty and save the surplus for a new, independent restaurant, leaving Lucky's behind as soon as possible. Lucky told her the Glavas brothers had the same idea. He said the businesses weren't traps, weren't factories, weren't eaters of employees.

But they ate the franchiser. On the way back to Sydney he stopped for lunch at the outlet in Mittagong and heard the news: on Monday, John Bakris in the Canberra business had been arrested for assault after attacking a difficult customer with a rolling pin. The kitchens needed rolling pins for the one Greek dish on the franchise menu: Kefalonian meat pie (Lucky had plans to add stifado). The injured Canberra customer was still in hospital and Bakris remained in jail. John's family requested that Lucky visit Canberra and resolve the mess, or wire bail money, or make a call and come to terms with the victim's family. Yes, a phone call, a settlement, he might try something like that, maybe tomorrow. The job could be low-pitched, Lucky thought. You dealt with good franchisees, and then there were the violent and uncompromising and cruel, the Achilleans, after whom everyone picked up. The kind of men you wanted to forget. What a power it would be if Lucky could pick the men like Achilles at interviews and refuse them any position.

On the road, he gripped the steering wheel firmly and thought: I own this monstrous business, but I'm not a true leader. I don't know what I'm doing. I'm still an imposter. I've built a castle that exposed me. The structure ought to be stronger, higher, gleaming.

Once back in Sydney, he went straight to the Stanmore restaurant, managed by Valia, who put away her apron and sat with him in the booth where they'd have about ten minutes together. Lucky apologised. That afternoon he'd arranged a meeting at the Quay with five men from Isaacs Incorporated, a Melbourne company that manufactured drink flavourings. There were nine Lucky's cafes already operating in Sydney, and twelve elsewhere in the state, and Lucky no longer spent any part of his day behind a stove, instead scouting for properties and meeting distributors and bureaucrats and local council members, and visiting bars and restaurants and dance halls in the evening, wherever his business associates suggested a night out, more work disguised as socialising—an antic web of institutions and communities. Such meetings bored Valia. She declined to partake. In the booth at Stanmore, Lucky told her about Cowra, about Bakris, and he pressed his tired face to hers, and they kissed and he rushed off.

His meeting with the Melburnians, held in a conference room with mullion windows, unfolded like a commercial sacrament. They tried the red, blue, green, yellow, orange, purple flavours with beer, lemonade, water and so on—a joyless production he treated with affability. Each of the wait staff, all made preposterous, was dressed in one of the six colours. By evening's end, the Victorians were drunk and agreed to two months of free packages per franchise outlet, and Lucky didn't need to tell them about his condition of requiring one week to make a significant commercial decision. As the conversation moved from drink flavours to the subject of cricket (to Lucky's mind, the only thing worse than playing cricket was talking about cricket) he excused himself and drove home.

'Gonna surprise the wife, huh?' one of the Melburnians said, his lips purple from the mix of flavourings.

Valia sat in the lounge room listening to the wireless. She put down her glass with a gentle tap and stood.

'Where are you going?' she asked. Lucky was already in another room, searching for the Bakris family's phone number. Did the Canberra franchise have a phone number yet? He looked through his papers for their address. Valia came to the door and asked about the meeting with the drinks people.

Valia's figure, standing by the study door, turned rigid when he passed her and made for the bathroom to brush his teeth, to remove the rock candy taste the flavoured drinks had left in his mouth. Then Valia stood in the bathroom doorway and spoke to him. She said something he didn't catch. Years later he could remember how long the drive from Cowra to Sydney took that day, he recalled what he ate when he stopped in Mittagong, but he couldn't remember what Valia said while she stood at the bathroom door and he wiped toothpaste from his mouth.

'I don't think these new drink flavours will work,' he said. 'I made a mistake accepting the offer.'

'There's a lot missing from this marriage,' said Valia. 'You haven't heard a word I've said. You're too far into your own thoughts. Every day you're like this. You're somewhere else.'

'I did in fact hear you.'

'You're not present. I talk to you and you wander into another room. I start a conversation and you start up with something else. We have different lives. There's no proper connection here. Even simple dialogue: *Hello, how was your day? I'm good, what did you get up to?* We can't even do that.'

'This is a problem easily fixed. All that needs to change is my headspace.'

'We've had this conversation a hundred times. We keep talking about it and nothing changes. I've thought about it for years. You can't change. I can't stay in this marriage.'

'Because you don't love me?'

'Not the way I used to. A marriage should be more than this.'

'Can you take a week off? I'll handle the Stanmore restaurant and you can rest here.'

'Let me leave without trying to convince me to stay. Let me go without a scene.'

Lucky watched Valia carry the suitcase through the door and out into the street. An unseen train whinnied beyond the treetops. At the kerb, Valia looked left and right. Which way would she go? he wondered. Right, to the station? Left, to Bridge Road, where she might soon find a taxi? Where would the taxi take Valia? If Lucky wanted to talk, how would he find her? Would she come back tomorrow?

Valia did come back. Then she left. And came back again. Then she left for good.

1965

1.

THAT SUMMER IN Sydney, which the newspapers identified as exceptionally hot and particularly profitable for the
restaurant industry, the Greeks played cards in a private
gaming room above a fruit-and-vegetable shop on Glebe
Point Road. Lucky arrived early. The house opened at 8 pm,
the first games began an hour later, and he stood alone with
his coffee at a table near the windows. Here the high tables
were for drinking; the regular tables reserved for cards. He
came early to see which players arrived together, to spot
friends or cronies who might soft play or otherwise collude
with each other. The room had a washstand sink, a stove
for the briki, a tray for bottles, another tray for glasses. On
one of the yellow walls hung a framed print of a painting,
unsigned, a nineteenth-century panoramic: the Battle of
Borodino. The door of the gaming room was locked and

a coat hung over the doorknob to cover the keyhole. Up here, above the fruiterer's shop, Lucky assumed they were adequately hidden from police and might only be identified from deep in the park opposite, through binoculars, by some marvel of spying.

He laid small bets. Gambling wasn't a problem for him yet; it wouldn't be that way for decades. To Lucky, the value of gaming was in the play, the action, the second act, the complication, regardless of the final result or whether his fortune was decided in terrifying speed, or over the course of several hours. Betting took him right out of the franchise world. The gameplay was drama; it was a bending of reality, a disruption, fantasy life adumbrated on a table. The play could be as overwhelming as sex. By 1965 it functioned, for Lucky Mallios, as a replacement for sex.

At the largest table he sat with five players, mostly sober-looking, all appearing a little pent-up, and he dealt the first game, making small talk. Lucky might have been the most well-known, successful man in the room, but his Greek—and this was obvious from the first word he uttered—was categorically the worst. For the most part he loved speaking his parents' language (Lucky's Greek had improved since the franchise started), but some nights it came as a relief when the conversation moved to English. It got to be oppressive the way some Greeks expected others to hold on to culture and language without error, like a treasure, two generations, three generations deep in a new country. The pride in depth of ethnicity. The shame in its lack. Any point-scoring about authenticity had long since come to bore Lucky. He no longer took offence. The idea of ethnic purity was a diaspora fantasy. Everyone in this room was a mixture of influences, a new type of person. They accepted their impurity or they didn't.

The air in the gaming room was blue with cigarette smoke. Before the second deal, Lucky asked about the players' heritage: three men at his table had emigrated from Kalymnos. Next to Lucky sat a Peloponnesian who absolutely refused to speak English. And there was someone else, who introduced himself as Alexander, from Ithaka, and he reminded Lucky of old Achilles Asproyerakas, in the way that Alexander's face seemed to express most thoughts and emotions he experienced. He said only his wife called him Alexandro.

'You know the Asproyerakas family?' Lucky asked. 'They're from the village of Vathi.'

'I hear of the man, Achilleas. I hear plenty about him.'

'His daughter, Valia, have you met her?' By 1965 Lucky didn't know where in Sydney she lived, or if Valia still lived in the city, or where she worked or if she worked.

'Don't know this one.'

'Tell me about Achilles.'

'What to say? He's a donkey. He's a disease. I'm trying to play cards today. Are you wanting to throw me off?'

Lucky folded and left Alexander in the game against the Peloponnesian and those two bet back and forth, Alexander's expressions alternating from apprehensive to grave, while Lucky—thinking about Achilles, whom he hadn't seen in maybe nineteen years—had the hardest time sitting quietly. At last Alexander lost the hand. He ashed his cigarette untidily while his opponent dragged an arm across the table, collecting the coins. Alexander turned to Lucky and said: 'You want to hear about Achilleas? He's living with my cousin Damianos, and he stays too long there. The man sleeps in a shed in the yard, says he's got nowhere else to go. It's not a Lucky's cafe. No offence to you, but my cousin does his own business. He doesn't want another person's fucking name on his shop.'

'Fair enough. I could have been modest and given the business another name. Too late to change now. Where's your cousin's place?'

'You know the Omega Cafe in Ashfield? That's the one. After Easter my cousin needed some painting done so he put a note in the window saying *Painter wanted* and next day Achilleas comes to the cafe, talking about Ithaka. Beautiful island. You've heard all that shit. That's how old man gets a job. But Achilleas says to my cousin that he will paint for no money—he only needs place to stay. Damian is a sucker; I say to him he's too nice. He puts Achilleas outside in a shed because that's where he has the room. The shed is not too bad for one person. Achilleas has bed, and toilet out there. And he does his painting of the walls—a bodgy job, a big fucking slop—and then he says he needs to stay a bit longer. He has nowhere else to go. Maybe he can chop some wood for the stove? But my cousin knows how to use an axe, he doesn't need someone to chop wood. Inside, Damian lives in the house behind the cafe with his wife and children. And in the morning Achilleas uses their bath, sitting in the bath making it dirty, leaving hairs. My cousin is trying to raise three children in this small place. I said I will come over and get rid of this man, make him trouble, but Damian says no, Achilleas too old, can't put this man on the street like that. But for sure you can put someone in the street. If they're not family, you can do it. We all know the rules. If you're not family, I'll put you out, like that.'

'Achilles can be difficult and dangerous. How about I talk to him? Maybe I can help.'

'Is it true he killed his daughter and burned down his own cafe?'

'That's false.'

'It's the story I heard,' said Alexander.

Ashfield wasn't far. Lucky lived in Stanmore and each morning he walked to the local franchise a few blocks away, on Percival Road, and said his hellos in the kitchen and went through a crooked door to a locked office with a desk and guest chairs and cabinets with labelled drawers. On the wall: an icon of St Vasilios (a gift from Valia; he was not religious). On his desk was an automatic electric speaker phone. When Lucky spoke to franchisees, a daily duty, he took notes and talked at the extension speaker box, which was ovoid and looked like the lidless eye of a marble head. He never raised his voice. Crazy to sit alone in a room yelling at a speaker the size of a stick of butter.

Before work the next day, Lucky visited the Omega Cafe, where he introduced himself to Damian and said he'd come to see old Achilles. With little more than a nod, Lucky was led into the yard, as if he were a repairman. Damian left him at the door of the shed. Lucky knocked. He couldn't let Achilles cause problems in another family. In each of his franchises, many of which were homes, he was determined that each family would avoid the fate of the Achillion.

Opening the door of the corrugated-iron shed, Achilles, his head shaved, his moustache white, his body thinner than Lucky expected, clad only in shorts, greeted his former son-in-law with the observation: 'You look rough. All droopy around the mouth.'

'How are you?'

'There's nothing wrong with me.'

'Do you need a job?'

'Not right now. I'm settled.'

'What about a new place to stay?'

'Maybe when it gets colder. Why all these questions? What are you doing here?'

'Look, these people, they're trying to run a business here, raise children, and you're getting in the way. Maybe you can do some jobs for me? I'll give you a couple weeks' work and we'll see how you go.'

'Work for you? Never.'

'Can you drive a small truck?'

'Are you talking about my eyes? I see perfect.'

'You'll be running some errands for me around Sydney and New South Wales. Starting day after tomorrow. Week after next you'll drive to Cobar.'

'That's in the middle of nowhere!'

'And you'll stay with me until I find you somewhere else.'

'Wait, who sent you here?'

'I'm helping you but not forgiving you. I'm doing this because you're Valia's father.'

'And Valia was the only woman for you.'

'Let's pack up your things.'

2.

That night, as they ate dinner in the Stanmore restaurant, Achilles asked why Lucky and Valia were no longer married, why they couldn't fix their problems, why they didn't have children, or go on holiday to an island like Ithaka. An acquaintance had informed Achilles of the divorce; some-one saw an article in the newspaper. Valia hadn't spoken to her father since the Achillion days. 'Tell me the truth,' he said to Lucky. 'I'm the person you talk to. We used to be family!' He wanted to know what went wrong, he said he'd thought a lot about how he'd made a mess of his own life. What he did to Penny. What he did to his family.

Achilles said: 'From people I hear that Valia has a child, a girl named Sophia. I'm a grandfather, they say. But Valia doesn't see me like that.'

'Is she happy, do you think?'

'How would I know?' said Achilles.

Lucky shook his head, shifted uncomfortably, rubbed the stubble along his jaw—all signs that he didn't want to talk about a subject any further. Other people knew these signals. Lucky's marriage to Valia was the most important and harmonious relationship of his life. What did that say about his other relationships? He remained attached to her, yet he was ashamed of this fact. Some people, even when you no longer saw them, even when you'd given up on reconciliation, even after years apart, you continued to share your life with them, and what they represented to you. They reminded you of your own potential. He couldn't speak to Achilles about this abundance of regret. Achilles was the last person.

'We can't talk about Valia,' said Lucky. 'Talk about anything else.'

'You stole my franchise dream,' said Achilles.

3.

Lucky gave Asproyerakas the spare room and kept him busy with little jobs. He courierised the old man. Achilles took soda fountain replacement parts to the Waverton restaurant. Moved a jukebox from Newtown to Kogarah. Hauled drinks to Queanbeyan. Then, as planned, Lucky hired a tow truck and sent his former father-in-law out west. First, to deliver an electric potato-peeling machine to the Lucky's outlet in Peak Hill, a town two hundred and fifty-four miles west of Sydney. From there, Achilles would drive north-west and pick up a used Holden EJ in the town of Cobar, towing the car back to Sydney. The franchisee in Cobar had offered the 1962 Holden in lieu of eleven monthly payments now in arrears. Lucky felt indifferent about EJs—he didn't like the congested sound of the engine, he didn't need a second car—but evicting a franchisee might result in making a family homeless, since the contract included the business premises plus adjoining house. He'd take the car, issue a second warning, and sell the Holden to a city dealership.

Achilles, leaving Sydney's city limits by 4 am, made good time to the Peak Hill franchise, run by the Rizos family, and he helped install the peeler in a shed outside. He loved watching the machine. It murmured, hummed, thudded and then ejected the peeled potatoes with a leathery squeak. These lucky bastards, Mr and Mrs Rizos, they had proper jobs, not this driving around like a servant to an ex-son. Cleaning the spectacles he wore for driving, Achilles said he would acquire one of these peelers himself if Lucky ever gave him a franchise. He told Mr Rizos that after the Achillion Cafe burned down he used the insurance money to build a tobacco shop. That was a big mistake. Inside three years the shop went out of business. I must keep going, said Achilles.

Next stop distant Cobar, where Stavros, the franchisee, did his best to appear composed about losing his car, and even helped secure the EJ to the truck, a task in which both he and Achilles were untrained. With profanities held between his lips, Stavros said, 'Give my regards to the American. Tell him it's tough out here. He should be the one to visit next time.' Like many of Lucky's franchisees, Stavros referred to the boss as 'the American'. They pronounced him foreign, not-Greek, part of a diaspora distinct from theirs. It wasn't Achilles' job to tell Stavros he needed to smarten up, to make do, that the restaurant's fortunes could be life or death for his marriage and family. According to the conditions of the franchise contract he and his family should be out of the cafe. No one had given Achilles good advice. Fuck Stavros, he thought. The cabin of the blue Holden, fatigued with stains and tears, smelled rank and reminded Achilles of a little goat. He wound down the front windows of the EJ on both sides to air out the car on the way back home. If he avoided any kangaroos, if he drove fast, he could make the trip to Sydney in nine hours.

Still heading towards Nyngan, the wide dirt road pinched at the centre, Achilles noticed smoke fluttering from the cabin of the Holden EJ. He was, for the time being, smoking cigarettes again. It was temporary and he justified it this way: if he didn't smoke on this assignment, he would have been bored out of his mind, might have lost concentration and run off the road. Achilles watched his mirrors as smoke now streamed out of the EJ's wide-open windows. He smacked the dashboard with his left fist, said, 'What? Fuck God!' One of the cigarette butts he'd flicked out of the truck window must have curled around and landed inside the cabin of the Holden. Black smoke in knots and braids poured from the EJ, like a gag in a circus car.

A car overtaking him leaned on the horn and signalled for Achilles to pull over, but he shook his head. How could he extinguish the fire out here? Pull over and urinate through the window of the Holden? He bent forwards over the steering wheel, leaning away from the fire burning a few metres behind him, his weight down on the pedal.

Nyngan was, what, forty-five minutes away? How exactly did cars explode?

Automobiles coming the other way flashed their lights at him, honked their horns, while the cars behind kept well back. The driver of one passing truck yelled out: 'YER ON FIRE!'

Achilles hardly slowed down when he entered the town, looking for the fire station. The station wasn't on the main street. As he swooped into a U-turn at the end of the road, a man came off the footpath waving, holding a hat in one hand and pointing to the street perpendicular. Achilles turned again and drove where vaguely directed—he could smell the burning EJ: after the U-turn the blue smoke filled up his cabin, inducing tears.

He stopped out the front of the station and ran from the truck as two firemen in overalls moved with hoses towards the fire. A column of water now plunged into the Holden's windows and streamed out dirty through gaps in the doors. Achilles, at a safe distance, sat in the gutter and watched the water tunnel through the truck and he thought of the firemen and what lay at the back of their minds each morning, before he turned up bearing a sedan aflame. They must, he thought, have felt a warranted pride in their work. They didn't carry the sack in someone else's money scheme: they were free from profit's consequences. They didn't create problems: they solved them. They didn't lose property: they prevented further loss.

The police required Achilles to stay overnight in Nyngan to answer a few questions about the ignited car he brought to their town. The tow truck, the local sergeant added, would need to be looked over by a mechanic and declared roadworthy.

'This is wrong,' said Achilles. 'I don't need to pay any mechanic. I can drive off now if I want.'

'I can detain you.'

'What for?'

'Public disorder. Suspected stolen car. Et cetera and so forth.'

Achilles took a room in the busy Royal Hotel and, needing to get away from everyone, he went swimming alone. At the riverbank he found a suitable place to strip down. A grassy spot swollen as if filled with water. Achilles removed his shirt and pants and waded in, laughing to himself and shivering in his underwear. He kicked his feet and sent ripples to the riverbank. He had no idea what they'd named this river. The cold warmly clothed him. It fitted to his sore back and settled at the neck, like gentle hands on his shoulders. His feet bounced over hard mud and the wire of gum tree roots. A brown dusting over the water. Kangaroos ticked through scrub on the opposite bank. After a swim he planned to have dinner at the Lucky's outlet in Nyngan. Achilles took pleasure, a little, in the sounds he made when his hands and feet broke the surface of the brown water. Then he swam to the centre of the river, into a gnarl of moving debris, which he couldn't see, which netted him, pulled him gasping under the water.

Downstream seven miles, the shipmate on a wool barge discovered Achilles' corpse tangled in the exposed roots of a lilly pilly tree.

4.

After their divorce Lucky and Valia met again on several occasions. Their meeting at Achilles' funeral in 1965 can be described briefly, because they barely exchanged a word. The service was held at St Constantine Greek Orthodox church. After the burial at Rookwood Cemetery, Lucky approached Valia to say he had tried to help her father. She said she was glad he tried. For years already Lucky had been in regular mental contact with her: for years he'd received make-believe consultations from her, imagined guidance about the franchise, advice about the way he dressed and the character of the people he met. More recently he tried to imagine Valia's house and his mind flashed to a garden, a view of water, and a child saying, *Mummy?* At the cemetery he said she looked good, and Valia did not smile. In the background stood her husband, whose existence was still difficult for Lucky to welcome or even acknowledge, whose name—Robert—he would have chosen to forget, if that were possible. And her daughter, Sophia, almost two years old, did she wave at Lucky after the funeral service? She waved. Goodbye.

1971

1.

IN THE FIRST week of August, Valia received the following letter:

Dear Valia,

Twenty-odd years ago I gave your former husband all the money I possessed in the world. You and he didn't squander that gift as I have squandered all of my gifts, such as they are.

I have not included my address on this letter because I've decided to take my life soon. Please do not try to contact my family.

But I owe you the truth. This is difficult to write. For a long time I've lived with my crime, and the shame has been unremitting and crushing. The truth is that I'm responsible for the death of your sister, Penelope.

In effect, I killed her.

I am responsible for the fire at the Cafe Achillion. But I did NOT intend to kill anyone. My objective was vandalism. I wanted only to damage your business because you and Lucky appeared happy, and to me, at that time, the happiness of others felt like a great injustice. These days I feel differently: my unhappiness is a form of justice. A great deal of my life has been a disaster, but nothing I've done was worse than the death of Penelope. I could not regret a thing more.

I suppose I am a murderer. I gave you that money out of guilt, thinking I could unburden myself.

You should be aware that I have written an identical letter to Lucky. I am aware you are no longer married.

The truth, I hope, has some value.

Live in peace.

Ian Asquith

2.

On the phone Lucky suggested they meet at the Stanmore restaurant; Valia said it didn't matter where. In preparation he bought a new shirt, visited the barber and went for a run early in the morning, seven laps of the Camperdown cricket oval. His staff waxed the floors and put out new tablecloths. Of the thirty franchises, the Stanmore joint remained his favourite, the most realised in its resemblance to the Achillion. Above the counter was the sign: OUR MOTTO: CLEANLINESS AND CIVILITY.

Following an untraceable rumour, all the franchisees suspected that the Lucky's empire, if it could be called that, began with a benefactor. Not an inheritance, but a gift. There was disagreement concerning the size of that gift and the reason it had been bestowed. Relying on hearsay, some wondered if Lucky had acquired this benefactor during the war, through an act of trickery or bravery.

After reading Asquith's letter of confession, a message that bombed away Lucky's day-to-day preoccupations, he waited for Valia to get in touch, despite a definite urge to pick up the phone and call her, which he somehow pushed to one side. Lucky didn't want any contact that was unwelcome. He went to bed full of trepidation. Probably, if Asquith was on the verge of taking his own life, he had mailed the two confession letters about the same time. Or maybe Valia hadn't received any letter. And maybe Asquith hadn't killed himself. For a few days Lucky cancelled all meetings, all his planned visits to his other outlets, and stayed either at home or in the office, near a phone, expecting—hoping—to hear Valia's voice again at any moment. In the mornings and afternoons he rang various Sydney franchises, in case she'd called one of his other businesses and left a message.

'We must meet,' Valia said when she called him at home.

The day she was due at the cafe, the employees were instructed not to disturb them, and the staff did their best to avoid looking at Lucky and Valia overmuch, pretending not to know who she was when she turned up and the pair modestly embraced, before sitting at a booth. Her face loomed olive and cold. Lucky looked at the back of his hand, the bumpy spots.

'Of all the cafes,' he said, 'this one is still my favourite.'

'Tell me the truth,' said Valia. 'Did you already know Ian Asquith had set the fire, or did you even for a second suspect him before receiving that letter?'

'I would never have accepted his gift. He would be in jail.'

'All this, your success, begins with Penelope's death. With his money you bought three cafes.'

'Yes,' he said. Lucky felt contaminated by the letter. The contamination spread to all his businesses.

'If there were any justice, this place wouldn't be here. Someone should come in and throw you out.'

'What do you want me to do? Tell me.'

'My grief for Penelope was painful and frightening.'

'I was there.'

'Admit that this business is an offence to Penelope. And to me!'

Everyone in the cafe heard Valia shout. Lucky knew her anger was coming. For days he'd drifted about waiting for this moment. Was it a moment? Or was he stuck in her contempt forever?

Poor Vasilis 'Lucky' Mallios, hated to the end by his ex-wife. He is survived by no one.

'Yes,' he said. 'This place is built on her death.'

He thought Valia would get up and leave but she didn't move from the booth.

'Why do you think this monster took his life?' she asked.

'In the letter he said his life was a disaster,' said Lucky.

'I didn't know the man. I sent him a postcard a few months ago. My supplier for the sundae dishes is English and I asked them to do me a favour and find his address. Then I sent Asquith a postcard of the Lucky's restaurant. I said thank you. It was something I'd been meaning to do for a long time.'

'Had you spoken to him before?'

'I wrote to him years ago, at a different address, when we got those first restaurants. Do you remember? He didn't reply.' Then Lucky's control slipped: 'I miss you, Valia. So much time has passed and it hasn't stopped.'

'I'm sorry you have those feelings. But I came to talk about the letter.'

There was a distance in her voice that Lucky had heard before—when the marriage faltered and failed. He was soft. Her tone clawed into him.

He said: 'Do we know for sure that he's dead?'

'I contacted the British consulate and enquired about him, said he was an old friend, said I'd heard a rumour he died, and a few days later they confirmed it. Let's get this straight: will you go to the police?'

'Will you?' Lucky asked.

'I don't see the benefit of this getting out. Not for you or me or the franchisees. Who have you told?'

'No one. You?'

'Robert,' said Valia. Robert, her husband—Lucky still loathed everyone with that name. Valia continued: 'I came here to tell you that I'm going to destroy the letter that Mr Asquith sent me. Penelope is dead. This Asquith man is dead. It's finished.'

'Then take this too.' And Lucky handed her the letter he'd received.

'I'll burn these when I get home. The letters are not going to turn up in ten years' time, you understand?'

'It's up to you what you do with them.'

'Goodbye now, Lucky.' She rose from her seat.

'No! Stay. How is your daughter? How is your husband? Tell me about him. What does he do?'

Valia shook her head gently. She wasn't going to talk about her family.

He said: 'I have something to ask you. I'm opening a new cafe in Bronte. We don't have occupants yet. It's a good location, near the beach. Lots of people walking the street down there. And you can take the cafe for nothing. Change the name if you want. That goes without saying. You don't want my name on the sign. Only problem is that there's no house out the back. No rooms like the Achillion.'

'We don't need it. We don't want your help.'

'You should think about it.'

Lucky put up his hand, called to the staff for some menus.

'I'm going, Lucky.'

'Think about what I said. Please. Will you come back in?'

'I won't set foot in a Lucky's restaurant again. We'll never have anything to do with your business.'

The menus arrived courtesy of a meek waiter who retreated after hearing Valia's last sentence.

'Let's meet again next week and talk,' said Lucky. 'But not in the cafe next time. We'll go sit on a bench somewhere. Is that a thing we could do?'

'No, we can't.'

On the footpath they did not embrace. The space between them expanded and Valia turned and walked past the tobacco shop. The green sign of a coal cellar, an Italian baker, a bookstore. Leaves and pollen flew everywhere. Lucky, watching through the window, took a deep breath and held it for a long time. Of course he loved her. Permanence in the face of life's transience.

1975

1.

TWO INVESTORS, SHIRLEY and Sam Gibson, wife and husband, had contacted Lucky a few months back. 'Excuse this call out of the blue,' said Shirley when she called him one Monday morning. They had a significant proposal, she said, an idea they wanted to discuss with him in person, next week perhaps. But Shirley called again two days before that initial appointment and cancelled (something had come up), and since then Shirley and Sam had cancelled four meetings with Lucky, all at a day or two's notice. As a rule, if anyone cancelled on Lucky more than twice he told them to go fuck themselves. He kept making an exception for the investors—that was how they introduced themselves, as 'two people who make a living by investing in other people's businesses'. After each postponement they sent him a case of wine by way of apology. Lucky had a feeling that something good was about to happen with Shirley and Sam.

In his office cabinets Lucky kept documents on each franchise; the deeds stayed with lawyers. The problematic cafes massed in Lucky's mind. The Blymaki family, in the suburb of Erskineville, had suffered break-ins of late, with cigarettes and drinks stolen; Nikos Dimostenis, unhappy in Oberon, shut his shop on weekends; in Queanbeyan, Helen Kalasoudas couldn't break even; down in Mildura, Jim Melemenis got himself into trouble with the Italians; Mick Papacostas and his brothers were playing too much dice in Camperdown; and the Kostarelou boys of Fairfield had turned their Lucky's restaurant into an old-fashioned kafeneio, where women and children were unwelcome. Once a week or so, Lucky drove into the city to see the bookkeepers. He called it 'the paper run'. They said forget all the other problems, his loans for new constructions were the biggest worry. Loans massed like a lump in the throat.

Lucky Mallios was getting tired and he welcomed new ideas on the franchise, a new structure, partners, saviours. For the fifth time a meeting with Shirley and Sam was arranged and this appointment they kept. He went to their offices on Hunter Street and, on level four, the investors' secretary showed him to a meeting room, where he shook hands with Sam, who wore what looked like a school tie, and a light yellow-suited Shirley, who gave off an energy that sprawled and seemed to contain her quiet husband. They both looked to be in their late twenties.

Lucky peeled off his blue jacket and hung it over the back

of a chair. Once all were settled, Shirley pointed at the wall behind Lucky, where they'd pinned up sepia-toned maps of six states and the Northern Territory, moving left to right from the most populous state to the least, with little black toothpick flags planted over each map. About twenty of these black flags spidered across the wall. With two hands Sam pushed a grey folder across the table to Lucky, who didn't pick it up. Real professionals handed objects to each other. Already he didn't like Sam.

Shirley spoke: 'On the maps we've marked possible Lucky's restaurant locations. We've done our sums. We plan to expand the business, perhaps even twofold. We want to bring in a payroll system, too, in line with how franchises function in the US. Respectfully, the business is a little outdated.'

'With payroll systems,' Lucky began, and this was a subject that came up now and then, 'I'd be at the mercy of payroll operators who could overpay and underpay staff, depending on how they screw up that month. The monthly fee is easy. It's worked for me.'

'It's antiquated,' said Shirley. 'You're paying too much for that ease.'

The overhead fan began to squeal, sending little bolts of tension into the air, before slowly the mechanism returned to its normal hum. Dimples appeared on Sam's cheeks. The young man's eyebrows were raised the entire meeting, his forehead creased. His expression, smarmy or anxious, was difficult for Lucky to read. Shirley, the speaker, the leader, seemed to enjoy getting to the point.

'How long you two been in the restaurant game?' Lucky asked.

'What's important is that we understand strategy,' said Shirley. 'That's what you should pay attention to. We've done the research. As it happens, we own a few retail spaces in the city. And we part-own an afternoon newspaper, the *Sydney Daily Post*.'

'I don't buy that paper,' said Lucky. 'It's low-grade stuff.'

He opened the folder in front of him: inside were addresses, estimated property values, estimates for yearly turnover, spreadsheets he couldn't comprehend, graphs that baffled him, and a new Lucky's logo, which wasn't half bad. He flicked through the papers, as if rummaging for something he couldn't find.

'You want a stake in the franchise?' Lucky said. 'I'm kind of intrigued. How much?'

'Not a stake—we want to acquire the Lucky's franchise outright. There's a figure on the first page of that document. That's what we're offering. And it's a generous offer, all things taken into account.'

All things? Lucky turned to the first page. The figure was enough to pay his creditors and take a brief overseas holiday.

'You must be joking,' he said.

'We understand exactly what state the business is in,' said Shirley. 'We know a great deal about the situation with Phoenix Construction. We know what it's cost you. We know the banks. We're giving you an opportunity to walk away.'

'Do you ever say anything?' Lucky asked silent Sam.

'I do numbers,' Sam said. 'Shirley is the more creative half.'

2.

Phoenix Constructions was a bankrupt building company formerly owned by Alexander, the same man who'd entered Lucky's life at a clandestine gaming room in Glebe in 1965, and who until recently had been Lucky's closest friend. At least once a week, Alexander would bring his wife Maria and their four children into the Stanmore restaurant, their dinner on the house, and Lucky felt welcome to turn up unannounced at their home for a drink or dinner, for games in the backyard. Alexander's eldest son, improbably, liked reading about baseball and Lucky, when he returned to Chicago for his mother's funeral, bought mitts and bats and Black Sox caps and children's jerseys. 'Don't give money to them,' Maria used to remind Lucky. She didn't want her children fixated on money. The kids called him Theie, or Uncle, or Mal, a reference both to his surname Mallios and the word for hair, *mallia*. Lucky's curly brown hair, cut once a year, had become a kind of trademark. On weekends, the two friends went to pubs and restaurants, though it must be said their time together, away from family, did not devolve to scandal or debauched play, for Alexander was resolutely monogamous (he quietly confided that Maria had once had an affair), and while people freely assumed that Lucky, in his off hours, buried himself under an avalanche of sex and skilfully concealed incredible exploits, the truth remained ordinary, if not stark. He worked, he saw Alexander, he attended franchise events. In this way the days of the week were taken. There might have been room for someone like Valia. Late at night, in closed restaurants, Alexander listened to Lucky talk about his ex-wife, about what happened at the Achillion, about how he worried about franchisees in regional areas where the wool trade was in decline, and how vitally important the business was to him, how some days it felt like a reason for living, how sometimes he felt like walking away from it all and going to live someplace like Ithaka.

Lucky wanted to mix their professional lives. He saw this step as natural, an expansion of their friendship. He decided to open nine new franchises, and he contracted Alexander to construct them, bringing the total number of outlets to thirty-nine. Here, in their contract, the Platonic ideal, the improvement on the cursed Achillion: to be in business with people you chose, people who were *like family*. Alexander signed with uncanny assurance. Phoenix Constructions began work.

Afterwards, Lucky told himself that maybe Alexander had secretly hated him all along. Or maybe he wasn't up to the work. Or maybe the subcontractors were to blame, or maybe this or maybe that. Whatever the case, in early 1975, after several dry months, it rained heavily in Sydney and the surrounding region and every one of Alexander's roofs failed to withstand the downfall. The walls had the look of stained aprons. Water drowned the restaurant floors and the vinyl came up like wet pages. Further north, the roof collapsed on the new franchise in Forster.

In a phone call to Lucky, a structural engineer read from his written report, which described the roofs as 'lightly conformed' and the walls 'incorrectly mortised', and four of the nine buildings 'appeared to be moving in a downward motion'. Astounded Lucky, in a call to Alexander, asked: 'Did you build these joints with fucking glue?'

Soon Alexander stopped answering the phone. Phoenix Constructions engaged a lawyer. Again Lucky visited each of the nine new restaurants. Looking for every crack, gap, lean, mistake, betrayal. Finding all such problems before him. They may as well have been built on the edge of a cliff. They may as well, all nine, all uninhabited, have been derived from some old offence of Lucky's, some wrongdoing at the start of his career.

In June, Phoenix Constructions declared bankruptcy. The repairs were yet to be paid for. The new franchisees were still not trading. And there were loans: massing and frightening loans.

3.

Lucky asked Shirley: 'Is Alexander involved with your business?'

'Never met the man. And Christ, we don't want to. But we know that he's started work again. He's running a building company set up by his cousin, a cafe owner in Ashfield. The new company isn't called Phoenix Constructions, but, well, you get the idea.'

'Someone should have told me that. My lawyer, for example.'

'We respect what you've done with the franchise. You're a visionary. We mean that. But what we're going to do with this business—I promise, it's going to make you proud. We'll keep the Lucky's brand name. It will be your company, in a sense.'

'It won't be mine. Don't insult me.'

'People will think it's yours. They'll credit you to some degree.'

'Do you think I'm going to give up everything I've gained through long and painful experience?' said Lucky. 'That it counts for nothing?'

'You're in enormous debt, Mr Mallios. You're in financial pain,' said Shirley. 'We can make that pain go away.'

The look of pity on Shirley's face knocked Lucky flat. Or maybe it was a mask and she was enjoying the transaction. Lucky couldn't tell; he folded; he forced out the words.

'You've beat me,' said Lucky.

'Thank you,' Shirley said softly.

'But I want to keep one cafe,' said Lucky. 'The Stanmore branch will remain wholly under my ownership, free to do with as I please. I still need to earn a living. I can't retire on this bullshit sum of money.'

'One single cafe,' said Shirley. 'The contract we draw up won't allow you to turn that into a second cafe with the same name.'

'I'm back to one.'

Shirley and her husband stood up, with Sam almost knocking over a glass of water in the process, and they came around to Lucky's side of the table to shake hands. Lucky didn't want to touch these devils. Up close he noticed that Sam was out of breath and sweating, and he had a blond wart near one ear. Shirley said she'd walk Lucky out of the building, and find him a taxi.

'Forget it,' said Lucky, and he left the room, accidentally slamming the door, and rode down in the lift alone. The wind bit down on his cheeks as he waited to cross Elizabeth Street. Cars squealed as they braked at low speed and each of his steps was a strange, cramped, expressive lurch. Lucky had difficulty grasping the fact he was no longer in anyone's presence. The fact he'd lost. From the city he went to his business in Stanmore, where he gave his chef the remainder of the day off. That night Lucky cooked the dinner service. He didn't know what else to do. He did not know how to do anything else.

4.

Some weeks later, Lucky did confront Alexander over his unforgivable negligence and betrayal.

It had occurred to Lucky, as he sat in his last remaining cafe, that Alexander would never dare walk through those doors again, and since Lucky had no wish to repair the friendship, they might leave it at that. They lived in different parts of the city—Lucky in the inner west, his old friend in the south—and were unlikely to run into each other on the street, or in a pub, or in a gaming room, because Alexander no longer played cards. But after a period of stewing, Lucky had to know what happened, and why.

He waited in his car down the street from Alexander's home, listening to the echo of doors around him, the neighbours coming home from work, the metallic gasp of handbrakes, while Lucky lit so many cigarettes that he wondered, by the last smoke, if he might run out of breath when he started speaking or when things came to blows. It was dark when Alexander arrived. The streetlights were dim and badly distanced: three houses shared a single light source. Lucky got out of his car and shouted Alexander's name, and they walked towards each other, stopping a safe distance away. Lucky couldn't make out the expression on his former friend's face.

'Why did you do it?'

'What?' said Alexander.

'You fucked up my life, and now you're back in business. It doesn't mean a thing to you, does it?'

'You don't have children. You don't understand.'

'I understand, mate. And let's talk about families, since you love your kids so much. I'm going to break your nose and when your children ask what happened to your face, you tell them I busted it because you love them so much.'

He launched forward and grabbed the shoulder of Alexander's jumper, and with his free hand he punched the traitor in the nose. They swung at each other, they wrestled: Alexander was the larger man, more experienced in violence, and only Lucky's halo of rage closed this advantage, leading them finally to a stoppage, an impasse, both men bleeding from the mouth, and Alexander, gratifyingly, from the nose.

'Stop! I've lost my wedding ring,' he said. 'It was my father's ring. And my pappou's.'

In near total darkness, Alexander dropped to his hands and knees and felt his way over the patch of road where they'd been wrestling. If Lucky had wished, he could have taken a run-up and kicked Alexander full in the face. The option appealed to him for a moment. Then he decided it would be cowardly. He bent over and, squinting in the dark, Lucky too looked for the lost heirloom, yet with a strong sense of impatience, a stopwatch in his heart. After the ring turns up, he told himself, we'll return to the task of breaking Alexander's nose.

'Found it,' said Alexander after several minutes. 'Now what?'

He got to his feet, clutching the ring inside his fist. When Lucky heard these words he turned and, hunched and drained, his mouth numb from the blows, shuffled back to his car and drove away. They did not meet again. For years, when unexpectedly possessed by the Alexander-related sadness and rage he did not nurse but could not escape, Lucky imagined what might happen if he bumped into him on the street, in a pub or at a wedding. Came the time, decades later, that Lucky wondered whether they'd recognise each other and, if they did, whether he'd stop to acknowledge Alexander at all.

2002

1.

SHIRLEY AND SAM proposed they conduct the interview in Drummoyne, at one of their pubs—busy, expensive, recently renovated—where the kitchen served Isan food. The pre-World War II building was called the Ashenden and stood on the corner like a stately home, the balconies brisk and ornamental, the downstairs windows touched with a dark tint. They sat in an upstairs dining room: pine-wood panels on the walls, tables separated by stone urns, vines overhead, surf music. Shirley apologised for the slow service. Emily didn't see any problem. While a waiter refilled their wineglasses, Shirley turned to Sam and mentioned the recent closing of a hard cargo dock in Sydney Harbour.

'I reckon it's come three years too late,' mumbled Sam, and scooped a wad of coconut rice into his mouth. Under Emily's probing, Shirley explained that their fathers and grandfathers had been dockworkers and expected Sam to continue in the trade. Shirley and Sam had better ideas. They maintained a curiosity about stevedoring and kept up with news of the trade, the heritage they'd rejected.

'I'm interested in how Lucky lost all his money,' said Emily.

'He was a gambler, you're aware?'

'I heard, yes.'

'I hope he's completely honest with you about that part of his life,' said Shirley. 'The man had a real problem for a while. I know for a fact he lost twenty grand in one day playing roulette. This would be, oh, not long after the Third of April. Maybe if you're a big deal, like a Murdoch or Packer, you can drop that kind of money. Not if you're Lucky.'

'He told me about a construction deal that went bad. Then you came along with an offer. How much did you pay him for the franchise?'

'How much did Lucky say?'

'He wouldn't say. But I get the impression it was a low figure.'

'Lucky got himself into debt. He'd taken things as far as they could go,' said Shirley. 'And we arrived at the right time. It's a shame if he still regrets the transaction. But we've all moved on, haven't we?'

'Please note that we expanded the franchise successfully,' said Sam.

'And we kept the two or three Greek dishes Lucky put on the menu. Back then those cafes were known for not serving Greek food.'

'What was the precise figure for the franchise sale?'

'We're not going to tell you the precise figure. That's confidential. And we've all moved on, like we said. We closed the franchises . . . when?' She looked at Sam.

'In '91,' said Sam.

'We wound up the restaurants because people didn't want to eat that way anymore. They wanted Thai, Sichuan, whatever. They want to sit in an old-fashioned pub and eat good food. Look at this place. It's paradise. Sure, Lucky's was an institution. Part of history. But it had its time. By 1991 three-quarters of the businesses were loss-making. Food culture changed. We moved on from the old cafe diner thing.'

'We offer what people want—that's all we've ever done. It's not complicated,' said Sam.

'Also,' said Shirley, 'the generation of kids who grew up in those cafes, most of them didn't go into their parents' business. They went to university. They turned middle-class, the second generation, and maybe that was the whole project in the first place. I don't know—ask Lucky.'

'It would help a great deal if I knew the sale price,' said Emily. Obviously they were hiding the price for a reason. Maybe there was some other way she might find out the sum paid. She felt good. She felt things were within reach. Like when a task seems difficult or impossible for months and then it suddenly doesn't; like you've squeezed out all the nagging and worrying.

'Can't do,' said Shirley. 'We'll give you something else instead. What do you want to know?'

'Lucky doesn't talk much about the start of the business.'

'We don't know much about his life before Lucky's,' said

Shirley. 'There was a rumour that he came into some money and that's how it started.'

'How did he come into the money?' said Emily.

'There were two rumours,' said Shirley. 'One was that it came from an insurance scam, which doesn't fit with Lucky's character. The other rumour we heard was family money.'

'We can't verify this,' Sam put in. 'It's hearsay from another time.'

'He hasn't told me about an inheritance,' Emily said. 'I'm aware his parents weren't wealthy.'

'He'll tell you what he wants you to know,' said Shirley. 'You can't blame him for wanting to control the way his story is presented. For you it's an article. For him it's his life.'

A waiter brought out another bottle of wine, but Shirley waved it away and asked for a bottle from the Otago region. Emily stared off, thinking about the rumour of an inheritance; yes, she made the pieces fit. She was relying on Lucky, and he was still screwing things up. She had relied on her husband, and he fucked up. She needed Liam to be her friend, but he couldn't be that person.

Shirley and Sam posed, tricked out in their success, their sense of who they were, wanted to talk about the expansion of the Lucky's franchise. How they got rich. Shirley and her husband thought they were the story.

2.

Two messages arrived while Emily was at lunch, and she checked them once back at the hotel. First voicemail:

Lucky reminded Emily about the taping at the studios the next day, which started at 10 am. And there was a voicemail from Michael: he sounded close to tears. It was a short message, during which he said he hadn't slept much. 'I don't know if I love Therese,' he finished.

Emily still had credit on the Go Bananas international calling card. She called her mother in Ipswich.

'How are things with Michael?' said Heidi. 'Is he making amends?'

'There is no mending, Mum,' said Emily. 'When Ian was in Australia, did he give anyone a large sum of money?'

'No idea, darling. I know he had money in Sydney, apart from his salary, and that was a sum his family gave him when he graduated university. He mentioned that he'd squandered it, but God knows what he spent it on. I don't want to know! I remember he said his family weren't too pleased. But in general they weren't pleased with him.'

'Let me get this straight: he didn't receive financial help from family in his later years because he lost that initial sum in Sydney?'

'Oh, I don't know, this was a long time before I met him. I know Ian came back from Australia with nothing to his name. From that point I suppose his family feared he'd only lose whatever they gave him. They managed that fear by cutting him off. If his brother and sister were alive, you could ask them. But they probably wouldn't tell you. Horrible people.'

'The misuse of inheritance was the reason why he fell out with his family?'

'No, there were many reasons. The Asquiths were high achievers and he certainly was not. He could be unpleasant. These rifts in families don't have one source. They don't come from one event. At least they didn't in mine and they didn't in Ian's.'

'The money, Mum—this is something else you didn't tell me!'

'Honestly, Emily . . .' Heidi took a breath. 'I didn't tell you he wrote a poem or play that went nowhere, and that he was bad with his money when he was a young man—like a normal young person. He also had a large mole next to his nipple.'

'The money he lost could be important.'

'Important how? It could be a nothing sum.'

It was almost dark outside. Bands of red sky pushed into the distance on Emily's tenth day in Sydney. She called Lucky and said she couldn't make the taping. Sorry. She had to be somewhere else tomorrow. Explain later, couldn't talk, had to go, bye—giving him no opportunity to speak. If necessary, she could narrate the events of *Wheel of Fortune* without needing to be there, in the studio, without giving Lucky, the liar, the stage he wanted. He hadn't given Emily what she wanted. All she'd asked for was the truth about her father and the facts about the franchise.

Lies and silence and repression: she needed clean air, someone straightforward.

2002

1.

THE DAY ARRIVED.

The shallow basin in Lucky's bathroom was pale blue and jutted out from the wall like an open drawer; the soap dish had once served as a butter bowl in the Stanmore franchise; the mirror was small, as he preferred, large enough for a head and neck. He disliked bathrooms in which one wall was half-mirror and you saw yourself from all corners. That modern design in which you were part of the effect. He shaved slowly, pausing to stretch his skin and check for cuts. There had come a point after which stubble and beards no longer suited Lucky and he duly shaved every morning. There was an age after which he regularly cut his hair, never again letting his curls reach the length that once suggested youth extended and music and classical statues. Instead, disordered hair now signalled self-neglect and delusion.

All Lucky could do was attempt to appear neat each day. Would the *Wheel of Fortune* make-up people bother working much on him?

A ringing phone raised him from this shallowness. His number was listed in the telephone directory: he let the past discover him here in this rented flat. It might be someone calling to catch up, or Emily, or a *Wheel of Fortune* producer, or a loan officer revisiting former applications and having second thoughts.

Joanna Matfield introduced herself and explained that Henry Matfield was her son. She allowed a pause after saying the name. This was the moment when some people walked away from her, when they hung up the phone. Lucky could picture her at the coroner's court, her feet dropping like she carried an injury, her torso long, her hair short and black. At the time he watched her like she might have some answers.

'I received a call from a reporter,' said Joanna. 'Someone writing for the *New Yorker* magazine.'

'I like Emily,' Lucky offered. 'Did you give an interview?'

'After the shooting, our lawyer advised me and my husband, Adam, not to contact you or the families, not to speak to the media. But Adam is dead—it's been a few years now. I would like to speak publicly about what happened. No more hiding. I want to apologise to the people who lost someone in the cafe.'

'I trust Emily completely.'

He would like to hear that conversation, to sit between Emily and Joanna. He had questions of his own. Henry fucked up his life, too. Take away Henry and the cafe could still be open, all those people alive. Sophia might be running the place. All of it could be hers.

'Are the families of the victims angry with you? Have they contacted you?' asked Lucky.

Joanna said: 'The victims' families have the right to feel any way they want to feel about me. They've been hurt in the worst way.'

'What will you say about your son?'

'Henry believed the world owed him things. Plenty of people are like that, but with him it was an extreme trait. It's true we fed that problem in some ways.'

'What do you mean?'

'We didn't give him every little thing he wanted—of course, you don't do that with a child. But when it became apparent that he had mental health problems it was easier to give in. In secondary school his health got bad. One day he skipped class and called me at work. He said he knew what was wrong with him. He said he had been flying out of his body over the streets, singing the song of everyone's lives, and he wanted to know if it had been on TV. Sometimes we didn't know what to do. You could say we never found the right thing to do. I wrote his year twelve essays. He wanted to pass. We made sure of that. I told myself that he'd missed so much school on account of his difficulties that he deserved some kind of assistance. As soon as he got his driver's licence he crashed into a parked car, a minor thing, and my husband went to the police station and took respon-sibility. When he got lost driving around Sydney—and this happened all the time—he'd find a phone booth and call us in a rage, demanding directions. As if it was our fault he got lost. Every problem he encountered was someone else's fault. He wanted money. He wanted me to write his job applications and put them in the post. We did that for him. He had this thing inside him, this narcissism or whatever it was.'

'Did he get help?'

'We tried to get him help from when he was fourteen until he was well into his twenties. Psychologists. Psychiatrists. At the age of twenty-one he was committed for the first time. There's a stigma around mentally ill men: that they're all dangerous, that they turn out to be antisocial or criminals. That's not fair. My husband, Adam, had depression all his life. With Henry, I don't know how much of the shooting could be attributed to his illness, and how much was this anger underneath everything. I don't know how to measure all the parts of him. I think every time he wanted something from the world he put himself on a path towards a disappointment that he resolved by lashing out. Always with words. And then he'd reset, and run off again towards a new meltdown. Eventually he found a job, he moved out. He bought a gun.'

In an instant Lucky's mind could open to the Third of April, and again, as he held the phone to his ear, he saw his friends' and customers' bodies on the floor. The police let him go as far as the entrance, the maw of the black hole, the suck of a great whirlpool distorting the past and the future. They'd already taken Sophia away. Now he sought to place Joanna in the scene. 'I have wondered: where were you that day?'

'I was at work when Adam called. He said I should come straightaway to the Lucky's cafe. He said something happened to Henry. I didn't ask questions. I left work and in the car I heard on the radio about a shooting incident in Stanmore, and I felt immediately that Henry was responsible.'

'And when you got to the restaurant? I didn't see you.'

'But I saw you from a distance. The police kept us away from everyone. I asked the policewoman if my son was alive, and she said: "Yes." Then Adam said to me: "It was Henry. He killed those people." We expected him to turn up at the house that night. We were frightened.'

'I thought he'd turn up at my place.'

'I feel responsible for the person he turned out to be. When I think of Henry now, I don't feel love towards him. I feel responsibility. Perhaps that is love. Perhaps we could have monitored him more closely after he moved out, convinced him to move back in with us. But the arguments were never-ending. He threatened to kill himself. He called us scum, nobodies. He said our lives were pathetic and we disgusted him. Whenever he felt bad, he started arguments. Underneath that was violence. We know that for sure now. But I suspected it then.'

'I think about the Third of April practically every day. I go over and over what I should have done instead of what I did.'

'I've come to believe there can be no full understanding of Henry. I've chosen to trust God. Maybe He understands why it happened. There's nothing else I can do.'

'He came to my house on the Third of April,' Lucky said. 'Why he visited you is unclear to me.'

'I'm sure it would have been better if he'd shot me and left everyone else alone.'

'Don't say that. You're needed here.'

'Maybe I could have stopped him,' said Lucky. He was shaking; he moved the phone from one hand to the other. No one, not Sophia, not the families, not the police, had ever laid blame at Lucky's feet or expressed anger towards him. That didn't change his own feelings. 'Henry wanted to come in for a drink. He wanted a job at the restaurant. I could have given him those things and it might never have happened.'

'I don't know about that. There are questions about Henry we can't ever answer. Perhaps faith can help you, Lucky?'

'I don't think it will. It never has. I'd prefer to live in a different fantasy.'

'Like what?'

'That things can change. That tomorrow my life will be different. That I still have some link to the life I almost led.'

2.

From the studio doors a queue of *Wheel of Fortune* audience members stretched across the footpath and onto a grassed area, where the line formed a concentric rill that ran murmuring along, interrupted here and there by producers and interns handing out bottled water and chocolate bars. As directed by the letter headed 'What to Do as a

Contestant', which arrived the previous week, Lucky went straight to the door and presented identification—an expired driver's licence. He wore a white shirt, a tie, and a brown blazer. He carried a small suitcase in which he'd packed a change of clothes, assuming he would proceed past the first episode.

Inside the studio building, Lucky was met by the producer Dan, who was all pseudo-sincere remorse for being a few minutes late. He kept running his hands through his hair and touching the stud in one of his ears. Lucky felt as if he were meeting him for the first time: the producer had the manner of someone who dealt with scores of different people every day and didn't remember anyone who wouldn't be sticking around, who wasn't important. Dan asked several 'funny old questions that are a require-ment of my job', such as: Do you have children? Are you involved in current libel suits or other litigation?

Dan asked: 'Do you have a gambling problem?'

'Not anymore.'

'Thank you for being honest with us. When did you stop gambling?'

'In 1998.'

'Congratulations. Wow, what an achievement. My aunt had a poker machine problem but now she's sober. Maybe that's the wrong terminology. Whatever, she's good now. Do you feel prepared? You can't prepare for *Wheel*, though, can you? That's what I love about this show.'

'Before I got on the train I took beta blockers and Valium and a small glass of brandy. For nerves. I get some nerves.'

'Gosh, nothing bad's ever happened to anyone who mixed Valium and alcohol before appearing on television.'

'Are you being sarcastic?'

'To tell you the truth, we don't often select contestants who are well into their seventies.'

'I understand,' said Lucky. 'They look old.'

'Also, we try not to overdo the sad stories on *Wheel*. Obviously the history of Lucky's is, you know, heart-breaking, but my producers tell me you have loads of vigour. That's the word they used. You bring that to the table, right? And you can be likeable? Because this is television and you have to take us with you.'

Dan brought him to a room stuffed with couches and tables covered with drinks and plates of sandwich wraps and cupcakes, and filled also with the day's players and their plus ones. Lucky asked when he was going to meet the host of *Wheel of Fortune*, Marjorie Sorenson, and Dan explained the host wouldn't have any contact with contestants until taping, because she liked to convey on camera that feeling of meeting someone for the first time. In about thirty minutes, make-up would arrive, wardrobe would sign off, and the first three players would go to the stage and compete in front of an audience. One last thing: Lucky's tie wouldn't work on camera; it might clash with the backdrop. Let's get rid of the tie, said Dan.

'I should talk to the other contestants,' said Lucky. 'Find a way to get an edge.'

'Why don't you sit and relax?' said Dan, before leaving the room. 'Don't try too hard.'

'Hey!' Lucky said to a teenager pouring himself a glass of orange juice at the refreshment table. 'Do you know the rules of *Wheel of Fortune*?'

'Yes,' said the boy. 'I'm Stan. I'm the carryover champion.'

'Good for you.'

'He loves words,' said Stan's mother, putting an arm around the child.

'I always have, sir,' said Stan.

'You like word games, huh?' Lucky said. 'Can you name the five properties of a verb?'

'Yes. No. What are they?'

Lucky said: 'Good luck.'

The crew tested bells and buzzers in the studio down the hall. Lucky didn't talk to other contestants, all busy with their plus ones. He waited: a long shudder. A make-up artist arrived and sat him down before a mirror, where she addressed the spots on Lucky's face, covering them with an impeccable, beatifying, almost golden varnish. He had never worn make-up before.

'You are really good at this,' he said.

The make-up artist, Jennine, said, 'I know. Who'd you bring today?'

'Oh, she couldn't make it.'

'Never mind. Now, remember when you get out there: you have a story to tell. And stop touching your face.'

In 1996, *Wheel of Fortune* retired its host of more than a decade, 'Baby' John Burgess (whose stout moustache reminded Lucky of the heroes of the Greek War of

Independence). Baby Burgess moved to a rival network, where he devised his own show, *Burgo's Catch Phrase*, leaving the wheel to a former talkback radio host, Marjorie Sorenson, whose TV experience included daytime panel shows and an award-winning *60 Minutes* segment in which she took a reporting team along for an endoscopic screening that yielded negative results but which had the stated purpose of raising bowel cancer awareness. No colleague or acquaintance referred to her as 'Marg' or 'Margie' or 'Maggie' more than once. Worst of all: 'Mags'. In newsrooms she was known also for her brief letters to the editor in which she lightly chastised columnists and TV reviewers who'd referred to her as a 'former shock jock'. The transition from Baby Burgess to Marjorie was notable, also, for a change in format: Marjorie had demanded that the puzzle board hostess be retired from the show, because she deemed the role to be sexist ornamentation. Under Marjorie, the relation of host to contestant was that of celebrity to non-celebrity, parent to child.

Dan came to the door: 'Everyone, time to rock-and-roll.'

On the way to the studio, the three contestants walked in a hurried cluster and few words, nothing expressive, rose in that bubble. Lucky and Stan and the third contestant found their positions behind the wheel. The audience applauded and the plus ones were ushered to their seats in the front row. The room was bright and cold. The red light went on and Marjorie moved in silks and gabardines to the podium, her hair resting on shoulder pads that looked like flattened petals.

'Back once again, it's my favourite time of the day!' said Marjorie. She briefly introduced each of the players, mentioning their names, home state and city, wanting extra information only from Stan, whom she described as the whiz kid from Wangaratta. Stan said that with his winnings he'd like to buy a boat and sail across the Pacific Ocean with his dad.

'Ideally,' said Stan, although Marjorie didn't ask him to elaborate, 'I'd like an ex-coastguard boat, or border control. I want those big lights that sweep around.'

'Young man,' said Marjorie, 'let's see if you can make your dream come true.'

In the Marjorie era of the program, the slot began with an opening round in which players spun the wheel and solved one puzzle, followed by three speed rounds, sans wheel, in which the winner was the first to buzz in with the solution. The three contestants then played four spin rounds, after which the winner played a bonus round, alone, in which the wheel featured gift prizes such as appliances, home computers, an outdoor set. On the first spin (category: Musicians) Stan hit *Lose a Turn* and the audience, as one, sighed for him. The third contestant, Joan, a pharmacist from Geelong, bought a vowel and guessed an answer (Cocteau Twins) that was several letters short. Stan couldn't help but smile and bounce on his heels a little.

_ _ E _ _ _ _ _ _ _

_ _ _ _

Lucky spun the wheel for $100, the lowest possible amount, and correctly guessed Thelonious Monk. The board flashed; the winning-answer sound effect blared like bells tossed in an electric net. Marjorie held up her hands as if to say, *Never heard of this Monk guy? Me either. Moving right along.* Then Lucky won every puzzle in the three speed rounds (formerly called Toss Up rounds, but Marjorie hated that phrase). This unusual feat—controlling all speed rounds—had occurred only five times in Australian *Wheel* history, said Marjorie, relaying information from her earpiece, but, unfortunately for Lucky, on none of those occasions did the player go on to win the game and play a bonus round. Maybe, she said, things would be different today?

Gameshow staff brought drinks for the contestants as Marjorie announced a commercial break. Lucky waved away all refreshment, checked the buttons on his shirt, touched the space where his tie had been knotted, and he gave a thumbs-up to Dan, who waved back.

By the final round, Marjorie looked clearly thrilled that Lucky was crushing his opponents. When he finally had a spin, young Stan rolled *Bankrupt* and said sorry to no one in particular. The pharmacist from Geelong stared at the wheel with what appeared to be impatience. Lucky finished his first episode with the winning total sum of $6700, and from the bonus round, the final puzzle, he collected a Never Out Of Bed linen set.

'Now, Lucky,' said Marjorie, 'where have you been all my life? You were born to play this game.'

'I've been a pensioner most of your life,' said Lucky.

'Lucky is a perfect name for a gameshow contestant! Could you tell us how you got that nickname?'

'I joined a band when I was eighteen, but some of the guys didn't think I was good enough to play with them. They said I was lucky to be in the band. There you go. It's a cruel nickname.'

'Love it. And it stuck. Say, you're not the same Lucky as the fella who owned those restaurants, are you?'

'That's me.'

'No way!'

The red applause light blinked and the audience applauded with extra enthusiasm.

In the program's Marjorie-era incarnation, contestants who won four episodes in a row would then, if they made it to the bonus round of a fifth episode, play for a prize of $300,000. According to *Wheel of Fortune* temporality, this was known as a carryover champion's 'Day of Fortune'. In the era of *Who Wants to Be a Millionaire?*, the more established but lower-rating gameshows began to offer bigger cash prizes, and gone were the days of long runs by carryover champions: audience research showed that viewers grew sick of a player after five episodes. They were regular people, the contestants, not performers. Some of them were strange indeed, not too likeable. On *Wheel* you got four slots and a Day of Fortune, which Marjorie called 'the big dance'.

Marjorie told Lucky: 'I want to hear more of your story but let's talk again tomorrow, shall we?'

The audience applauded again as the sign blinked. One of the producers whipped his hand around in a whirlpool motion. Young Stan burst into tears at the podium and a security guard stood in front of his mother and prevented her from consoling him until the shot was cleared.

Dan rushed out of the studio and a stagehand informed everyone there would be some adjustments to the set before the next game. The audience were given snack boxes and ushered into the foyer, and from the foyer they marched down a hallway to the network's courtyard, pausing to show the day passes they wore around their necks to a security guard who smiled and nodded. No one from the audience got close enough to ask for Marjorie's autograph. They offered Lucky his own little dressing room: he changed clothes and, when he was decent, Dan came inside.

'You surprised a lot of people,' said Dan.

Lucky said: 'Did you see Stan? He nearly shit his pants out there. Kid needs to learn how to lose.'

'Marjorie likes you,' Dan said.

'She's a rabid right-winger and it's in their religion to like small business people.'

'I'd put money on you making the Day of Fortune, if my employment contract allowed me to do that.'

In the second episode, flanked by an art teacher at a Launceston high school and a Brisbane real estate agent with a blonde, Ingres curtain of hair, Lucky took the first four puzzles easily—Thing, Phrase, Famous Painter, What to Do In Queensland—but he had trouble speaking clearly into his microphone and, when Marjorie called a commercial break, Dan took this opportunity to give Lucky a few words of encouragement. Before they restarted taping, Marjorie waved to a small girl in the front row. Men in the audience touched the collars of their shirts.

Dan said to Lucky, the board leader by $2100: 'Speak up. Don't get stuck in your head. Look at the wheel, man, and be confident. Imagine it's the shield of Achilles! Know what I mean?'

The next puzzle fell in the What Are You Doing category. Lucky spun for $800 and straightaway bought a vowel, 'I', because about seventy-five per cent of What Are You Doing puzzles began with a gerund.

_ I _ _ I _ _   _ _ _ _   _ _ _ _ _

'I'd like to answer this,' said Lucky.

'Feeling lucky, Lucky?' Marjorie asked. 'Sorry about that. Are you sure you want to guess this? It's early days.'

'I believe it's *Singing show tunes*.'

The board lit up with letters.

'What in the world?' said Marjorie, leaving the podium to stand next to Lucky. 'Did someone put something strange in your coffee this morning?'

'I didn't drink coffee today. It makes you sweat in pressure situations.'

'Now, Mr Lucky, we ought to clear something up for our audience, shouldn't we?'

'I think so.'

'For anyone who wasn't watching yesterday, you are *the* Lucky of the Lucky's restaurant chain, which most viewers over the age of twelve would remember?'

'I am.'

'I used to love going to those cafes when I was a girl! That was *real* old-fashioned food. How could I forget those milkshakes and the icy pineapple drinks? Where can I get a Lucky's meal these days?'

'You can't. There's not a single Lucky's restaurant left.'

'Nooo! That's a shame. Good memories, though. Please spin the Wheel of Fortune, sir.'

He brought up *Lose a Turn* and the audience groaned. A group of people sitting to the left of Dan cheered and whooped and called out the name of the next contestant, the Brisbane real estate agent, who, when asked about her hobbies, said she'd almost finished her doctoral thesis in linguistics. Almost finished, she said again. Marjorie laughed like she hated her. The real estate agent leaned forwards and spun $500 first, and $400 second, and third $300, and solved the Event puzzle—*Dinner and a movie*. The seventh round progressed much the same. Lucky watched the real estate agent spin large and win letter after letter. Marjorie's face hardened. The Brisbanite accumulated $900 to nail the puzzle (Rhyme)—*Go with the flow*.

In the second spin of the final puzzle the real estate agent hit *Bankrupt*. 'Yes!' someone in the audience cried. Marjorie offered a few words about the capriciousness of the Wheel of Fortune—and yet she pronounced this volatility the same thing that made the game exciting ('So fun,' she said) and the reason *Wheel* was the longest-running gameshow on national television.

Marjorie asked the art teacher from Launceston what she'd do with her winnings.

The teacher said she wanted to visit Rome with her husband and walk the Via Appia.

'All right,' said Marjorie, 'anything's possible if you make it all the way to the big dance. We're looking for a fictional character.'

The art teacher bought an 'A' and guessed 'D'. On the next spin she bought 'E' and asked for 'N'.

A _ _ _ _ _ _ _ E   _ _ D D E _ _

_ _   _ _ _ E   A N D   _ E A _ _ _

The art teacher's eyes closed in search of the answer. There was silence. Marjorie looked at her index card. 'A fictional character, a fictional character,' said Marjorie, who repeated herself when she wanted you to hurry up. Dan had warned all the contestants about this signal. The art teacher spun the wheel again. She hit *Lose a Turn*. Lucky let out an audible breath.

'Lucky!' said Marjorie. 'It's your time to shine.'

'I believe so,' he said. He spun three times for a total of $1800. He guessed *Aphrodite goddess of love and beauty*.

Marjorie reminded viewers that Lucky was only two episodes away from a Day of Fortune. Swing music, faddish that year, played over the PA.

3.

During the break between the second and third games, Lucky left his dressing room and went out to the courtyard with the rest of the audience. The clouds were breaking apart and rain pooled on the new paving stones. A passing train scattered the conversations, after which Lucky could hear some audience members talking about him. Their voices were louder than usual, after all that time watching other people speak. They liked him. They didn't like him. Was he on the spectrum? He was super old. Notice that Marjorie hadn't mentioned the shooting at his cafe?

The sky was a grimy colour, a pile of unwashed sheets.

From the sound of Emily's voice last night, when she called to say she couldn't make the taping—a flat voice in which there was no trace of acquaintance—Lucky knew that she'd discovered something. Had she already spoken to Sophia?

Nearby, the rigger and cue card guy were smoking, and drinking cans of cola. They shot four episodes twice a week. The changeover between eps was scheduled to take forty-five minutes. The crew was usually set in thirty.

Lucky won the third show without difficulty.

4.

For the fourth episode, the audience, as instructed by Dan, clapped a little harder than before. Marjorie made small talk with Lucky and the camera stayed on him, as if trying to crack his composure. Next to him was a contestant on holiday from England. The other was a bank clerk. They meant nothing to Marjorie. She reminded viewers that Lucky was one episode away from his Day of Fortune.

Lucky's hand shook as he spun for the first puzzle, the wheel ticking down to *Lose a Turn*. The English tourist and the bank clerk hooted and clapped with extra vigour because they now had a chance. Marjorie didn't bother asking Lucky's competitors about their lives or plans. The bank clerk, a man with a small bald head, won the first and second puzzle. The show halted for commercials. Lucky went to the toilet and Dan waited for him outside.

'Bad vibe right now,' Dan said when Lucky emerged. 'This bald guy is good. He tested off the charts. But you're the kind of contestant we want. Well known by name but also a mystery. A kind of celebrity but broke. And you've got a purpose. We like people with a mission. It's not too late for you to enjoy Day of Fortune money.'

Then Lucky got another turn: he gently spun the wheel and the stagehands shot each other amused looks and one of them gave Marjorie the okay gesture high above his head, meaning Lucky didn't need to redo the spin. They knew he was trying to game the wheel. He rapidly solved the next two puzzles, which might have been written for him: Food turned out to be *Potato salad and grilled octopus*. Classic Movie: *Midway*. (As the audience clapped, Lucky recalled the horrifying scene in which the pilot burned alive before crashing into the ocean.) He knew he solved these puzzles a little too quickly, didn't spin as much as he should have, perhaps because nerves were getting to him. Marjorie cut to a commercial and touched the bow on the side of her wrap dress, called for the director. People from make-up attended to the players, gave each of them bottles of water to sip from—sip, they said, don't spill the drink. The cameras rolled again.

'Everyone, if Lucky wins this final puzzle he returns for the big day, the big dance. If he loses tonight, he doesn't qualify. Lucky, tell me: what would you do with that potential jackpot of three hundred thousand dollars?'

'I'd open a restaurant. A new Lucky's.'

'What? No way! You're starting up the franchise again? I'll be your first customer.'

'I don't want to start a full franchise. One little business in Sydney.'

'You're not wealthy, are you? Let's make that clear to viewers out there.'

'The cafes didn't make me rich. And I made some bad decisions.'

'Ouch. We won't ask you what those decisions were! Or will we?'

'I sold the franchise for less than it was worth, put it that way. Also, I had a gambling problem. Many Australians gamble to an unhealthy degree. If you do gamble too much, and you're watching this, please seek help. That's what I did.'

'Thank you, Lucky. You have a good heart. Tell us about your plans for the new restaurant.'

'It will look like the old ones. And there's a woman who used to work at one of the cafes. As you may know, a man came in and shot people at my cafe and this young woman, she survived. I won't say her name, but maybe she'll be the manager of this new restaurant. Because, look at me: I'm too old to run the place full-time.'

Along with Marjorie, the audience made an *awwww* sound.

Marjorie said: 'Of course I remember the Third of April. A tragedy for our city. All right. Spin the Wheel of Fortune, sir. We're all hoping you come good here.'

The category was What Are You Doing. He guessed 'N' and 'G' and 'T'. He bought 'A'.

G _ T T _ N G _ _ _ _ _ _ _ _ _ _ _ _ _

A _ _ _ _ _ N T A _ _ _ _ G _ T

The English tourist started to look around with excitement, like she knew the answer. Lucky shook his head, like there was a mistake on the board. Marjorie's head pulled slightly to the right: she did this, Lucky thought, whenever someone was relaying lengthy instructions through her earpiece. The instructions, presumably, were to give the contestant some time to find the solution.

'Think, Lucky. The category is What Are You Doing. Have you ever done this? Or, has this ever happened to you, all of sudden? If you win today, you know what tomorrow is. But no pressure, right?'

'I know the first word,' Lucky said, and he spun the wheel once more, landing on *Lose a Turn*. Marjorie threw up her hands as if to say, *I did what I could*, and she told viewers she'd like to come back and ask Lucky on-air about the tremendous life experiences he must have had, but this was a gameshow and what can you do? The bank clerk was next. He rolled *Bankrupt* on his second spin. The tourist took her chances and kept spinning until the board was near complete, except vowels and a couple of consonants.

'Someone knows the answer,' said Marjorie.

'I'd like a Fortune Day of my own,' said the tourist.

'And what would you do with the money?'

'I'd keep travelling!'

Marjorie looked unimpressed by this answer. The tourist spun until there were only vowels left.

'You have to solve now,' said Marjorie, barely suppressing her delight, and the tourist solved. The answer was *Getting pulled over for a broken taillight*. Her total score: $12,600. Lucky's score: $12,800.

'Lucky, my good friend,' said Marjorie, 'we have to play a bonus round for gift prizes from our sponsors, but I can confirm you're coming back for the Day of Fortune!'

Dan leaped from his chair, applauding with the rest of his aisle. In a few minutes the crew would finish taping for the day, the audience would be given gift bags. Tomorrow, Wednesday, was Day of Fortune. Lucky held up his arms, his eyes closed, and to himself he said a few words the boom could not pick up. Cue swing music.

1992

1.

LUCKY AND VALIA fell for each other a second time. They reconciled, they began a new relationship, but ran out of days. They started again too late. In October, she called him at the restaurant to say she had stage IV pancreatic cancer, diagnosed three months ago, and she'd recently stopped a course of chemotherapy. Lucky understood she was calling to say goodbye, but he didn't accept this conversation as a farewell: he asked if she were available to meet the next day. Valia said she was. He asked if she could leave the house. She definitely could. Valia gave him an address, and the next morning he took the day off and drove to her home in Ryde. All this time, forty years, he'd wondered where she lived in Sydney. Valia met him at the door in sneakers and straw hat, ready to go out. She didn't feel fantastic, she said, but not terrible either. Today would be a slow walk to a nearby park.

'You look better than me,' said Lucky, not yet knowing what to say.

Her house, half brick and half siding, with steep gabling of varying angles, ran back to a point where Lucky could make out a grapevine trellis and an olive tree beyond, reminding him of the Achillion's backyard. As a result he couldn't much associate the place with Robert, her late husband. Lucky had seen Robert's death notice in 1987 but, with painful determination, he didn't contact Valia to offer condolences, presuming they wouldn't be welcome, conceding his motivation was not entirely pure. On the walk they avoided their shared history and spoke about what Lucky considered neutral topics—food, movies, his impending holiday in Greece, her trip the previous year to the Northern Territory—and there was such a strong sense of ease between them that he assumed Valia would ask him inside once they returned to her house. Their faces, their words, their every projection had about them the same sense of surprised reciprocity. After talking for thirty minutes, Lucky knew he could spend all the remaining days of his life with her.

Here was this thing he had kept; at last it could be used.

They would go inside, thought Lucky, and go to bed. They might not make love; it didn't matter. It would mean everything to lie down next to Valia again. But on the footpath outside her home, while he was looking up at her front door, he stepped in newly laid dog shit. The black stink of the turd passed through his heart. Valia, her cheeks shaking with laughter, removed her broad hat (her hair remained unaffected by the treatment) and she watched while he scraped off his shoe in the gutter.

'Can you believe that happened?' he said.

'Come back tomorrow,' said Valia. 'If I feel a little better, we'll have something to eat.'

'We'll go to your favourite restaurant.'

'If I'm hungry. It's up and down.'

The next day he knocked on the door and for a moment they stood on the porch in their good clothes, looking at each other. Lunch was an unusual scheme. They went to their favourite restaurants, one after the other, ordering light. First, Valia's choice: a seafood bistro. Then to a taverna that Lucky had discovered the previous year. What they didn't eat they took home. Finally, Lucky made them coffee at her house. They avoided the subject of Achilles. Ex-husband Robert was mentioned only indirectly: he had three children from a previous marriage, and they'd been raised in this home, along with Sophia, and at their mother's house in the Blue Mountains, which was bigger, and where they had their own rooms. For the first time Lucky heard the stepchildren's names. He'd imagined their family as comprising a decent husband, the extraordinary wife, and the children, mostly sublime. Nothing she said denied him this old picture. But he didn't need to hear a great deal about the past. They weren't catching up. They were racing towards happiness and death. And there was too much past.

Valia did mention the fire at the Achillion: she had told her daughter Sophia about the letter from Ian Asquith.

She should know what happened to her aunt, said Valia. Lucky left the subject in the air. Valia let it drop.

That afternoon, at the door, she asked: 'Why didn't you marry again? Did you find anyone?'

'No, I didn't love anyone else,' said Lucky.

'But how is that possible?'

Lucky didn't answer; he didn't know the answer. He shook his head. But if he was here, at Valia's home, had he truly failed in love?

The following day he called and asked whether she thought it was a good idea for them to see each other again.

'I think so,' she said. 'I think it's the best idea I've heard in years.'

'It is? I'm supposed to be leaving on Friday but I'll cancel my holiday.'

'Don't cancel. You're away only ten days and I'll be here when you get back. Yesterday I told the home care nurse you had a holiday already planned. I'm not going to die in the next month. That nurse has seen a lot of pancreatic patients and she says I'm doing much better than most. I will be here next year, I think.'

Six days later Lucky returned from overseas, cutting short his trip. He'd thought of Valia more than ever before: on this, his second visit to Greece, he couldn't enjoy himself. The good food was wasted on him. When he opened the window of his room in Ithaka and saw the harbour, the water as smooth as hotel sheets, the little homes of Vathi like Venetian toys, he still wished he'd never come; when he shut the room for his afternoon nap he knew that someone was missing, that he'd made a great mistake and should return immediately to Australia.

In Sydney he found that her condition had worsened, and Sophia had moved in to care for her mother. Lucky wanted to see Valia every day; he hoped to continue what they'd started.

'Let's not plan anything yet,' said Valia. 'I'll call in a few days and you can come visit.'

Valia did call and ask Lucky to come over, and that day she looked emaciated, as though she hadn't eaten since they last saw each other. Her olive skin now yellow, her lips pale. They sat on the couch watching *Wheel of Fortune* and the news bulletins, switching channels in the ad breaks. Valia found it hard to speak: mucus seemed to simmer up her throat and she spat it into a bucket at her feet. Sophia came in and out, emptying the bucket. The kettle whispered in the kitchen. The windows were open. When she fell asleep on the couch, Lucky carried her to bed and she woke up as he lowered her onto the mattress.

'You understand, Lucky, I am dying now.'

At the front door, Lucky said to Sophia: 'Valia needs some sustenance. Later tonight you could wake her up and somehow get her to eat.'

'Mum can barely swallow food,' said Sophia. 'And even when she does, she can't keep anything down.'

'Then she needs to be fed through a tube in her stomach.'

'I've asked and the doctor said no hospital in the city will do that for us.'

'If we arrange a feeding tube, somehow, Valia will regain some strength, and then, who knows? Maybe we can restart the chemo. If we sort out the problem with food, we can turn it all around.'

Two days later, Sophia called the restaurant in Stanmore to say her mother had died. At the time Lucky had stepped out to find change for the cash register. Sophia asked the waiter to give him the message.

2002

1.

EMILY FOUND A table at the window of the cafe in the shopping mall. A full taxi rank lay adjacent to the cafe, the drivers slouched in their seats, windows down, their arms slung on the doors like swimmers clinging to the side of a pool. Sophia, who'd suggested the location, arrived and sat with a handbag on her lap, her hair a little wet, and Emily recognised the mint and cetrimide smell of the same shampoo that she herself used in London. It was still an incredible notion, to Emily, that here was a stranger, the survivor of the Third of April, and you could ask about her life and she would tell you a story.

Sophia looked at Emily, evaluating her. What did she see? No, Emily was growing tired of this question, of looking outside herself for a sense of herself as if it were a sound way to feel part of the world, to be in another person's company, when it was a metric for undervaluing or overvaluing everyone.

Sophia said: 'Lucky called and said he felt comfortable around you, like an old friend.'

'I like him too, but at times I wonder whether he's being entirely truthful with me. At first he lied about his gambling.'

'He fell to pieces after the shooting, like me. Christ knows how much money he pissed away. You know what happens to gamblers—they lose. He's ashamed. He lies because of shame.'

And his lie about Ian Asquith, was that out of shame, too? 'Another thing, and this isn't for the *New Yorker* article, Lucky said he didn't know my father, but I suspect they might have met each other. Does the name Ian Asquith sound familiar to you?'

'It doesn't,' said Sophia, and she appeared convincing, seemed genuinely not to register the name. On the walls of the cafe were fan mirrors and walnut veneer panels, which created a gloomy mood of seniority, like the business was here first, before the taxi rank, before the mall.

'I had to ask. Now, I want to understand your connection to Lucky: he was your mother's first husband. When did you start working for him?'

'After Mum died, Lucky offered me a job, because at the time I was out of work and I had a small child. I was a single mother. My half-brother and half-sisters wanted to sell Mum's house straightaway and split the money. None of them live in Sydney. We sold the house and my money went into childcare and rent and bills and I needed a job. Lucky came through. The shifts were flexible. He's good like that.'

'He and your mother stayed in touch after the marriage ended?'

'No, but they were close at the very end. Lucky held a candle for about forty years.'

'I wonder what it was like for Lucky, to have those feelings for so long?'

'I'm sure it fucked him up. Me, I don't give a shit about my ex-husband. Exactly zero feelings.'

'One day I might reach a similar point with regard to my husband.'

'Things are bad?'

'It's a mess,' said Emily. 'Can we talk about the Third of April? Are you sure about this?'

Sophia nodded.

Emily said: 'Henry Matfield was a regular customer.'

'He would come in and sit with a coffee and stare at everyone.'

'When he came to the Lucky's restaurant on the Third of April, you were in the kitchen, is that right?'

'I heard a gunshot and a second shot soon after the first and I looked through the kitchen pass and saw Henry. If I'd been on the floor I probably wouldn't be here. One of the cooks—his name was Chris—he said to me, "Go out the back." And that's what I did. I was hiding the whole time and I could hear what was going on— forty-something gunshots.'

'You hid in a refrigerated room behind the kitchen,' said Emily. She didn't want to pop question after question at Sophia for the duration of the interview, but to intermittently bridge the talk with plain statements.

'That's what Chris meant by "out the back". There was no door between the coolroom and the kitchen because we were constantly going back and forth during a shift.'

'There was a backyard.'

'There was a tiny outdoor area big enough for a couple of bins. Sometimes the chefs stood out there and smoked. In the yard there was a door into the lane, but I didn't have the key, and there was barbed wire at the top of the fence. If Henry opened the door to the yard, he would have seen me. And Lucky had an office in that building but the office door was locked. There was also a bathroom: a customer was shot on the toilet. The poor bloke was sitting there on the toilet with his pants down. The coolroom was the best place to hide. It was small. There was no window. Chris was right about that.'

'You were in there a long time—until the police arrived. I realise this sounds trite, but it's impossible to imagine what that would have been like. What did you do in the room? From my reading, there's no detail about what you did in there.'

'First I sank to the floor and curled into a ball. The space was tiny. I flinched when the gun went off, and whenever I moved I could hear my feet hitting this bucket. I was terrified that he'd open the door and see me there. The gunshots kind of got louder every time. They sounded like a hammer on the ground right next to me and that pounding sounded bigger and closer. After a while I changed position. The coolroom door opened inwards and I turned towards the door and pressed both feet against it and with my hands braced myself against the back wall of the room. I was pushing so hard against the door my legs were shaking by the end. And it was fucking cold. I was wearing a thin dress and sandals.'

'Henry walked right past the coolroom.'

'Yes, when he shot the man in the toilet. It didn't occur to me that Henry would ever stop and go away. I had this idea that he was lurking in the kitchen, waiting for me to come out. And then he'd get me.'

'What else were you thinking about?'

'Just sort of fear. And I thought of Mum and Dad. I thought I would die and leave my son without parents too. I had this sense of my three-year-old boy's loss. This flash of his perspective. That was a feeling of horror, too, like that sound of the gun.'

It occurred to Emily: did Ian Asquith, when he thought about ending his life, have similar flares of a child's grief, or was he only thinking about his own pain?

She asked: 'A policewoman called Sharon Hand found you. I contacted her but she declined to be interviewed. Could you describe what happened?'

'Long after the gunshots stopped I heard these voices, men and women sort of barking at each other like they were angry, but then I heard the police radio walkie-talkie thing, which is when I knew it was over. The cop opened the coolroom and saw me there, and she helped me up and we walked through the cafe. The other police were saying, "Don't look down, close your eyes," and that's what I did, since there were bodies blown apart on the floor. I kept my eyes shut until we got outside. Then we went down the street into a park, where police vans were set up.'

'At that point, did you feel relief?'

'No, I was afraid that someone was going to start shooting at us. We were out in the open and I was sure he was there and would shoot at me in the street. I had this strong feeling like he was waiting for me, hiding somewhere with a gun. I told the police we needed to go somewhere safe right now because I was sure he was going to come back. I was afraid I was going to be killed.'

'You went home?'

'The paramedics checked me for hypothermia. I went to the station to give a statement. When I went home my son was there; someone had picked him up. And two policemen stayed overnight, while I lay awake listening for noises. No one knew where Henry had gone.'

'When did you see Lucky again?'

'The next day he knocked on the door but I couldn't talk to anyone. People from the media came to the house. I let the cops come in but that's all. Yeah, I don't know when I spoke to Lucky again.'

'How did you get through the months after the Third of April, emotionally?'

'It took everything I had to get out of bed. I didn't know much about depression before. Like, I had all these questions

I couldn't answer. Why couldn't I deal with it and get on with things? And I mean, I was "the Third of April survivor", as they say—did I even have a right to feel bad? Eating was hard, and sleeping. I had this pain in my stomach and I kept going back to the doctor saying that I thought I might have been shot that day in the restaurant, when I was still in the kitchen, but no one had ever detected it. I had this fear that there was a bullet lodged in my stomach. And the doctor kept saying it was all in my head. He was a bit of a cunt. He hadn't seen anyone like this before. But, yeah, something was wrong with my thinking. I began to grind my teeth. Never did that before. By 1997 I had split my upper molars and premolars, busted them like they couldn't be saved. I ended up needing partial dentures. At the age of thirty-six I needed false teeth, like I was a junkie or something. I used the last of my victims-of-crime compo for dentures.'

'How are you doing now?'

'A few months back I lost my job at the district sewage treatment plant. Don't look at me like that!'

But Emily wasn't looking at her any particular way.

'Matter of fact, it was the best job I ever had,' said Sophia. 'People think the plant was terrible work.'

2.

In late 1999, Sophia came back from the mall with food poisoning. She drove home with the back of one hand over her mouth, and once inside her apartment she felt dizzy, and the air seemed much hotter, the smell of everything stronger. After vomiting in the bathroom, she pressed the flush lever and her false teeth fell into the toilet bowl. The flushing blue water quickly resolved—her denture had been washed away. Sophia laughed as if it were happening to someone she didn't like. Then she looked at the bathroom floor, and the dismal green towel hanging behind the door. What if all she could ever be was the person she'd already become?

That same day Sophia called the district sewage treatment works and explained about the missing false teeth. How expensive they were. How she didn't have a job per se.

She said: 'Is there anything you can do for me?'

'Sure we can—these things happen all the time,' said the voice on the phone, which went on to advise Sophia to wait two days before visiting lost and found at the North-West Sydney Sewage Works. 'Once a week we find personal items at this end, when we drain the filter tanks. You'd be amazed by what turns up. And you'd be horrified.'

On the suggested afternoon, Sophia stood at the gates, watching shift workers arrive. The smell of fuel drifted over the building with a mote-strung breeze. A sewage plant employee named Gerry came to meet her and escorted Sophia inside, pointing out they had ten minutes maximum to find the missing false teeth. His workday was ending.

'This is interesting work you do,' she said.

'Think so?'

Inside the treatment building, Sophia could hear sewage water in the process of being washed. The long vibrations made her want to press her ear against the wall and listen to the hum. Lost property was stored in a cupboard near the lunchroom, all the rescued items kept inside large Tupperware containers on wire shelves. Sophia saw a tray of spectacles, and two boxes of car keys. Maybe someone had thrown their wife's keys in the toilet. What people did to each other no longer surprised Sophia.

Gerry pointed to a box on the top shelf. 'Your teeth might be up there,' he said. 'I'm supposed to watch in case you steal anything.'

'Fine if I try them on?'

'If you're willing.'

There were about thirty sets of dentures in the rattling box, most of them old and cracked. Sophia had the sense that certain pairs, those stained grey and black along the base, belonged to people who were now dead. She touched these lightly. There were two partial posterior dentures; she couldn't tell which was hers by looking at them. Maybe someone else ground his or her teeth until they cracked, until the nerve was exposed, until they had to be extracted because they couldn't afford an alternative. Gerry turned away and scratched his head while Sophia wiped the teeth with a handkerchief and tried on the first pair, then the second.

'Perfect fit,' Sophia said.

'Happy we could help.'

'Is it hard work, retrieving these objects from the sewage filters?'

'It can be hard on the stomach,' said Gerry.

'I'm guessing you don't need a particular trade qualification for this kind of labour?'

'Why do you ask?'

'Then it's easy?'

'Easy as you like. People learn on the job. Why?'

'Because I'd like to apply for work.'

Sophia could think of no better job than rescuing precious objects from the city's stream of shit. She put this in more formal terms in writing and posted the letter. Sophia wanted to be the person you visited when something important had been swallowed up. She wanted to be there when people came looking for the stuff they'd flushed away.

The sewage works offered her a job.

3.

Three months before her interview with Emily, Sophia had been sacked from the treatment plant. The state budget insisted on a ten per cent efficiency dividend across all utilities and the Sydney Water Corporation responded with a small program of job cuts. The plant manager told Sophia that she was the first to go because she was the last person hired in her department. An old-fashioned way to go about things, he said. A bullshit way, said Sophia.

'I lost my job this year, too,' said Emily.

'But you're working again? For a magazine that sends you overseas? Lucky you.'

Sophia said that earlier in the day she'd interviewed for a position at a garden centre, but it hadn't gone well. She wished she could do it over. The problem was, Sophia hardly slept the night before, her mind wouldn't switch off, and at the interview she lost her train of thought several times. Then some questions she couldn't answer, her brain like jammed machinery. That morning she wasn't a functioning adult. Afterwards she went home and slept two hours and woke up to restart the day and she kicked herself for failing her kid. Sophia needed a job: anything would do. Nine weeks ago, the landlord of their townhouse raised the rent to a ridiculous amount she couldn't afford. Now she was on the waiting list for government housing, but that would take at least a year. Until she could get some money together, Sophia and Jamie were staying with a friend. Jamie's father was entirely out of the picture; when the relationship ended, he moved back to Italy, where he was a citizen, and where he could avoid being policed for non-payment of child support. The international treaty on child support, said Sophia, was a real piece of shit.

'I'm sleeping on my friend Nicole's couch, and her two girls share a room, leaving Jamie a room to himself. If the situation gets unpleasant we'll move on. And knowing Nicole, it will probably get unpleasant.'

'When did you last speak to Lucky?'

'He calls and we chat. I like the guy. I guess I'm the daughter he didn't have. But, see, it's not good for me to talk to him—I want to be free of the shooting, everything about it. After this interview I don't want to talk about it anymore. People ask me about the Third of April. It doesn't stop. At work, at barbecues, wherever. At the fucking job interview this morning they asked. People are curious about death and mayhem.'

'Do you feel at all that some good came out of the Third of April? That it contributed to critical mass that, after Port Arthur happened, led to gun legislation being changed?'

'Maybe that's true. But do I turn to that fact when I'm struggling with things in my mind? Not on bad nights.' She looked at her watch. 'I'm almost out of time. I need to get a bus to Jamie's school and bring him home.'

'I have a car,' said Emily. 'I could take you to pick up your son and then drop you anywhere you like.'

'As long as you don't write a word about Jamie.'

4.

Emily's essay for the *New Yorker* would never be published, nor filed nor finished. Three months from now, Emily would be working on the piece, with some difficulty, in her Kensal Green flat, when the call came from Liam. The flat was furnished much the same as before the separation. Michael subtracted his clothes and books and a few bookshelf trinkets, such as the little bell he'd used as a boy, whenever ill, to summon his parents, and the ice hockey puck he'd bought on a childhood holiday to Canada, an object that he considered to be a lucky charm. Liam would call to say he had some news. He'd taken a job as a staff writer on a well-resourced technology magazine, a role he thought was 'the right move at the right time'. Unfortunately, and Liam paused after he announced the word 'unfortunately', his replacement had scrutinised the commissions for the food issue and made a difficult decision about certain articles in the pipeline. Liam tried to make it sound as if Emily's wasn't the only piece spiked. Liam sounded half in the bag; he slurred and repeated himself. He suggested she pitch the piece elsewhere, said it was a story he'd like to read one day. The magazine would pay expenses: the managing editor had signed off on all receipts and a kill fee of seven hundred dollars. When he'd run out of things to say, Emily thanked him for calling and said goodbye.

5.

The school had yielded up its restless population, aged between five and twelve years, and most had been collected by parents or babysitters or otherwise dispersed via bus. The wail of kids leaving school had scattered; a few children waited in the shade—their voices moderate, the riot gone out of them—they leaped to their feet when a parent approached. Among these pupils: Jamie, sitting on his bag, reading a large-format book about the Battle of Waterloo. Before his Napoleonic phase, Sophia explained, Jamie was mad about medieval Japan; before that, he'd loved Greek myths.

An adult stood behind him, a lanyard around her neck, arms crossed.

'Not again,' said Sophia.

'What again?' said Emily.

'That's Hannah, the vice-principal. She's taken a special interest in Jamie. She thinks I'm a loser.'

'I don't think you're a loser,' said Emily.

'Come with me,' Sophia said. 'Pretend you're my friend. You're supportive.'

Hannah moved towards them with the quick strides of the highly productive, Jamie trailing behind. To begin, she praised his reading habits, and they all looked at the boy in what appeared to be a consensus: this was a nice, smart kid.

Hannah said: 'But we have other topics to discuss.'

'Other topics?' Sophia said warily. 'Keeping in mind he's eleven years old.'

'Jamie has brought his pet snake onto the school grounds.'

Sophia turned to her son. 'You have a pet snake?'

'For a few weeks,' Jamie said, 'give or take. Since we moved.'

'Does Nicole know you've brought a snake into her house?'

'She doesn't know about Louis II.'

'Who's that?' asked Sophia.

'The snake's name is Louis II. He was a French king also known as Louis the Stammerer.'

Hannah said to Jamie: 'You don't have much of a stammer anymore.'

'I do voice exercises.'

'Where is this bloody snake?' said Sophia.

'At Nicole's house. Under my bed. In a box.'

'You're a sensitive kid,' said Sophia. 'Snakes are not pets for sensitive kids.'

Jamie said: 'What if I'm pathologically sensitive, like Franz Kafka?'

'Like who?' said Sophia.

Emily interjected: 'You've been reading Kafka?'

'Yes. Well, not exactly. I've read about him online.'

'Kiddo, the snake has to be removed,' said Sophia. 'Do you know what would happen if Nicole found out? We'd be homeless!'

'She'd kick us out because of Louis? That's bad.'

'Anything's possible with Nicole. Where did you get the snake?'

'I bought it online.'

'You don't have any money!' said Sophia.

'I've got a little money.'

'I know a good veterinarian in this area,' said Hannah. 'Absolutely a vet will know what to do with a snake.'

'I'm not destroying Louis II,' Jamie said.

'We'll see,' said Sophia. 'We have to remove the snake. Appreciate your vigilance, Hannah.'

Hannah made a point of shaking Emily's hand.

'Your accent—you're English? Where from?'

'London.'

'Oh, I lived in Clapham for seven years. Loved teaching over there. Miss it often. Always something to do in that city.'

They returned to the car, the doors banged like stones on the roof. Sophia sat in the back seat with her son. 'What is going through your head?' she demanded.

'I'll tell you: Louis is a small non-venomous python. Yesterday I took him to school and today a teacher found out. People in my class talk too much.'

Sophia said: 'Other kids will see a pet snake as a sign that you're weird. And it gives me no pleasure to say that.'

'It's not a sign of anything,' said Jamie. 'I may just as well forget what they think.'

I like this kid, thought Emily. He could teach me something.

Jamie said: 'Louis II is my best friend.'

'The snake will never be your best friend,' said Sophia.

Emily started the car and Sophia gave her a few directions; the rest would be given on the way.

Jamie said: 'Louis is my friend and I'm worried about him. He's stopped eating.'

'You have a dangerous pet!' said Sophia. 'He's stopped eating because he wants to eat you! He needs to make room in his belly for a little human. Think about it! I've heard of this behaviour.'

Emily said: 'You shouldn't love something that will only disappoint and hurt you.'

'Okay, but no,' said Jamie. 'Pythons don't stop eating in order to prepare themselves to eat small humans. That is snake scarelore. It's a total myth. Anyway, he couldn't eat me. He's a small non-venomous python. It would be physically impossible for him to swallow a person, even if he wanted to. He's about as thick as three of my fingers.'

'You will need to say goodbye to Louis,' said Sophia.

'Anyway, I think he's stopped eating because he doesn't like the frozen mice I buy him. I've tried five different sizes: large, hopper, fuzzy, pinkie, and half-pinkie.'

'Frozen fucking mice!' said Sophia. 'Where are they?'

'What's a hopper mouse?' asked Emily.

'A little bit fuzzy, but not large,' said Jamie. 'I keep them

317

under the bed in a bowl that I fill with ice cubes at night. But the bowl isn't cold enough. I think the mice are turning and Louis knows that.'

Sophia said: 'Right, you've brought a live snake and dead mice into someone else's home. If Nicole discovers these creatures she will suggest we leave. She doesn't like animals. She's scared of dogs. She's not a nice person.'

'You said she was doing us a favour.'

'Charitable people can also be horrible,' said Sophia. 'Don't be fooled.'

On the main road they passed a shoe factory, a row of dusty, shuttered warehouses for importers of food, and a bunker-like building covered in pebblecrete, which was the sewage treatment plant where Sophia had worked. Emily turned off the highway onto uncrowded streets; she drove around a yawning man on a bicycle, a pair of girls on rollerskates. Nicole's house, grey brick and brown roof, stood on a corner, on a street in which the driveways were almost touching. Next door: a long, flatbed truck, empty except for a few bags of cement.

'Here's how this is going to work: we go in and get the snake and the thawed-out mice without Nicole seeing,' said Sophia.

'And without harming Louis II,' said Jamie.

'Are you afraid of snakes?' Sophia asked Emily.

'Maybe a little,' she said.

'Why would you do this?' said Sophia, shaking her head, turning to Jamie. 'You're a smart kid.'

'I'm interested in reptiles, Mum,' said Jamie. 'I saw one for sale and I went for it.'

'I'll take Louis away,' said Emily, and they all got out of the car and Sophia led them to the front door, turning the key, calling out to her host. 'Hi, Nicole! I've brought a friend back with me. Five minutes and we'll be out of your hair.'

The home struck Emily as distinctly Nicole-focused. As you entered, on the wall was a framed caricature of Nicole, with comical distortions applied to her chin and hair, all done in black-and-white except for her diamond-shaped red lips. Alongside this illustration hung a signed football jersey and photographs of Nicole singing, and diplomas, awards, citations, photographs of Nicole in Elizabethan costume. Novelty items on a sideboard: beads, decorative plates, ceramic echidnas, ashtrays in the shape of comic masks. Jamie put his hands behind his back, as if he didn't want to touch anything in case it broke. Sophia explained to her friend that Emily, a journalist, had been helping Jamie with one of his assignments and recognised talent in the boy.

Nicole said: 'Really? What sort of talent?'

'Academic,' said Emily.

'I thought he was underachieving.'

'That's where Emily comes in,' Sophia replied, sitting down with Nicole.

Emily and Jamie entered a bedroom where cardboard boxes and stacked chairs were pushed up against one wall. Sophia's television and VCR and portable stereo bunked in one corner of the room, their cords all bundled together. In the midst of the clutter was Jamie's single bed.

'Mum says she needs only four hours sleep a night. That's why she took the couch,' said Jamie. 'She claims she doesn't need to sleep much when she's not working.'

Emily asked: 'How did you get money for the snake?'

'Lucky gave it to me.'

'Thought you didn't see much of him.'

'We don't. I called Lucky and said I wanted some shoes to play basketball and he was like, "Sure, kid," and deposited the money in my Junior Savers account. But I changed my mind about the basketball team. I'd rather have a snake. Maybe I've said too much. Don't tell Mum about Lucky and the money. She'll hate him and he's a nice man. I'll say I traded football cards for cash at school. That's the story. You think it's an okay story?'

'It's fine. It's clever,' said Emily. Jamie stuffed a package of mice in her handbag.

In the backyard, Nicole's daughters jumped on a trampoline, two counterforces rising and falling, their blonde braids flapping. Emily closed the curtains. In the wardrobe, behind a pile of video cassettes and an untidy bundle of clothes, was a large Tupperware container that housed Louis II. Jamie carefully lifted the lid. The snake did not move.

Jamie said: 'Their bad odour is perhaps part of their self-defence mechanism. It's discharged from their cloaca. The smell doesn't trouble me.'

Further dispersing a stink that reminded Emily of foot odour and rotting tomato, the boy tenderly lifted his pet out of the box and laid it on the bed. The doona was pale blue and it quaked as the snake began to move. Emily sat on the bed and covered her nose and mouth. Louis II turned and scuttered over her hand and coiled around her wrist. She closed her eyes but it seemed as though she could see right through her eyelids and perceive his shape.

'He likes you,' said Jamie. 'He identifies you as a friend.'

The snake moved up Emily's arm, and his skin was soft, textured glass. She had expected him to be wet or slimy because she imagined all scaled animals felt a little like fish. Instead Louis II was dry and smooth. Not mucky but not pleasant. From the bedroom, she could clearly hear Sophia and Nicole's bright voices all caught up with each other; they were talking about movies. Emily tucked in her chin when Louis wrapped himself around her neck. The impulse to tear the snake off her body, to tell the boy she couldn't do it, sorry, was constrained by the thought that she needed to be part of this undertaking.

'He definitely likes you,' said Jamie.

'Don't say that again. Give me one of your mother's jackets.'

'But a jacket will look weird,' said Jamie. 'It's hot today.'

'Get a scarf,' Emily blurted out. She took a breath. 'If Nicole asks, I'll say I'm feeling cold. We'll say I'm sick.'

'Cool,' said Jamie, and he snatched up one of his mother's long scarves and wrapped it around Emily's neck, entirely covering Louis II.

'Now what? Are you going to kill him?'

'I honestly don't know what next,' said Emily.

'Please don't throw him in some bin. That would tear my heart in two. Will you call Mum tonight? We should know the outcome, don't you think?'

As Emily opened the bedroom door, she heard the prolonged thump and crash of the back door, which indicated the two girls were inside. As they tore up the hallway, one of them bumped into Emily, disrupting the scarf.

'Amelia and Clio, meet my mother's friend Emily,' said Jamie. Both girls sniffed at this new adult before them. Something smelled bad, their expressions seemed to say— where in the world did this stranger come from?

Emily informed them: 'I have a cold. You might want to stand back.'

'Poor thing,' said Clio, as Emily moved off down the hall. 'Hope you get better soon!'

Near the front door, Emily announced: 'I'm away now!'

'You're going already?' asked Nicole. 'You could stay for dinner, if you like.'

Emily said goodbye and kept her chin firmly tucked into her neck, sinking her range of vision. Nicole's turquoise shoes were the brightest objects she could see. The snake clasped Emily's shoulders tightly as she burst down the steps and hurried across the lawn, a stiff shadow moving towards the street.

Sophia came to the open window of Emily's car. 'Part of me wishes it was a venomous snake that could bite Nicole. Then Louis would be his own solution. What will you do with it?'

'I still have no idea,' Emily said as she started the engine and Louis II curled around her torso. The next day it occurred to Emily that she ought to have pulled over further down the road and put the snake in the boot, but at the time, hyper-aware of the creature's presence, all she thought to do was keep driving to the centre of this unfamiliar city, hoping to be struck by some useful thoughts regarding Louis II's fate. Inside the car, the snake unravelled and lowered itself, like a slow tentacle, onto the floor. Emily said: 'Oh, fuck this, really!'

She changed lanes, merged, and turned onto a gridlocked highway, the traffic as neat as the aisles of a supermarket. Louis II lay somewhere in the footwell. Emily implored him to stay away from the pedals. The phone rang inside her handbag and she reached over, but caller ID didn't recognise the number, which happened with overseas calls, meaning it might be Michael again. His divorce psychodrama happened to be a crisis that involved her, but one which was not much like her own. She let the phone ring out. A voicemail arrived and at the next set of lights she listened to the start of the message—'It's me. It's early in London. I need to tell you something important . . .'—before the traffic moved again and so did Louis, sliding up the door and onto the seatbelt anchor. Emily dropped the phone back in her bag. Louis rolled down the strip of seatbelt until he rested snugly in her lap, as if he were in on the story of her marriage. The traffic stopped and she called Lucky.

'I can't talk for long because I'm driving and I have a python in the car.'

'A what?'

'I've got a *snake* with me. A reptile. I met Sophia and we discovered her son Jamie secretly acquired a pet snake and they needed to get rid of it.'

'Then bring the beast over!'

323

6.

Emily drove with one hand on the roof grab handle, one eye on the snake in her lap. She left the highway. She knew the way: she passed fences covered with tags, concrete walls cracked and streaked, here and there scaffolding, new and narrow buildings, convenience stores, corner hotels, a cricket field hidden behind gum trees.

Outside Lucky's building, she parked and picked up the snake, holding it in her upturned palms as if it were a ritual offering. Which it was, in some sense. Delivering the snake here would solve a problem for Sophia, for Jamie, and for Lucky. Emily dropped the bag of mice in a bin on the street. They did smell bad; they had turned. Louis was right to refuse them.

'Fuck's sake,' she said when he opened the door. 'It was in the car with me for almost an hour.'

'I've got him now,' said Lucky, and he took Louis to the couch, placing the snake beside him. In this position, Lucky did not move, except to speak. 'You talked to Sophia? What did she say? You can tell me.'

'We talked about the Third of April. And then this happened.'

'The snake belongs to me now? What do they eat? Cockroaches?'

'Mice, which apparently come in various sizes and you'll need to keep them frozen. Its name is Louis II. Sophia and Jamie are staying with a friend, and the friend would not be thrilled if she discovered the snake.'

'The thing was a burden. I can help her with that. I'll take care of it,' said Lucky, as the snake moved behind his shoulders, going for the late afternoon sunlight at the end of the couch.

'Can you ring Sophia and tell her you have Louis?' said Emily. 'I have to leave and make a call.'

'This is the perfect gift,' said Lucky with an interested smile. 'They can come and visit and Jamie will play with his pet.'

Emily looked at the snake as it took a U-turn along the top of the couch, stopping to peer down at Lucky. Poor Louis II's eyes looked like stones. Lucky lifted both his hands in surrender as the snake playfully swished down on top of him.

Emily didn't ask about *Wheel of Fortune*, didn't ask about the sum of money that had started the franchise. That would happen later. Her mind was elsewhere; she knew something was coming. In the car, parked near Lucky's building, she called Michael.

'I have something important to say,' he said. 'Therese is pregnant. We're going to have the child.'

'That's that then,' said Emily, after a terrible pause.

This twenty-second phone conversation brought an end to the bumbling dialogue of their breakup. If Therese weren't pregnant, Emily and Michael might have trapped each other in unpleasant conversations for weeks or months or years, once she returned to London. It was a common process of separation—the inconvenient and unwelcome calls, getting in each other's way, coming at each other with this week's ideas about what went wrong in the marriage, or how things might be put right again, or, worst of all, how they'd learned to get over each other, how they'd made their peace. Attachments were exceptionally complicated. Now he would have a child, but not hers. He'd plunged into another life.

Isabel, the hotel receptionist, must have seen the look on her face, because she came out from behind the desk and swept across the lobby to ask if Emily was okay. Emily said she was great, thank you. In the room she opened her computer and began a letter to Michael. She was finished with dialogue but she needed the final word. She began a letter to him, a Word document, about Therese and the new pregnancy, about Emily's thwarted attempt to fall pregnant, about Bion of Smyrna, about the great question mark of her father, about Michael's lack of passions, his lack of warmth, about the tears she was crying, about the fact she had fucked Liam and the sex made her realise that she didn't want to live the rest of her life sleeping only with Michael, about the crappy flats they'd rented and the money they failed to save, about the years she wasted on the subeditors' desk, about her failure to write a book, about the fact she'd never loved anyone but Michael but never felt intense love coming from him, and how she didn't think she deserved true devotion, and didn't have the courage to go out and find such feeling.

Emily finished writing at 3 am and, without rereading her words, without reflection, she deleted the document.

Destroying the unsent letter also completed it. Her arms hurt below the elbow: a subeditor's muscles and tendons. She lay on top of the bedcovers, thirsty and hungry, drained of everything but mostly of love. And she began to perceive the future beneath her.

1994

1

IN WHAT AMOUNTED to semi-retirement, Lucky visited his cafe once a day, after lunch, staying for an hour or two. He lived nearby in the same two-bedroom house he once shared with Valia, keeping that second room as a study, cluttered with silver from the old cafes, and gewgaws from the early days of the franchise. The buildings in Lucky's street were all uniform, the road narrow, the second storeys slightly set back like the fire step of a trench. He supposed the street's architect had been a World War I veteran and had unconsciously or otherwise reproduced, in Sydney, the trench architecture of the Western Front. Lucky liked to speak in terms of idle theories, secret meanings, and there was a time when these ideas amused his employees, including Sophia.

On the second of April, the day before the shooting, he went down for dinner and told Sophia about his idea for a film—a big-budget thing that would never be produced, obviously, but which he felt should in some way be expressed. To begin, Lucky said he believed that religious belief could be located somewhere on the psychotic spectrum. The film's premise: a vaccine for psychosis is developed and all of a sudden the world's religiosity starts to decline. It would be a conspiracy movie, a thriller, in which the big churches bribed governments and pharmaceutical companies, and various heads of state were assassinated, their murders each solved, and all the machinations unravelled by a detective, a lonely nihilist with a widow's peak—that sort of thing. Sophia nodded through the shit-talk, brought him coffee.

She said: 'I know about the fire and Aunt Penelope and the money.'

'Yes. Right. It was weak of me not to have mentioned it.'

'Part of me feels like I'm betraying my family by working here.'

'I don't want you to feel compromised. I don't want you to be part of something that makes you feel uncomfortable. I don't want you to work somewhere else, either. Are you quitting?'

'I don't know. I needed to bring up the subject. The fire, the money. It's like something we never recognised. We should recognise it. Like, it happened.'

'If you want to quit, it doesn't affect our friendship. I'll give you two months' pay, if that's what you need. But you're the best worker I've ever seen. You could have this business eventually, if you wanted.'

'How do you think about the fire?'

'That money was a poison in the business. I live with it, but that load is all mine. It shouldn't be yours. It should be a secret.'

The next night, he told police that Henry Matfield came to his home at 4.25 pm: Lucky could be precise because at the time he was watching the final round of *Wheel of Fortune*, an unusually tight game, full of blunders. He thought about letting the doorbell ring until the visitor went away, before Henry started banging on the door and calling out in a deep, serious voice, as if some accident had occurred on the street. That afternoon Henry looked like he'd been on a bender that ended thirty minutes ago, despite the fact he didn't drink alcohol since booze mixed unpleasantly with his medication for depression and epilepsy. Lucky knew such details because Henry, when he came into the cafe, shared his personal business with people he didn't know well. He kept asking for work at the restaurant and Lucky kept putting him off, claiming that most people were not suited to hospitality. Lucky supposed the young man was lonely, a disappointment to others, and that he disclosed intimate details because he wanted to draw strangers closer. Perhaps this had worked in the past—maybe compassionate people had taken an interest in Henry before he eventually wore them out.

Henry bowed with theatrical delicacy when Lucky opened the door.

'How do you know where I live?' asked Lucky.

'I followed you yesterday,' said Henry.

'You shouldn't do that.'

'Scary, isn't it?'

'If I see you, I see you at the cafe, all right, we can talk there.'

'Sorry, mate. But I don't feel good.'

'Go home and sleep. Have something to eat. Focus on your job. Where do you work?'

'A shit demolition company. But can I help you with something today? I mean, a job around the house maybe?'

'Right this minute?'

'Yeah, right now. Or later. I can come back tomorrow? Like an odd job or whatever for extra cash.'

'Later in the month I might need someone to take broken furniture from the cafe to Tempe tip,' said Lucky. For years he dwelled on this point in the conversation, identifying his perfunctory offer of a future errand as his first chance to prevent the Third of April. Given a single minute he could have drawn up a list of tasks for Henry, keeping him busy for the rest of the day and for weeks afterwards.

'Later in the month? That would be awesome.'

'You have to take the furniture to the tip. Don't dump it on some street corner.'

'I wouldn't do that. Can I come in for a drink?'

His second chance: Lucky almost let him in. He did hesitate, he did think about talking to the kid, making him coffee and advising him to concentrate on turning the part-time demolition job into a full-time thing. Forget about the restaurant and pleading for piecemeal work. Why not move towns? Sydney is expensive. But Lucky said: 'Not right now.'

'Why not?'

'I'll see you at the shop.'

'The people at your cafe don't like me, do they?'

'Rubbish. See you later, yes?'

The police claimed Henry had the rifle and ammunition vest already in his car, likely in the boot. According to the timeline, he could not have driven home before visiting the restaurant. Then why did he knock on the door? Police speculated: perhaps Henry was looking for distraction, or he wanted to spare Lucky's life and on the way to the cafe he checked the restaurant boss was at home. Or he knew perfectly well that Lucky would be another person who wouldn't give him what he wanted, and the visit might serve as propellant.

Peering through blinds in the front window, Lucky watched him cross the road and get into his hatchback, the car radio booming with the cackle and bark of football commentary.

2002

1.

TIME FOR MAKEUP again. Lucky Mallios, his face loose and expressionless, his eyes closed, sat before a mirror framed with fluorescent tubes. That morning in the shower he had shaved his face by touch, without a mirror, because he decided it was too much to confront his reflection on the Day of Fortune. Jennine, the make-up artist, worked on the shaving rash across Lucky's neck. His posture kept deteriorating as he sat in the chair.

'You look totally stressed out,' Jennine said.

'Right now I need to block out irrelevant thoughts.'

'Such as?'

'I made a lot of mistakes in my life.'

'You can't talk like that, mister!' said Jennine. 'You're about to win three hundred thousand dollars. You're getting that money!'

Earlier, in an attempt to prepare himself for the television studio environment, for the bright lights and cold air, for the ramping up and maintaining of audience enthusiasm to a degree that was unnatural, he left Louis II with fresh water in the flat and took a train to Circular Quay, where he sat on a bench outside the Museum of Contemporary Art. He watched as the sun came out from behind a cloud and shone on the Opera House tiles and made them look brand-new.

'Nearly finished,' said Jennine. 'No plus ones again?'

'Didn't invite anyone. They'd make me nervous. Put me off my game.'

Last night Emily had practically dropped the snake at the door and gone elsewhere; she didn't ask about *Wheel of Fortune*, and he didn't know what exactly Sophia had told her about the Third of April, or Valia, or the fire at the Achillion. After the game he'd call them; after the game, they'd all know more. After the game—another alarming thought—he'd need to buy frozen mice for poor Louis. Turning from the mirror, Lucky opened his eyes to the encouragement and embraces his opponents were receiving from their plus ones. Dan knocked on the open door and leaned in, standing on one foot. The green room's coffee machine made a whizzing sound like a worn-out refrigerator.

'We're ready when you are—whoa, nice! Looking good, Mr Mallios. Time to go, sir.'

'The game's not supposed to start for another hour,' said Lucky.

'We have to shoot some background material. Your background. Hasn't anyone told you? No fear, it'll be the easiest thing you do today.'

Lucky and Dan crossed the hall and went up a flight of stairs, down a hallway, and found another flight of stairs that climbed above what Lucky supposed was the *Wheel of Fortune* studio, and they walked along another hallway, past executive offices, until Dan pressed a lift button, and they went up one level to a roof garden with resort-style outdoor furniture. A view of grey terrace houses and the lustreless trusses and tubes of new apartment buildings. Present on this rooftop: Marjorie and a camera crew.

'What's this?' said Lucky

Dan then stepped aside, holding his breath, signalling for Lucky to walk ahead of him. The sound guy whispered something in Marjorie's ear. She waved Lucky forwards, and he moved towards her. She explained: 'What we're about to do is assemble a package about your background, so viewers get a sense of who you were and what you're all about, in real life, away from *Wheel*. To be honest, that personal colour stuff gets lost a bit in gameplay. Plan is, if you win today we'll run a background segment on *Wheel*, like we do for all Day of Fortune winners. Also, the network's current affairs section might use the footage for a piece on Lucky's and the Third of April. That would air around the time of the anniversary of the event. We all share content now. It's network policy. We've streamlined the entertainment and news divisions.'

'Maybe during the rugby league half-time you could run a two-minute segment on the massacre,' said Lucky.

'As it happens, we do run breaking news at half-time,' said Marjorie. 'Everyone does. But I note the sarcasm. Lucky, I'm sorry for what happened on the Third of April. I'm sorry for your losses.'

He'd heard these words a thousand times. He knew when sorry was just something to say in the face of all the suffering.

'You're going to shoehorn a segment about a mass murder into a *Wheel of Fortune* episode. Is that in good taste?'

'Look, it might not run if you don't make it through to the bonus round.'

'Did you speak to the victims' families?'

'Couldn't get them. Couldn't get the survivor either, Sophia. They all said they weren't available and that's understandable. It was a long time ago. People want to move on. Anyway, we don't need a tonne of voices. We've got you.'

'I understand why Sophia and the families knocked you back. You're a gameshow.'

'The news is entertainment. It's the leading form of entertainment. And entertainment shows can offer us news. Prime example is right here. The Third of April is a big deal, a proper trauma in this city. We can't avoid it.'

'On *Wheel of Fortune* you can avoid it.'

'The shooting is part of the Lucky's story. I've been doing this a long time, mate. Viewers pay attention to serious news presented in a soft format. We're respectful of people's pain. That's what you need to keep in mind. Can we do this?'

Lucky turned around and put his hands in his pockets and muttered and the crew started filming. Marjorie, blinking politely, assured him it wouldn't take long, and she kept on assuring him until his face moved from indignation to something more neutral, until his eyes stopped moving between her and the cameraman to her left.

Marjorie: 'Henry was a regular at your cafe in the months before his rampage. Did you suspect anything?'

'If we'd thought he was dangerous, we would have barred him from the restaurant.'

'Even for people like myself, who have the fondest child-hood memories of Lucky's cafes, the first thing that comes to mind when we hear that name is—well, a terrible, senseless crime. How does that make you feel? I know that ownership of the franchise had changed hands, but you founded the company, and that last restaurant belonged to you, and it was your name up on those signs. It must weigh on you.'

'It's difficult to feel proud of the franchise after everything. I feel like I failed.'

Marjorie smiled: it was the quote she wanted.

'It's Day of Fortune: what will it mean if you win this money and open a restaurant with the only survivor of the shooting?'

'I've already answered this in gameplay.'

'Let's try again. You're half an hour away from potentially winning three hundred thousand dollars. What does the jackpot mean to you?'

'It means I'll be able to do a good thing.'

'Oh, Lucky, you must have helped many people.'

'Not the people I loved the most.'

'Done!' Marjorie said. 'We can use that. See how easy that was?'

Dan nodded, gave the thumbs-up, and Lucky sat down on the outdoor furniture and Marjorie crouched nearby and placed a hand on his knee and reminded him he knew how to play the game. He was as good as anyone she'd seen in that studio. Her perfume reminded him of roses and molasses. Describe the scent in a three-word phrase: *smell of victory*. Or: *nursed in luxury*. Or: *dazzled by fame*. Marjorie checked her watch with a tiny motion, and patted his hand.

'Good luck, big guy,' said Marjorie. 'We want to use that footage on *Wheel* so I'm counting on you to win. You got this. And don't stay outside too long or you'll have to go back into make-up.'

2.

Dan found his usual seat in the front row. Red lights, intro music, and Marjorie arrived at the podium, her hair styled differently from twenty minutes ago. She took a moment to explain the rules of Day of Fortune to Lucky, who nodded, understanding the explanation was for the benefit of viewers unfamiliar with the format. On the bank of screens behind the contestants the figure of $300,000 flashed for a few seconds. Someone in the crew stomped on the pedal of a fog machine and sent a comet of theatrical fog across the set. Lucky leaned over the wheel. He asked for the letter 'M' in a five-word phrase.

M _ _ _ _   _ _   _ _   _ _ _ _   M _ _ _

He tapped the front of the podium because he knew the answer.

'I'd like to solve. The answer is *Missed it by that much!*' Lucky said.

'Terrific,' said Marjorie. 'Say, Lucky, is it true you sold tongue sandwiches in your franchise? That tongue on toast was one of the early big-selling dishes?'

The crowd made the sound of *ewwww*.

'At first they were big sellers, but we replaced tongue with ham once ham became affordable.'

'Delicious. Moving on. Ratings are falling as we speak.'

Lucky lost all three speed rounds. Phrase: *You can do it.* Game: *Futsal.* Film: *The Emperor's New Groove.* He wasn't in the game. He saw himself at home watching this very episode on TV, thinking where did they find this old guy?

'Our champion has stumbled!' said Marjorie. 'We'll be back after this break.'

She went over to Lucky and punch-patted his arm with her fist, before chatting to the other two contestants. Lucky looked unhappy, stretched his legs, trying to loosen a knot.

A Brisbane law student named Franco spun a total of $3400 and solved the next puzzle. Famous Actor and Role: *Errol Flynn as Robin Hood.* Lucky clapped and grinned and doffed a pretend cap to blank-faced Franco, who rolled *Lose a Turn* on the next puzzle. No one in the crowd sighed for him. Someone called out Lucky's name. A silver-haired childcare worker, Mel, coolly rode the wheel to $2400, almost filling the board. Famous name and title:

A R T H _ _   W _ L L _ S L _ _

D U K _   O F   W _ L L I N G T _ _

In the audience, Dan threw up his hands to gesture that there wasn't anything more he could do. Someone smothered a cough. Franco the law student moved in discomfort. Then Mel, who'd banked $2100 in the three speed rounds, rolled the wheel to *Lose a Turn*.

'Oh no!' said Marjorie. 'This is tearing my heart to bits. Lucky needs to land some cash.'

Lucky brought up $1000. 'I'd like to solve this. I'm ninety-five per cent sure it's *Arthur Wellesley Duke of Wellington*.'

'Bravo! Now we have a game. Two more puzzles. Our carryover champion Lucky needs to win both of these to capitalise on his Day of Fortune.'

Lucky, refusing to meet Marjorie's eye, paused before he spun the wheel. He called out a letter.

'N.'

He rolled again. He nominated 'G'. After the next spin he called for 'V'. Then 'S' and 'T'. Aspiring barrister Franco bunched his hands into fists and clamped them under his arms. Mel, of the Adelaide Hills, assumed a look of distaste. Lucky's eyes were closed in data-search. He saw the answer in the colour of gold and a font similar to the franchise sign.

'Lucky? Lucky!' said Marjorie.

'Yes?'

'Give me your next letter now. Game on, mate.'

'C.'

There was silence. Dan mouthed the words 'fucking fuck'. The category was What Are You Doing.

G _ V _ N G   _   _ _ S _ C _ N

_ N   _ N S T _ _ _ _ N T   _ _ _

C _ _ _ S T _ _ S

'I know the answer,' said Lucky. 'But—'

'Then give us the answer! Now is the time for solutions!'

'The answer is *Giving a musician an instrument for Christmas*. But the word "musician" is misspelled on the board. I think you've made a mistake.'

'Let's have a look, shall we?' said Marjorie, and she waved magically at the board, which lit up:

G I V I N G   A   M U S I C A N

A N   I N S T R U M E N T   F O R

C H R I S T M A S

'Dear Lord, I see what you mean,' she said, turning to the audience. 'That puzzle can't go to air. That's a DVD extra, people. That's why it pays to be in the studio audience!'

The director looked at his notes. Dan got out of his seat and scooted over to Marjorie. He shook his head; she shook her head. A new puzzle was required. Lucky's winnings for that phrase were erased and he gave up an unpersuasive smile. He looked like he'd lost the game already. Marjorie, genuinely upset, apologised briefly for what happened, said she was proud of Lucky for being a good sport about everything. Nothing like this had happened in all the episodes she'd hosted. Nothing ever went wrong on the board. She hugged him. The audience's grumbling continued for a few minutes. The cameras rolled when they went quiet.

The category was Book and Author. Lucky turned over seven consonants and then rolled *Bankrupt*.

'Total disaster!' said Marjorie. 'Oh my, this *truly is* a Greek tragedy.'

'I've lost,' said Lucky.

'It ain't over yet, mate,' said Marjorie.

'It would be a miracle to come back from here,' said Lucky.

'Miracles happen on this show,' said Marjorie. 'Next up: young Franco.'

Franco eyed the wheel, looking for the dangers. The answer to Book and Author, which he offered after two spins, was *The Tree of Man, Patrick White*.

Mel solved the next puzzle on $2100. After three spins she nailed the category Things: *Three wishes*.

'And there we have it, boys and girls!' said Marjorie. 'Mel the childcare worker from Adelaide wins today's game and goes through to the bonus round. Before we take a quick break I'll say so long to our other contestants. Goodbye, Franco. And here's the biggest cheers to the magnificent Lucky. Awful to see you hit a critical *Bankrupt* on Day of

Fortune, but I have good memories of those restaurants, if that means anything to you.'

'It does,' said Lucky.

'And I promise to be your first customer if you do open that new restaurant.'

'I'll keep you posted,' said Lucky, his voice and expression bare of affect.

Marjorie threw her cards in the air. None of the contestants shook hands. The *Wheel of Fortune* rigger turned the confetti cannon away from Lucky and towards the applauding audience.

2002

1.

WITHIN THE NEXT month all the prizes would arrive: the bonus-round takeaways, the consolation gifts. What would he do with a SkyBound Stratos trampoline? At this time Sophia did not have a backyard. A new microwave was coming: he could use it to defrost Louis' mice. The Never Out Of Bed sheet set was on its way. Two boxes of Tasmanian wine, all bubbly, arrived that morning. The day after the Day of Fortune. Emily was coming over and her questions were frightening, unavoidable. Lucky needed to change his shirt before she arrived, the perspiration like a sign of acceptance: he'd run out of artifice, energy, pride, restraint, fear. He was finished, finally, with the feeling of defeat. He did have time for changes. The afternoon sunlight cast a glazed orange dinge over the street.

~

The snake was wriggling around somewhere in the apartment, he told Emily as she sat on the couch. The last time Lucky saw him, Louis II had been curled like a bowline in the sink of the laundry closet, doing whatever snakes did after a meal on a hot day. The snake diet was an atrocity. Lucky switched up the speed of the ceiling fan and told her about the *Wheel of Fortune* experience, all of it: the four slots he'd won, the Day of Fortune, the manipulations of Dan and Marjorie. Emily wrote in shorthand in her notebook.

'Will they run that lame package about the Third of April?' she asked.

'Couldn't get a definite yes or no there.'

'I want to ask about a rumour I came across this week. You started the franchise with a sum of money you received as a gift or an inheritance.'

'This is true,' said Lucky, forcing himself to look at Emily. 'Your father gave me the money in 1946.'

'Lucky, Christ! How many times did I ask you about him?'

Emily leaned forward on the couch as if to seize something on the coffee table.

Lucky had tried to give her nothing. Still she tunnelled towards her father, day after day.

Here was an answer. Here was a story Lucky told himself for many years before he understood the truth.

'There was a fire,' he said. At the Cafe Achillion, in 1946, and his sister-in-law died, he explained. Her name was Penelope Asproyerakas. He spelled the surname. She had applied to university; she wanted to be a scientist.

345

There was a fire and the police identified arson as the cause, but they could not find the person responsible. How hard did they look? At first they questioned Lucky's father-in-law. Then they spoke to cafe owners elsewhere in Sydney, Greeks who might have held some grudge against the family. It was easy to imagine the arsonist committed an undetectable crime, but it was easier to imagine the police gave up the investigation early, supposing it to be the result of an unfathomable feud among migrants. Ian Asquith must have read about the fire in a newspaper. A year or so earlier they had met in a bar, but they weren't friends, they weren't anything to each other until the destruction of the Achillion. A few weeks after the fire, Asquith tracked down Lucky and offered him a large sum of money to rebuild the lost business, or to use the gift however he and Valia saw fit. They assumed Asquith was rich—he gave that impression—and could afford the sum. (But he wasn't rich, said Emily. He must have given you all the money he possessed.) Asquith returned to England and he never wrote to Lucky, never responded to letters. He wanted the gift to be a secret. That was all he asked. Now Lucky apologised for his fidelity to this request. He didn't know Asquith. The money and the secret were their only ties.

'That's why he made the painting,' said Emily. She did not write the story down; she didn't need to. 'He did an important thing.'

'That must be why.'

What good would the truth do, after all this time? Lucky thought. I don't want to bring more pain into the world.

'I need to be careful of the stories that people tell me,' she said.

'I have paperwork. I'll show you the paper. Give me a day to find it.'

Emily put her head in her hands and—Lucky could not tell if she sobbed. He could see plainly enough that she had been given what she'd wanted and he didn't think it decent to watch another person engulfed by the completion of a long passion. He went to the bathroom and washed his hands. At the fridge he checked on some food he prepared that morning and, while fixing a bowl of olives, his intercom buzzed and he rushed over to the console near the door and let in the visitors downstairs.

'Another prize from *Wheel of Fortune*?' asked Emily.

'Do you need to be anywhere this afternoon?' asked Lucky.

Emily spotted Louis II among the curtains near the television.

2.

She'd already seen her future, or glimpses anyway. New settings, new questions. By the end of that year, Emily would move to Sydney and apply for dual citizenship, being eligible for an Australian passport on account of her mother. She would work at a bookstore and, nights and weekends, write a book about the aftermath of the Third of April. All the families spoke to her. She earned their trust, she made a practice of showing them passages of the manuscript, ensuring she had their consent to tell the story. In the brief afterword she mentioned her father's gift to Lucky, and the fact that her understanding of trauma and unrecoverable loss began with bearing witness to Ian Asquith's death.

3.

Jamie entered the apartment ahead of his mother, scanning the white tiles for the snake, finding Louis in a belt of sunlight behind the television set. Lucky had filled his bath with wood shavings, expecting the tub to serve as a lair, but Louis twisted his way around the bath, poked around the tap, and slithered out for some place better. Maybe that room was the wrong temperature. Not enough sunlight. Snakes, suddenly the most important animals to Lucky, were organically strange and discerning. Probably they required an elaborate terrarium. Lucky needed to go back to the pet store. Jamie could be of assistance. That was something they could do. For his guests Lucky set down a plate of savoro—fish cooked in vinegar and currants.

'This was my mother's favourite dish,' Sophia told Emily,

'It's Greek but h-h-has traces of Roman cuisine,' said Jamie. 'Ancient Romans liked to a-a-add currants and vinegar to f-food. Sorry.'

'It's okay,' Emily said. 'Good fact.'

'Don't ever apologise for your speech,' said Sophia. 'It's this drama with Louis. It's stressed you out. It brought back the stammer.'

'Is L-Louis eating?' asked Jamie.

'He loves the fuzzy,' said Lucky.

He poured wine into glasses on his crowded side table, where no one had noticed them among the silver sundae dishes and engraved sugar bowls and other franchise leftovers. All of these Lucky's creation. All of these saved from the second great fire. He took what he could from the final restaurant, and he went home. At home, many boring and lonely nights passed, as occurred for all humankind: he thought of such community in his solitude. Today it was time to resolve that anomaly. Lucky, his face a picture of anxious concentration, brought drinks to his guests. He told Sophia and Jamie that yesterday and the day before he'd performed as a contestant on *Wheel of Fortune.*

'I wanted the money to start a restaurant,' he said, before they could ask him about the result. 'I wanted another chance. I wanted to do something the right way, without any horrible flaws. And I wanted you to manage the place, Sophia. But that's not going to happen now.'

'I'm too old for hospitality,' said Sophia.

'I tried to save Penelope. I tried to save my marriage. I tried my best with the franchise. I tried to stop gambling.'

He held up his glass and they drank, and Lucky, who'd tried also to keep his flat cool and dark all day, opened the curtains to provide more sunlight for Louis II. The sky was the blue of a computer screen and Jamie brought his pet into a warm spot near the door. The afternoon felt quiet for a moment: the snake hardly moving; Jamie taking in the books and knickknacks on the shelves and sideboards; Sophia finishing her wine. Emily gazed at a postcard Lucky handed her, a souvenir given to customers at Lucky's franchises in the early 1970s. Here it was, the photographic model from which Ian Asquith had painted his suicide picture. She'd looked at her father's painting thousands of times: his image was better than the postcard; he'd improved upon the composition; she saw the tells of pride.

'We should make this a regular thing,' said Lucky. 'Come visit Louis II, and I cook your favourite dishes. On Sundays, like family.'

Sophia held out her empty glass, which Lucky promptly refilled.

'What's this box?' said Jamie, holding up a clarinet case he found slotted between the wall and a bookshelf. 'Is it snake-related?'

'It's a clarinet.'

'I want to learn that instrument!' said Jamie. 'You could give me lessons.'

'I can't pay for lessons right now,' said Sophia.

Emily put down the postcard, stopping herself before she fell too far into Asquith-thought again. Maybe she knew all she would know about her father. They waited for Lucky in silence, with a close attention that he interpreted as doubtful confidence. Sophia waved her hands for Lucky to go ahead, hurry up, play.

He thought he'd need a full hour in which to decide the tune, and another hour to give a polish to his playing—never much to begin with. His guests didn't have that kind of time. He bought the instrument long ago, a few years before the Third of April, and had not once played the thing, not a single chuckle from the clarinet. He told the salesman at the store on Parramatta Road it was a gift for someone else, a friend who'd expressed an interest in one day taking it up. The clarinet was a memento, an insignia, unspent capacity, ancient armour. An object he wanted hidden at home. Of what good use was it? He unlatched the case.

AUTHOR'S NOTE

THE STORY GOES that in the eighteenth century a man
with the surname Asproyerakas left his home in southern
Kefalonia and settled in the village of Vathi on the neigh-
bouring island of Ithaka. In Vathi, he acquired the nickname
Pippos because he had a habit of calling out *pip-pip-pip*
while feeding his brace of ducks. Eventually, my ancestor
adopted Pippos as his real name.

The Asproyerakas family in this novel bears only a slight
resemblance to my own. Still, I've come to think of the
characters in these pages as kin. I will miss them.

ACKNOWLEDGEMENTS

MY DEEPEST THANKS to all my family, especially: Thalia Pippos for her endless love; Marina and Simon Bollinger for showing me the way; and George Zacharatos for my first lessons in Greek literature and mythology. *Lucky's* is dedicated to my partner, Renee Brown.

Thanks to my publisher, Mathilda Imlah, for her belief in this novel; to Georgia Douglas for her generous work and support in a difficult time; to Ali Lavau and my agent, Jane Novak, for their guidance; and to Anthony Macris for our long conversation. I thank Zora Simic for her faith that the day would come.